HELP
YOURSELF!

EDITED BY JIM FEAST,
RON KOLM AND ALFRED VITALE

HELP

YOURSELF!

THE

UNBEARABLES

ISBN: 1-57027-104-6

As always, dedicated to Tuli Kupferberg,
Hakim Bey & Rollo Whitehead.

Book design: Ben Meyers

If you wish to contact the Unbearables or any of the individual contributors,
or if you need crediting information or the publishing history of any of the
texts that comprise this volume, please write or fax us c/o Autonomedia.

Autonomedia
PO Box 568 Williamsburgh Station
Brooklyn, NY 11211-0568
Phone and Fax: 718.963.2603
www.autonomedia.org

Printed in the United States of America

CONTENTS

TESTIMONIALS ON COPING FROM POP CULTURE ICONS!

TIPS AND HINTS ON MAKING RELATIONSHIPS WORK!

USE GROUP THERAPY FOR PERSONAL GROWTH!

SUMMING UP FOR SUCCESS!

Graphics Credits

The Third Wave of Self Help:
Why We Think You Need This Book

JIM FEAST

"Why do people love actresses?" Michael Carter asked, hunched over a pool table at the Shandon Star as he lined up a shot.

"Because they are employees whose inner and outer lives, as long as they are in front of a camera, are determined by someone else," Carl Watson replied.

"Think how complex that is," bart added, having topped off another mug from the pitcher. "A woman leans across the breakfast table to cuff her screen hubby: the skittering hand, the puffiness under her eyes: these are not chance, but calculated effects dependent upon makeup girl and acting coach."

Huberman threw out, "An actress is a woman whose every flinch is scripted."

Alfred, drinking orange juice to assuage a bad liver, brought us back to the topic at hand. "That gets to the heart of self help books. Their message is that you will be successful to the degree you allow yourself to be permeated by an alien will."

Ron K had to disagree. "You mistake the point entirely. Sure, the author got rich from whatever capitalist endeavor he found himself in, but it was by his own method, arising from his own unique personality, which is, of course, unrepeatable. The readers, who are not stooges ..."

"All three of them," from Lorraine.

" ...see the author's success story as an adventure, and read his book to vicariously share in that adventure."

Randall handed Ron a cue stick, cutting his rant short.

"I guess Ron means," Tsuarah explained, "that self help books are true stories which people read as fiction."

"Like they do everything else," Arthur Nersessian said, coming in and bringing some of the December 7th coldness with him.

It was time for some background, so resident history buff Mike Golden stepped up to the plate. "In 1935, Huey Long was assassinated, killing a lot of dreams. Remember his program 'Share the Gelt?' He promised to pass a law that prohibited individuals or families from owning more than $15 million. The rest would be confiscated and divided up among the poor."

"And don't forget EPIC," Randall threw in, pointing his cigarette like a pencil.

"What's that?" Maynard asked.

"Upton Sinclair's campaign in California. He felt the government should seize non-operating farms and factories and hand them to the unemployed to operate democratically."

"With the movements like those crushed," Golden continued dolorously, "people turned to self help books. It was a crying ..."

"Shame," Thad offered. Golden's last words had been buried in the hubbub when the Kolm/Randall team lost to the two Michaels: Carter and Topp.

"... need of the time," Golden repeated. "Everybody was asking, 'How can I get a job when 30 million are out of work?' The book stalls were filled with titles like *I Made a Million Selling Rotten Apples*."

Carol pointed out a man in a back booth reading the *Racing Form*. I sat up, startled, at first thinking he had a pair of antlers affixed to his noggin, but, looking closer, I saw it was the shadow cast by a broken, unlit chandelier that dangled from a chain like a brace of ducks

"Reminds me . . . " she muttered. I didn't catch all of what she was saying because I turned to hear the bard of Phoenicia pontificate.

Sparrow, sipping a Kiddie Cocktail through a tiny straw to placate his bad pancreas, was fuming, "The trick in the '30s was this. You had to know that only losers read self help books. So if you really wanted to snare a job, your best bet was to convince all the other applicants to read the same stuff the losers were reading."

"Like what books?" Witz asked incredulously.

"One of the books that comes to mind," Sparrow returned, "stole the wisdom of the East and offered it as a way to climb up in the corporate world. It was called, *Kowtow: The Ancient Chinese Art of Bootlicking*."

Sam Delaney took some innings, "In the '60s, the second wave of self help books appeared, spearheaded by two good German doctors: Herbert Marcuse and Erich Fromm. It was a peculiarity of history that these men, who'd worked through the '30s in the Karl Marx Institute in Frankfurt and then fled to the U.S. to escape Hitler, would end up on the best-seller lists, still slugging it out over the exegetical niceties of *Anti Duhring*, but now couched in terms of salesmanship."

"What were they disputing exactly?" Benderson asked.

"Psychoanalysis. To Fromm, Freud, who had become mired in conservative beliefs in his old age, had begun as a crusader championing the equality of all human potentialities: political, economic, sexual; each would add its beans to the ultimate coffee cup of ripened individuality."

"The end result," Bonny threw in cynically, "being couple enrichment programs, EST and Esalen." She was smoking cigarillos like a hot wok, the haze getting in everyone's eyes.

"And Marcuse?" asked Savage, one of the few who seemed to be paying attention.

The old man, who was wearing dark glasses and a beret, had gotten up, shed his antlers and toddled to the pay phone up front in the Shandon (which had recently changed its name from The Cupping Room). Stubby pencil in hand, he checked off something, maybe a racing form, as he talked. Then he slung the receiver back in its cradle, and exchanged his beret for a green croupier's visor which he took from his pocket.

"Where Fromm felt *Civilization and Its Discontents* signaled Freud's reactionary turn," Delaney went on, "Marcuse said it contained a hidden barb. Freud wrote that the repression of sexuality caused peevishness and other disorders, but was inevitable, *as long as* the daily grind was necessary for society to continue to produce what was essential. But what if, Marcuse asked, due to cyberization, we could still keep the goods humming out, but didn't need to work all that much? In that case, the instincts no longer had to be kept down. If they were, it was all unneeded surplus repression"

I glanced back to notice the old man was now taking down a cue. The way the Shandon Star (AKA The Homestead) operated, if you wanted to play on its one pool table, you put your name on a tally board. Each winner played the next person in line.

Scutti fielded the ball, really getting into the line of reasoning. "So, every corporation could reduce working hours to four a day and install squash courts and orgy rooms!"

They were getting into utopian speculations, but I had turned my attention to the pool game. The old man played badly, scratching his first shot and making other flubs. He stopped to talk to his opponent, Thad Rutkowski, and then I saw each of them opening their billfolds and laying a few twenties on the side. Breaking the next rack, the old man cleared the table.

Our conversation had been getting lively, but an event at the bar stopped us in our tracks. A stoop-shouldered man, shoved in between Maurer and Sirowitz, who had been talking to himself, suddenly stepped back, whipped out a gun and placed it to his temple. All the Unbearables backed away; but the old man with the cue stick inched forward, speaking low. In a moment he had thrown his arm around the gunman; in a second moment was buying him another round, deftly removing the pistol from his grasp and stowing it in his cummerbund. Did I mention he wore a weathered, roomy tuxedo?

José brought us into the next inning. "How is our book going to be any different from all the trash out there? Self help books now are all niche-oriented. There are environmental ones, *How You Can Profit from the Death of Planet Earth*; ones about relationships, *How to Date Fat Men*; and even ones aimed at pre-schoolers, *A-OK, B-OK*. They're all dreck."

"Our book will herald a third wave," Jill said, twisting her gray ringlets in her fingers. "It will synthesize the first wave's impossible dream that everyone has a part to play in the economy and the second wave's belief that each of us has a personality worth the development.

"Buy our book, we'll say, and you'll learn how to single-handedly destroy society and reconstruct it in a way most pleasing to yourself."

Everybody guffawed, but Jill was peeved. "Don't laugh. Burroughs talks about something similar in his *ReSearch* interview."

"Burroughs," Carol muttered. "*That's* it."

Kolm thundered back, "Our book will be larger than life. If the first wave came from outside the masses, and the second was sent down from above, ours will go right through them as bacteria shoot through a round of curdled milk turning it into Swiss cheese. All those air holes allow thought to freely travel through."

"Yeah, baby," said Dalachinsky, clicking his fingers, "We need a hip Titanic of a book that will slice apart the coagulated miasma of dupology."

Bonny extrapolated, "In the '40s reading material was swapped around. When you finished your paper, your *P.M.* or *News*, you left it on your subway seat for the next rider. So, for our book, I think people should pool their money and organize buying groups just as in the late '80s AIDS patients formed groups to buy illegal drugs that offered some respite."

"Why do that?" Kostalanetz asked.

"Because you can only emancipate yourself in a collective. None of our self help pieces will have any validity unless they are read in tandem with all the others in the anthology, just as none of our poetry is any good except when it appears with everyone else's."

That last line got no assent. Shalom seemed interested though, asking, "So are you saying people should share our book?"

Bonny said, "it must be read in an agora."

"I don't follow," Sandlin said.

She explained, "The old books might recommend you ask your boss for a raise. Fine, but our book stipulates you bring along 20 or 30 friends who crowd into the corporate office to offer moral support. Or if you find you can't tell your boyfriend what you want sexually, get 10 or 15 Unbearables to stand around the bed for encouragement and advice to help you get off."

"I'm for that," Sharon said.

An elderly Oriental woman came in, her long white hair coifed up and fixed with what looked like a doily on top. Her yellow slicker was crusted with salt. As she approached the old man, I saw her lined face ignite with great humor. He got up to meet her and they stood close enough for me to eavesdrop.

She said, "You're not drunk. Tell me you're not drunk."

"I only knocked down a few. Grab a stool," the old man said.

"We don't really have time. We've got to get a move on."

"I got you a present," the fellow said.

"I never *did* like your presents," she giggled as he handed her the gun. She dropped it in a pocket, adding something in Japanese. As they exited, he dipped his hand into a large tub filled with pickles in brine, scooping some out. They wiggled like minnows between his fingers.

"Somebody's got to buy another pitcher of this forty rod!" Tuli hollered, "I'm getting mighty dry here, mighty dry!" Carol volunteered the two of us.

As we walked to the bar, Carol said, "I'm pretty sure that guy who just left was the same fellow who was standing next to Burroughs in an old photo. I can't remember his name, though."

"That's easy to find out," I said. "He played pool so his name must be on the chalkboard." We went over to it and counted down the requisite names till we found:

~~ROLLO~~

I was shocked that our hero and exemplar had actually been among us, unrecognized, a theory made manifest, dovetailing thought and action in a consumate performance of self help. So it's in homage to Rollo Whitehead that we've assembled this collection of texts embodying the third wave of self-help.

SELF EMPOWER-MENT OVERVIEW: ADVICE FROM WINNERS!

CAPTAIN JACK EXPLAINS HIS BONG TO BILLY

8 Step Program to Becoming a Revolutionary

Sparrow

Most people say, "I am not a revolutionary. I am merely a liberal," or "I am not a revolutionary. I am just a Republican." Nonsense. Anyone can become a revolutionary. Just follow the 8 step program outlined here.

Step One: Revolutionary Epigrams

Every revolution was once a spelling bee.
Never be afraid to be *first*.
Most revolutions begin in the suburbs.
Save five cents a day for the revolution.
Karl Marx was not a Marxist, Edgar Allan Poe was.

Step Two: Saving For The Revolution

Each of us carries pocket change everyday. We receive this change by buying bagels and the *Cleveland Plain Dealer*. Or whatever newspaper we buy. We use this change to pay for further purchases of the day: an orange, a blowdryer, etc. What I am suggesting, however, is that we take just five cents and place it in a special jar labeled "For The Revolution."

Step Three: Your Revolutionary Diary

Your first decision as a revolutionary is what kind of Revolutionary Diary to use. A small spiral notebook that you buy for sixty-nine cents? An exquisite, hand tooled leather volume with Chinese lace paper? A stapled together mishmash of torn-up scrap paper?

Whatever you choose, write REVOLUTIONARY DIARY on the cover.

Don't feel obligated to write in this diary. After all, you are a revolutionary, you can do anything you want. You can leave your diary blank forever.

The important thing is that you now have a Revolutionary Diary. If you feel inspired, transcribe your plans and visions therein. What if you are as brilliant a tactician as Trotsky, yet only lack an avenue to transmit your tactics? Now you have that avenue.

Step Four: Your Political Soul

According to Christian theology, each person has a soul. The soul is unique and eternal. Wherever you go, you carry this soul with you. Your mind and body make decisions which affect your soul.

Political theorists believe we have a political soul as well. Deep within us our political soul reacts to every political event. We cry when a large plane crashes. We fear war. We despise our landlord. We feel compassion for a child in dirty clothes clinging to a blue-eyed doll.

How will you respond to your political soul? Will you cultivate it, or allow it to languish?

Step Five: Cultivating Your Political Soul

Consider a political tragedy—for example, American slavery. Imagine the face of each American slave, one by one. When you have seen enough slaves, envision the face of each American slave owner.

Feel your political soul enlarge.

Step Six: Becoming A Revolutionary

Having a large political soul does not automatically make you a revolutionary. A revolutionary believes in total change.

You must begin to believe total change is possible. You can start by changing small things. Take off your socks and put your right sock on your left foot, and your left sock on your right foot. The next time you buy toothpaste, buy a different type of toothpaste. When you make stew, add raisins suddenly to your stew.

Step Seven: Now You Are Almost A Revolutionary

Take out your Revolutionary Diary, and set it on the kitchen table before you. Feel the proximity of the revolution.

The revolution is coming closer, like a horse charging up a hill.

Step Eight: Going Into Seclusion

In the final stages of becoming a revolutionary, it is helpful to go into seclusion. (Often revolutionaries do this in prison, but that is not absolutely necessary.)

Find a secluded glen or brook, or lock yourself in your room.

Think of your favorite foods. Remember men and women you have slept with. Recall sermons you have heard in church (or synagogue, or mosque, or Shinto shrine).

We are set on the earth for a finite number of weeks. Then we disappear. Perhaps we return after that. Perhaps we go to Another World. No one knows.

With our limited weeks, how can we make this world more delightful?

The 7 Habits of Highly Ineffective People

LORRAINE SCHEIN

I was going to tell you about the book "Do What You Love, The Money Will Disappear," but I have decided to inform you about "The 7 Habits of Highly Ineffective People."

As the author says in the book's opening, "Before I go on, I recommend that you not see the advice I am giving you as a book." So, I suggest you see it as a can of Campbell's Cream of Mushroom Soup. (Actually, you should see it as a waste of good money instead, one that will provide superficial, tired management clichés soaked in New Age pseudo-scientific jargon, illustrated by many numbered diagrams and charts.)

The 7 Habits are ingrained habits of immaturity that move us progressively on an immaturity continuum from dependence to ingrained habit to annoying tic. All ineffectiveness lies in the correct P/PC balance — the Procrastination to Procrastinating Capability ratio. The 7 Habits are: 1. Procrastination 2. Sleeping 3. Anarchism 4. Window-Shopping 5. Poetry-Writing 6. Catalog-Reading 7. TV.

The first and most basic habit of the highly ineffective person is inactivity. This means that, as human beings, it is a waste of time and energy to take the initiative and do anything beyond getting out of bed and watching *Babylon 5*. It's a waste of time to do anything because effort only makes you more tired and leads to more disappointment or Chronic Fatigue Syndrome. So when an urge to do something strikes, follow these rules:

Always put last things first. When communicating, try to dither, and remember: Seek first to be misunderstood; then misunderstand. Mumble, whenever possible. To fully realize your aimlessness, it is important to write a personal mission statement of Tedious Platitudes, such as 1. I will be a cheerful elf. 2. I will floss three times a day. 3. I will not masturbate and floss at the same time in public. 4. I will take a flower-arranging class at the New School. 5. I will not read poems or other spoken word art for over 10 minutes at readings. 6. I will buy a Filofax and pretend to care about time management, but will actually fill the pages with the taped-in slips from Chinese fortune cookies.

Which brings us to how to fritter away your time. Time should be wasted on a Time Mismanagement Quadrant, according to the following principles: 1. Always read stupid self-help books like this, which will eat up many odd minutes of useful employment. 2. Always stay on unemployment for as long as you can. 3. Spend a lot of time attending anarchist meetings, and making Utopian plans for revolution with no practical methods of achieving it.

Visualization exercises can also help you achieve your mission. Here is one of my favorites: First, repeat "Every day in every way, I am getting better and better," while rubbing your stomach and visualizing a white light going on in your bathroom. Visualize going into the bathroom, looking for the source of the white light and notice that someone forgot to flush the toilet. Then SEE yourself actually flushing the toilet, repeating FLUSH FLUSH FLUSH each time. Surround yourself with the white light, because you forgot your bathrobe. End by calling on a higher power, like pi.

If you try these techniques, your circle of influence will bisect your circular reasoning and you will achieve the fuck-up/FU Win Some/Lose Some paradigm, while the author of the book will make thousands of dollars from speaking engagements to multinational corporations and write a sequel for more money.

Comment Baiser une Carte Postale Sans Risque de Microbes *

PETER WORTSMAN

Monsieur desires? the sultry card reader inquires. Tight-lipped silent type, you stick out your tongue and gurgle. The gentleman is well-tooled, she compliments to provoke articulation. Whereupon the tongue detaches itself and falls on the face of a pre-stamped postcard. It's her turn next and she willingly lends an ear. The two go at it like vermicelli in hot water. His eye on the action, the author pulls a heavy tome from the shelf (the Bible, Das Kapital, or the Brooklyn phonebook), raises it, solemnly reciting famous passages by heart, and blam! Another classic hits the dust. There you have it, ladies and gentlemen, evidence of love flatly taken in the act, legitimized by tradition and ready for delivery.

* *How to Fuck a Postcard Without Risk of Infection*

How to Attend Art Openings

Richard West

1. With a reservation if you have one and if not, you should pretend to or declare you were simply too busy to bother with such minor details.

2. When you enter the building, be the last to board the elevator so you'll be the first to exit the elevator and enter the room. Never walk behind anyone if you can help it and if you can't, drop back a few paces so you can dramatize your entrance.

3. Don't look at the art but rather position yourself strategically deep within the room preferably with or near important looking people but not too far from the *hors d'oeurves*.

4. Don't let people see you eat.

5. If you can't conceal your food, don't eat too much or you'll be suspected of having bad taste. Don't speak while you eat, it masticates your metaphors to say nothing of your company.

6. Avoid all people of lesser importance on the unofficial social register.

7. Avoid poorly dressed people as well as people who lack good image consciousness unless they are important artists or impoverished investment bankers.

8. When conversing with anybody, try to dominate the conversation and to end the conversation first. Remember: reject them before they reject you, it will make you appear more important.

9. If you must look at the art, try not to be observed doing so and try to avoid discussing the art.

10. If you must discuss the art, then pepper your platitudes with pompous phraseology, e.g., "The seasonal color hues give rise to the pixilated optical shimmer inherent in the point-less-istic period."

11. Relegate all discussion to sound-bites and hit and run conversations.

12. Remember, the important thing is to get invited to or information about the next party — the point of life being to be seen at the best events.

13. For maximum impression, don't show up anywhere. As soon as you show up, your importance declines in a direct ratio.

Under Any Circumstances

THADDEUS RUTKOWSKI

Don't put a dry bean in your nostril and poke it with your finger until you can't reach it anymore.

Don't stick a fork or other utensil into an electrical outlet or, in your own words, "Don't play with the plugger place."

Don't ride your bicycle at full speed across an active roadway without looking both ways or stopping.

Don't take a magnifying glass outside on a sunny day and incinerate ants.

Don't light a firecracker and hold it in your hand until it explodes and leaves a wet, circular blister.

Don't stuff match heads into a closed metal pipe until the device has the killing power of a grenade.

Don't place a shotgun shell on its end and hammer a nail into its firing cap.

Don't pretend you are shooting BBs at a paper target when in fact you are shooting at human beings.

Don't tie a child to the crossbar of a swing set and leave him to be discovered by his mother.

Don't bait your schoolteachers by giving them quizzical looks while they are trying to lecture on serious topics, like civics and physics.

Don't break into the school building through the rooftop trapdoor and steal as many video recorders as you can carry.

Don't stand by the highway and throw goonies through the windshields of passing cars.

Don't shoot songbirds with your .22 in a safety zone or even in a non-safety zone.

Don't argue with your parents so intensely that you get sent to a foster home.

Don't fight with your foster parents so much that you get sent back to your original home.

Don't disrupt a local wedding ceremony and make the newlyweds' relatives beat you like a piñata.

Don't knock on the door of a fraternity house with a baseball bat and shout, "Send out your biggest brother."

Don't antagonize a shirtless man by digging your fingers into his pectoral muscles and lifting him off the ground.

Don't say to the person returning the gloves you left at a bar, "If you can take them from me, you can keep them."

Don't get thrown through the bar's window in such a way that the glass leaves a gash down your back.

Don't park your car where it can be rammed by a vengeful road warrior.

Don't, as you are leaving for a new life in a different state on another coast, even think of coming back to where the trouble began.

Four pieces from Peops

Fly

HOW MUCH PERSONAL INFORMATION ARE YOU COMFORTABLE WITH REVEALING TO OTHER PEOPLE TO MAKE YOUR POINT?-OR MAYBE JUST TO GET SOMETHING OUT OF YOUR SYSTEM? - ARE YOU TALKING TO ONE PERSON WHO HAS YOUR CONFIDENCE OR ARE YOU WRITING A SONG FOR EVERYONE IN THE WORLD TO LISTEN TO? THERE ARE THINGS THAT PEOPLE SHOULD KNOW ABOUT BUT THAT DOESN'T MEAN THEY HAVE TO KNOW THE DETAILS OF YOUR LIFE & THAT DOESN'T MEAN INTERROGATE YOU - ITS ACKNOWLEDGE & DEAL WITH YOU THAT WERE BEYOND THEN TO BE REQUIRED TO ONLY WHAT HAPPENED THEN TO TALK ABOUT IT NOW -

THEY HAVE THE RIGHT TO HARD ENOUGH FOR YOU TO THINGS THAT HAPPENED TO YOUR CONTROL - BUT TO JUSTIFY & EXPLAIN NOT BUT WHY YOU ARE TRYING WILL MAKE YOU QUESTION YOUR OWN RIGHT TO FULLY EX PRESS YOUR SELF WHILE NOT FULLY EXPOSING YOURSELF. PEOPLE WILL TELL YOU THAT "YOU BROUGHT IT UP!" & THEREFORE YOU ARE EXPECTED TO ANSWER TO THEIR INTERROGATION OF YOUR PERSONAL DETAILS ... ITS UP TO YOU - YOU CAN BE POLITE OR YOU CAN TELL THEM TO GO FCK THMSELVS - JUST REMEMBER YOU ARE NOT OBLIGATED TO JUSTIFY YRSLF TO ANYONE ... DONT RESPECT SOMEONE WHOSE GOT NO RESPECT

MAY 18 - FLY·2K

I BROKE MY TOE JUMPIN INTO THE WELL OF A 48 IN THE CHICAGO TRAIN YARD - RUNNIN FROM THE BULLS - I HAD CAUGHT OUT & THE TRAIN I WAS ON WENT TO ANOTHER YARD & THEY WERE DOIN WORK ON IT SO I THOUGHT THEY WERE DUMPIN ME SO I RAN TO GET ON ANOTHER TRAIN & THATS WHEN THE BULLS SPOTTED ME SO I RAN BACK A FEW CARS THEY WERE COMIN WITH SEARCHLIGHTS SO I WANTED TO GET FAR BACK FROM WHERE THEY SAW ME - I CROSSED OVER SOME STRINGS & WENT FURTHER BACK TO WHAT I HOPED WAS MY TRAIN & JUMPT IN THE WELL OF THE 48 LANDED BUSTED MY TOE & FREAKT OUT FOR AWHILE - THE STRING WAS BACKIN UP TO THE MIDDLE OF THE YARD SO I DECIDED TO BALE - I HOBBLED OVER TO THE EDGE OF THE YARD & THEY SPOTTED ME I HAD TO SLIDE ON MY ASS TO THE STREETS BELOW & I WAS 100% LOST ON THE SOUTH SIDE OF CHICAGO ON A SAT. NIGHT - LOOKT FOR A LIGHTED AREA TO ASK DIREC- SHUNS & FOUND A LIQUOR STORE & BAR & INSIDE THERE WERE SOME OLD BLACK MEN SO I BANGED ON THE DOOR & THEY BUZZD ME IN - I ASKD DIREC- SHUNS BACK TO ASHLAND YARD & THEY SAW MY GUITAR & I ENDED UP PLAYIN SOME SONGS FOR THEM & THEY GAVE ME WHISKEY & TOLD ME HOW TO GET BACK TO THE TRAIN YARD...

I MADE IT BACK TO NYC I WAS ALREADY "REZO" SO THEN I BECAME "BROKE TOE REZO" - I FIRST GOT INTO OLD BLUES MUSIC WHEN I DROVE OUT TO CALI ONE WINTER WITH A VAN OF PUNKS TO GET SOME GOOD DRUGS - ON THE WAY BACK SOME ONE WAS PLAYING A ROBERT JOHNSON TAPE & I HAD NEVER HEARD ANYTHING LIKE IT CUZ I WAS A NARROW MINDED PUNK - WHEN WE STARTED DOING PIRATE RADIO I DID A SHOW ABOUT OLD BLUES MUSIC - THEN I GOT A GUITAR I CALLED IT "GREIF" CUZ I HAD JUST BROKEN UP WITH A GIRL - SO I STARTED PLAYIN THE BLUES...

WHEN I WAS 18 YRS OLD I WAS LOCKED UP IN A MENTAL HOSPITAL FOR 5 MONTHS... THE POLICE FOUND ME WALKING ON THE SUBWAY TRACKS I THOUGHT THE WORLD WAS GONNA END & WE WOULD ALL BE BROAD CAST ON PRIME TIME T.V. - I DID 2½ MONTHS IN A PUBLIC INSTITUTION & 2½ MONTHS IN A PLACE MY MOM FOUND CALLED "WORK LIFE" ... WHEN THEY PICKED ME UP I HADN'T SLEPT IN 2 MONTHS CUZ I GOT SICK & I HAD A REACTION TO THE PENICILLON THEN THEY GAVE ME PREDNIZON WHICH IS A HARD CORE STEROID & IT TOTALLY FCKT ME UP I COULDN'T SLEEP I WAS 18 YRS OLD IN PORTLAND GOING TO SCHOOL & I WAS A LUNATIC - IT WENT FROM STARTING A FOOD CO-OP TO CREATING MY OWN CURRENCY & DESTABILIZING THE AMERICAN ECONOMY - I STARTED THINKING THE RADIO WAS TALKING TO ME & BILLBOARDS - I'D SEE TOO MANY MEANINGS IN THE WORDS — AYAHUASCA - I WAS EATING THAT ROOT & STUDYING ANTHRO-LINGUISTICS I GOT SO I COULDN'T EVEN FINISH A SENTENCE - I WENT TO BERKELEY & MY FRIENDS THERE SAW THAT I WAS CRAZY & THEY CALLED MY MOM

I WISH I WAS A PIGEON IN THE SKY

WHY ARE THERE SO MANY SONGS ABOUT RAIN BOWS?

STOP THE DROOLING...

ALL MY FRIENDS... BOOKS FOR I STOLE & NOBLES AT BARNE TO WORK I WENT THEN WHEN I GOT OUT PUT ME IN "WORK LIFE 2½ MONTHS MY MOM WOULD SING ME IGGY POP SONGS — AFTER AN EX JUNKIE - SHE ONLY FRIEND WAS IRIS IN WHITE PLAINS MY

MY MOM SENT THEM A LANE TICKET & TOLD THEM O GET ME ON A PLANE — WAS STILL TAKING THE PREDNIZON DOING SIT UPS & PUSH UPS & ITCHING - I WAS CONVINCED THERE WERE ICROSCOPIC TRANSMITERS UNDER MY KIN - I WAS CONVINCED THE WORLD WAS BOUT TO END & THERE WAS A PLOT & WAS THE ONLY ONE WHO COULD SEE IT

DROOL - SO THEN THEY GAVE ME A NEW DRUG SIT & WATCH MYSELF THAT I WOULD JUST ME SO MANY DRUGS MONTHS - THEY GAVE WAS THERE FOR 2 WHITE PLAINS & I A WEEK LATER IN GAVE ME DRUGS & I WOKE UP LIKE THERE WAS A T.V. SET - THEY & THEY TOOK ME TO BELLEVUE WHERE ME & MY MOM CAME & SIGNED PAPERS FOR ME - EVENTUALLY THEY CAUGHT THEY HAD TO STOP THE TRAINS

I THOUGHT MY MOM WAS PART OF THIS PLOT SO I LEFT MY HOUSE & WALKED TO L.E.S. & COULDN'T FIND ANY ONE SO I WENT TO THE SUBWAY & WALKED THE TRACKS FRM 23rd ST TO CHRISTOPHER & I THOUGHT I WAS BEING BROADCAST ON THAT SHOW 'COPS' - I THOUGHT THE WORLD WAS GONNA END BUT IT WOULD BE O.K. BECAUSE WE WOULD ALL LIVE ON -ON T.V. ....

FLY - 1999

SASCHA MADE US ALL GO UP TO THE ROOF FOR THE SUNSET - HE COULDN'T STOP SMILING - 08/02/99

VERMONT THEN MINNEAPOLIS & PORTLAND - WELL ACTUALLY I GREW UP IN MINNEAPOLIS FIRST THEN I WENT TO VERMONT TO GO TO COLLEGE BUT I DROPPED OUT & I WAS WORKING FOR AN ANARCHIST ECOLOGICAL SUMMER PROGRAM & I WOULD TRY TO COME TO NYC TO TRY TO HELP WITH USEFUL ACTIONS LIKE IN MAYBE 1989 THE CUNY STUDENTS WERE OCCUPYING THE SCHOOL & WE CAME TO HELP THEM & IT WAS WEIRD - A COUPLE COMMUNISTS & COUPLE STUDENTS & US JUST WAITING AROUND FOR THE COPS TO COME & THEY DIDN'T - I WENT BACK TO MINNEAPOLIS CUZ MY MOM WAS SUICIDAL & THE KIDS THERE WERE DOING MORE INTERESTING THINGS POLITICALLY LIKE HAVING PUKE-INS - I WAS THERE FOR ABOUT A YEAR & A HALF & THEN I LEFT CUZ IT WAS JUST TOO HARD TAKING CARE OF MY MOM- SHE WAS REALLY DEPRESSED- I WENT TO PORTLAND TO GO TO COLLEGE SO I COULD BECOME REALLY SMART BUT WHEN I GOT THERE I MET SOME SCAREY STUDENTS & I COULDN'T GET FINANCIAL AID CUZ I WASN'T OLD ENUFF SO INSTEAD OF COLLEGE I GOT INVOLVED IN A FUCKTUP COLLECTIVE HOUSE, TRIED TO HELP OUT RAISING SOME KIDS- WENT OUT WITH A HIPPIE WHO PUT UP BLACK PANTHER FLIERS TRYING TO GET PEOPLE TO RISE UP!!! AFTER THE FUCKTUP SUPPOSED COLLECTIVE HOUSE I MOVED INTO A PUNK HOUSE & WE DID A ZINE CALLED ☆➚

"THIS IS A WINDOW THIS IS A ANIMAL" - I WOULD RIDE THE BUS AROUND PORTLAND & GIVE IT TO PEOPLE WHO LOOKED LIKE THEY MIGHT NEED A ZINE — I WAS TALKING TO MY AUNT IN SAN FRANCISCO WHO HAD A WEAVING BUSINESS & HER WORK LOAD HAD JUST DOUBLED SO I SAID I WOULD COME TO S.F. & WORK FOR HER IF SHE WOULD TEACH ME TO WEAVE - THE DAY I MOVED TO S.F. I DROVE THERE JUST IN TIME TO SEE HER COMPETING IN A WEIGHT LIFTING COMPETITION - SHE WAS AT THE TIME A US CHAMPION WOMEN'S WEIGHT LIFTER - BUT A COUPLE YRS LATER SHE DROPPED A WEIGHT & EXPLODED HER ANKLE - I STARTED DOING DORIS RIGHT WHEN I MOVED TO S.F. I DON'T WANT TO TELL THE STORY OF THE NAME BECUZ PEOPLE NEVER UNDERSTAND IT...

FLY. 09/07/2K CINDY AT MY HOUSE NYC

The Rolling Donut

Jim Knipfel

Being, as I am, well, blind, and working as a "journalist"—which only means that I write stories which appear in a newspaper, several of which having dealt with being blind—I wasn't so surprised when she called. I'd received calls like this before.

She gave me her name, which I promptly forgot, then went on to explain that she was a social worker, mobility trainer and an activist, who was making a documentary film about the blind, and wanted me to be in it. She never actually used the word "blind"—instead she used "visually-impaired"—which should've put the zap on my head immediately that I was dealing with one of *Them*. One of those insipid, correct-speaking morons who insisted on placing labels which only They seem to understand on the nation's retards and cripples. Nevertheless, I agreed to meet with her. I can be awfully stupid sometimes. I had dealt, and struggled, with people like this before—I'd spent the previous two years, in fact, clawing my way slowly through the nightmarish bureaucracy of the New York State Commission for the Blind and Visually Handicapped, and all I got out of it, really, was a recipe for how to make a nice casserole. Answering a few questions for a filmmaker seemed like a piece of cake compared to what I'd already been through.

When she showed up at the newspaper's offices a week later, she brought no movie cameras with her—which was strange, I thought, for someone making a documentary film.

We sat down at my desk, and she explained that she was indeed interested in making a film, but had never really done such a thing before, hadn't talked to anyone about how to do it, had no money to do it, but thought it might be a neat thing to try one day. She explained that right now, she was just going around, talking to various "members of the visually-impaired community" (which I don't consider myself), to gather up some of their stories, and see what sort of ideas developed. She had, it seems, no fucking clue where to begin with any of this..

Christ, another waste of time, I thought.

But it was worse than that.

She was a small, gray-haired woman with puffy, bulging eyes and a frog mouth. Probably in her early sixties. Something about the way she carried herself, the quiet, slow manner in which she spoke, was rife with hippie. I could smell it on her. Anyone who refers to herself as an "advocate" of anything was bound to be bad news. It soon became apparent that even gathering material for a movie was the furthest thing from her mind. No, she was on a mission. She wanted to *help* me.

"Here..." she said slowly (I think she might've been stoned, come to think of it). She reached into the large shoulder bag she was carrying and removed something, placing it in the desk in front of me. "Try this."

I picked it up and looked at it. It was a folding blind-man's cane. No big deal—

I had three of them at home, and one in my bag at work, to use after I left the bar that night. Only difference with this one was that the white tip was as large and as round as the wheel on a Tonka truck.

Blind-man cane tips come in several varieties. Your basic tip is just a cone-shaped piece of plastic. It's fine, except for the fact that it tends to get stuck in sidewalk cracks. Any uneven surface, in fact, will stop it dead. Myself, I use something called a "rolling marshmallow tip." As the name implies, it's about the size and shape of a marshmallow (one of the big ones), and is equipped with ball bearings, so you can roll it smoothly back and forth over bumps in the sidewalk as you shamble down the street. This thing, here, was like a fucking donut.

"Yeah, that's very nice," I said.

"It works better than what you're using."

"Uh-huh." She had been in my office for five minutes, and I was already bored nauseous.

"You can keep it," she said in that same, slow voice.

"Yeah, that's very kind," I replied. "Thank you."

"Try it."

"Pardon?"

"*Try...it.*" It sounded vaguely like a threat. I should have started whacking her in the head with the thing at that point, until she fled. But I didn't. I always make that mistake with people like her. Instead, I stood up, let the collapsible cane flop open, and rolled it back and forth across the carpet half-heartedly.

"Yes, that's very nice," I told her, trying to be as pleasant as possible, even though my jaws were beginning to clench up.

I could feel her staring at me. "But you're not doing it right," she said eventually.

Oh, Jesus. I handed the cane back to her. "Why don't you *show* me how to do it, then?"

"You see, I have a new technique, which works much better than yours. It covers more ground."

"Uh-huh." She stood up and demonstrated. Whereas the technique I was taught has the cane tap out a two-foot arc in front of me, hers seemed to involve tapping directly in front of the right foot only, which made little sense—what happens to the left foot? When she was finished, she said proudly, "See? It's better that way."

"I'll keep that in mind," I told her.

"Will you use it?" Her voice was full of desperation and yearning. It was pathetic. She was like a drowning Amway salesman.

"Yeah, whatever, I'll think about it."

"*When* will you start using it?"

"*Jesus*, lady—when I wear my cane out, okay? Then I'll use it. How's *that*?" I spat out the "that" perhaps a little too sharply. Hippies' feelings are so easily hurt.

She seemed satisfied with that answer, and a few minutes later, she left.

Two weeks later, she called again, with the same goddamn movie pitch. Did she think I'd forgotten? She asked again if she could come back and interview me. And I, again, agreed. To this day, I don't know why.

When she showed up the next time, she at least had a tape recorder with her. One of those ancient, top-loading Panasonic jobs with the heavy buttons. The case was held together with masking tape.

We sat down at my desk again, she pushed the record buttons, and then started talking. Not asking questions—just talking. About what a "magical" world blindness must create, and what a "beautiful" place it must be to live in.

I just sat there with my mouth open. What was this woman thinking? Who was she trying to help with this bullshit? While going blind never bothered me all that much, it was—and I've said this elsewhere—a royal pain in the ass. There's nothing "magical" about running into walls or tripping over boxes. And there was nothing "beautiful" in the struggle to stumble home from the bar every night.

"Look," I finally interrupted her monologue, "I have no idea what you're talking about. The only thing that's 'magic' about being blind is when somebody rearranges the furniture." It was a half-joke, which I didn't even understand after I said it. I was getting too furious. I hated these people who thought that the crippled somehow had to develop some kind of mystical powers in order to compensate.

"But I put on a blindfold once, and walked around my apartment, and it was amazing what—"

"Yeah, fine—" I cut her off. "You got to play at it for a little while. You also got to take the blindfold *off* whenever you wanted to. I can't do that."

That almost shut her up. I hated to resort to that kind of cheap histrionics, but for someone in her position, she sure as hell didn't know what she was dealing with.

"Are you using your new cane yet?" she asked.

I sighed. "No," I told her.

"Why not?" she asked, like a teacher asking me why I hadn't done my homework.

I, very patiently, and with as much kindness as I could muster, suggested that I'd had quite enough, that she should take her tape recorder down to the blind apartment complex on 23rd St., where they'd be more than happy to talk to her about what an "empowering" experience blindness was. Those people make me sick, too. She seemed taken aback, but left.

A week later, the threatening letters started arriving at the paper. Even though the letters were unsigned, she made little attempt to disguise who was behind them—all the letters made reference to the rolling donut cane she gave me.

I let them come. After years of being pushed to the edge by these people, I was glad to see that I had finally done the same to one of them.

Marble Tower

PETER BUSHYEAGER

There's a contest at work, an international competition among major corporations. Whomever breaks a five-foot-tall styrofoam egg in the correct way is the winner. Each corporation's egg is in a special color. My company's egg is navy blue, which the consultant determined is one of my strongest colors. I'm a "summer" person — the Classic type, with a tinge of Romantic. My other prime colors are burgundy, cadet blue, soft white to pure white, powder blue, pastel aqua, mauve, pastel pink, rose pink, orchid and raspberry. I must avoid green or cocoa-brown. Shiny or black is death.

My metals are silver or white gold — yellow gold would leave a coarse impression. If I were a woman my furs would be my hair shade or lighter, and my eyeshadow would be in soft, grayed tones. As a Classic, my handshake is firm and my eye contact direct. My collars are regular or spread, in the English manner.

It's the day before the contest, when each contestant is supposed to break their egg, gather up the pieces and fly with them to Brazil where the winner will be announced. I shut the door to my office, break the egg with a wood mallet and instantly realize that I've done it in the winning way. I move on to the next step of the competition: cutting letters of lunch meat that spell out our marketing slogan. It's slow going — the pressed ham is slimy and cut too thin. But eventually I finish the project, despite the fact that the slogan includes many "w's."

Then I lay out the letters on a board. I'm never able to actually put all the words together. I know each letter is there, but they keep flopping around and getting scrambled. Eventually, I put the letters in plastic ziploc bags, store them in a refrigerator and leave for home.

Twenty blocks from the office, I realize that I should have documented with photos the breaking of the navy-blue egg. Or probably shouldn't have broken the egg at all. Who will trust my word?

This is an anxious situation. Tomorrow I have to be in Brasilia and I speak poor Portuguese. That's enough pressure; how can I throw in a last-minute photo session as well? Should I reconstitute the egg and rebreak it at the competition? Would this be fraud? Would the egg break in the same winning way?

My mode of transportation back uptown: a seven-foot-long tubular foam pillow covered with fabric flecked with hard remnants of cotton bolls. I lay down on my stomach, the fabric scratches my belt buckle and the static that's created carries me on a thin monorail back to the office district.

Before I can open the door to my office, I run into Tina, the consultant, in her black silk pantsuit. She's apple-cheeked and blonde, and she's smiling in a way that makes her look stunned — that split-second after an unexpected slap. She is positive, excited and reports her observations to the Secretary, who every day writes her a check for $3,000.

"It's a team problem; we need a workshop," she says, and asks me to share my earliest memories of being on a team. My memory: a tug of war game at camp. I'm not sure if this incident, which comes to mind immediately, is a complete fabrication that meshes well with her workshop, or an actual memory that dredged itself up when bidden.

One thing's for sure. Everything I say, every expression of emotion or attitude will be recorded by Tina, then spilled out on the Secretary's antique roundtable like an old-fashioned ticker tape.

Tina has mastered the Rotarian, direct eye-to-eye thing. She can't make her voice boom, but she can appear out of nowhere in her flapping silk, striding fresh from a tennis court to the elevator that runs up the center of our marble column. Sixty floors up, she'll make an unexpected appearance through the elevator door that masquerades as a utility closet. Then she'll "light up" her eyes — just like my mother taught me before I went out on dates at 16 — by imagining a huge lottery prize or the most wonderful sex.

Building a Better Casket

Arthur Nersesian

At an early age Irving Malio found himself the proprietor of a dying business. It was the family funeral home and his father's untimely demise left him in charge. This was in the Cobble Hill section of Brooklyn, where the mortuary market was tight and competitive. Consequently, one had to be sharp to survive. Irving hired an innovative embalmer from Baltimore and took personal charge in the reconstruction of cadavers. With a fine eye for mood and variation, he watched his business quickly grow.

After a while, even though he charged more, those in the neighborhood who could afford it patronized him. Much of his clientele were underworld types and bullet holes were not infrequent. Unless one saw a bullet-hammered face before it had been worked on, Irving's artistic sensibilities could not truly be appreciated — the angle of a coffin, the application of a fragrance, the resculptured nose. Wax was his marble. His motto became: "Why have a closed coffin funeral, when we can keep it open?"

Soon the most mangled of the Northeast were brought to him: car accident cases, air-flight victims, the mauled and the bloated. One unfortunate had his nose and most of his face scraped off by a speeding cab. It made the cover of the *Post*. Malio arrived just after the ambulance. An optimistic paramedic had collected the dangling respiratory orifice and was applying CPR. For Malio time was money so he pulled the lad off the ill-fated and explained, "Boy, you got to learn when to do mouth to mouth and when to stick an apple in the mouth." The well meaning youth surrendered up the corpse.

Some time after the CPR incident, while a group of pall bearers were hoisting an unusually corpulent corpse, the body snapped through the coffin's bottom, plopping to the floor. Mourners shrieked. The incident turned nasty, and while watching his underlings scoop up the remains, Irving experienced an epiphany concerning the shortcomings of coffins. He later explained the problem to his embalmer:

"These coffins ain't gonna last."

"Huh?"

"I say they're no damned good."

"What?

"They fall apart before they hit the dirt."

"Right."

"What do you think we ought to do?

"Definitely."

"Definitely what?"

"I'm gettin some coffee — Want some?

He tried discussing the problem with others but none seemed to grasp it. One guy finally came back with, "You're scared to die, that's all right." But that wasn't it at all. It was the boxes. They didn't hold up for anywhere near eternity. And this was his profession, dammit!

One afternoon while stuffing a coffin he made a resolution, "No way am I going in one of these."

He mentioned this to the embalmist, who replied, "You gonna smoke, eh?"

"No, not like that." There seemed to be something hypocritical about being cremated, after all this was his craft and trade.

"Then you're going in there." The embalmist pointed to the coffin.

"No, not that either."

"What then?"

And Irving couldn't reply. This question obsessed him for the longest time. He began to suffer from an easily interpreted nightmare: He was drowning because the life preserver he was clinging to was defective. With fear, commitment and a lucrative enterprise providing the funds, he addressed the question passionately. He collected data and wrote people who prided themselves on these matters. Soon, with wires and toothpicks and papier mache, he was fashioning model upon model, little vessels designed to conquer the hereafter. Then a pile of mouse size coffins littered the house, each one better than the last, approaching that perfect container. Finally, one day, it was done, and once again he felt secure around his embalmist.

A couple of days later, though, at his Aunt Lucy's house, he overheard a TV program, *Star Trek*, and with the opening line, "Space, the final frontier," his heart sank. He was so crushed by the thought that his vessel might someday have to navigate the stars, he cremated his masterpiece.

To accept that the earth is finite and thus doomed to dust was hard enough, but that he, plain old Irving Malio, would have to create a structure to outlast it was confounding. Inevitably, he would have to deal with things like space and time and half-lives, so he consulted an astrophysicist, an astronomer, a geologist and a chemist. He spent hours on the computer, weaving his way through conflicting schools of thought and theory. He was noticed by the CIA, who dashed off a memo.

It bothered him how his hunt for the grail seemed to slink through so many classifications and subjects. Such craziness. But patiently, he pursued it. The final version was to be an oval, buoyant craft of golden luster. It was forged personally for him in Paterson, New Jersey, and the chemical makeup was never to be known to anyone except Irving.

Irving's quest occurred while he was still relatively young. No one was particularly concerned with his eccentricity: No children to find him weird, no wife to fret, no responsible neighbors to suspect. By the age of twenty-nine, Irving slipped his masterpiece into a Long Island warehouse on long-term storage. He took a bride, also Italian. They had children: two boys and a girl. The children went to school, Malio worked and his wife kept house. Happy times, sad times. They had good meals, watched lots of TV and immeasurably grew older and older. And one autumn afternoon, Irving died.

When the will was read, all realized that there was something about this man, some unusual potential, that no one ever thought he possessed. A clause of his will made an incumbance upon the distribution of his inheritance and benefits that Irving be buried in his special coffin.

The family decided that to save the cost of probate court, and since the coffin was already constructed, they would execute the last will and testament.

There were some difficulties in finding the coffin as the warehouse had burnt down and it was assumed that the box was destroyed with it, but it turned out the coffin was the only salvaged item on the insurance manifest. They had to stick Irving's body in refrigeration for a time, while they hunted down the coffin. In the interim the neighborhood heated up over the coffin question. Theories evolved, revolved: Fame? Art? Mental Illness? The coffin was eventually found in the dead storage department of the Museum of Natural History; nobody was quite certain how it got there. During the wake, it caused quite a stir. More came to see the coffin than the deceased. During the three-day wake, the funeral parlor, to judge by the type of people that came to observe, began to resemble an art gallery. One 'artist' even requested to lie down in the coffin, explaining that through this perspective he could understand the man and his motives. The ushers escorted the 'artist' out. The final verdict was that the coffin looked like a tarnished space probe.

After the wake, and all the fuss and fudget, when the procession finally delivered the coffin to the cemetery, the head gravedigger explained that the coffin couldn't be buried. By its sheer weight, it would crush the graves below it, and by its size it pushed into three future grave lots. On top of that, the gravedigger, a scholarly bull, cited both union rules and civil ordinance. They were in a pickle.

First, the guests panicked, then gradually they turned grim and silent. The gravedigger stood his ground leaning on a spade, waiting for them to load the coffin back into the hearse. When Irving Junior's wife learned about the impasse, she moved quietly up to Irving Junior's side and whispered, "We've spent five hundred dollars on caterers, for afterwards. We've got to leave dad here!" Irving Junior, who had the same resourceful mind as his pop, slipped the gravedigger a fin and that was that. The coffin was laid into the earth.

Three weeks later a shroud of grass grew over the gravesite, and it was as if the lot had never been disturbed.

A family of centipedes accumulated on the smooth surface of the shell, and on one occasion the littlest of them attempted to gnaw into it. He was the first of many organisms to do so, but for all of them it was to no avail. The gravedigger had predicted one thing correctly: within ten years, the egg caved into a grave below. This turned out to be that of Irving's mother who had not yet properly deteriorated.

One young groundskeeper watched as a clutter of squirrels pushed and pulled over something. By discoloration, it looked almost plastic. When the keeper shooed them away, he could hardly have guessed that the blue spongy pebble was the tip of Malio's mother's nose.

Exterminating the Angels

Rob Hardin

> "I believe my father has been unequally blamed for my failures. But surely, if he had given me the six-year-old homosexual 'blow job' oral stimulation that I was entitled to, like most other people get, I would never have taken LSD without his permission."
>
> —Herbert Mullin, schizophrenic murderer

One Sunday morning in a mangy East Burnside dive, Dornald Phortz awakened to the din of insects. The sound came to him slowly through a haze of dreamed applause. Piercing that haze was a thin and irritating sound—the clink of a music box muffled by desiccated gnats. "Dried pupae. How lovely," he thought. "Now back to sleep."

Groaning, he pulled the coversheet over his head. But the nattering voices continued to keep him awake. Then a tiny wingéd bastard dove past Dornald's ear, its shriek comprising a single, suicidal vowel. Reflexively, Dornald swatted it. Blood licked the crease in his palm.

His fingers twitched open like a defective power window. In his palm, he found a Cheerio halo that flickered as it vanished. Beneath it lay a minute disemboweled figure holding a cornet smashed flat. Its translucent wings were partly severed. They flipped and shivered in the breeze of Dornald's gasps.

A Lilliputian boot-heel dangled from Dornald's pinkie-nail. It wasn't the most agreeable sight to accompany Dornald's return to consciousness, but it was no worse than his usual vision of a triple-breasted Jesus nursing Mary Magdalene as she beat the Poppin' Fresh Dough-Boy with a car antenna bent into Hitchcock's silhouette.

Hissing, Dornald wiped the doll-thing's entrails on the bedpost. He was no more disgusted by the milky-white ooze than he might have been by a phalanx of iguana kidneys attempting to catapult themselves into his spittoon (and lately, that had happened a lot). He glanced at the clock, which read 11:30 A.M. If he hustled, he might make it downstairs in time for a cholesterol-rich breakfast.

Springing from his mattress into what he'd presumed would be the splendor of noon, Dornald found himself surrounded by a swirl of glittering insects. "Jesus Pillsbury Fuck!" he screamed at the infestation.

He recited a table of square roots based on the catechism, gazed into the swarm and followed its trajectory. It whirled past his mattress, through the open window and out into the sky, where tiny figures hovered—obliviously—with flimsy harps and tawdry firefly nimbuses.

"Wait a minute," he whispered. "Those things are only *wearing* human faces."

He headed for the can and vomited into his urine donga. He couldn't stop picturing the angels' obscenity. Their features were all camouflage, vestigal approximations, as insensate as the hypomorphic mutations of the tobacco budworm. Why, these micromorphs had less in common with men than sentient aspic. What was more, only he, Dornald Phortz, was equipped to deal with their infestation. Only he had anticipated the arrival of the chintzy cherubim. Only he was the progeny of a juggler who had founded a sex cult devoted to the pleasures of the unicycle. Only he had owned and understood the holy tome, *Embraced by Angels*, by William A. Burt (Signet Paperbacks)—superficially a tone-deaf medley of new age rumor, but to discerning peepers, a cookbook for divine insecticide.

Reaching into his pocket, Dornald pulled out a beaker, a lighter, a tube of mascara, a calligraphy pen, a plumber's glossary, a plastic dashboard cast of hands steepled in prayer, and a chunk of fluorescent pink chalk. He placed the objects on a nearby end-table. His copy of the angel cookbook lay under the bed. Carefully, he eased the well-worn paperback out of its hiding place. Dust-bunnies trailed the spine like a Fu Manchu.

" 'Making angel contact is a very personal experience,' " he read aloud, skewering a hapless seraph with his calligraphy pen. " 'You really need to be alone and at peace with yourself to get in the proper frame of mind.' " His voice was momentarily drowned out by a score of seraphs crushed with a well-aimed chunk of the *Plumber's Glossary*. Unfazed, he continued to read:

" 'It's very important to your well-being to spend quiet moments by yourself. After all, you are not alone.' " A cluster of seraphs landed on the table. He picked up the dashboard hands and aimed them at the tiny crowd. " 'An angel is only a meditative thought away.' " Helium screams issued from the seraphs as he diced their spines with the point of the praying hands.

But for all Dornald's diligence, there was one seraph who proved too agile for his mincemanship. It proved to be the most pernicious seraph of all.

Larger than the others, it rose from the table with apparent effort. Filaments of black smoke flowed from its tremulous wings. Its sclerae were as heavily veined as those of a dragster-crazed dybbuk by Big "Daddy" Roth. It glared at Dornald, veered perilously near, then swerved past his head. "The name is Michael," it rasped.

The seraph's bloated belly and dart-shooting tooter were unlike anything Donald had ever hallucinated. Its thorax, dark with densely-haired supernumerary legs, drooped just above Dornald's forehead. Its bug-toy trumpet, affixed with a miniature crossbow, depended from its hands. "Honk honk," Dornald mocked. Unfazed, the seraph dove at Dornald again. Cosmologically, it was clearly a Kamikaze proxy.

"Me or you," Dornald whispered to the flatulent phantasm. "Get ready to be pulverized into smaller segments than your nephew's compound eyes."

Eyes trained on the seraph, Dornald tore a shred of wallpaper from the dumbwaiter. He placed it in the beaker, ignited it with the lighter and swallowed the flames. Mesmerized, the seraph flew into Dornald's mouth. "Aha!" he thought as he bit through the seraph's head. "Love them barbecued wings," he said—savoring the tickle of gossamer on his tongue.

As soon as the seraph's body went slack, haloed bees materialized and surrounded Dornald's head: Huge, fuzzy hymenoptera with human tongues in place of stingers.

"Don't you dare interrupt me," Dornald warned. "Your camouflage doesn't fool me for a moment. The Amazing Criswell was right: You're all butterflies with grafted bat-ears in place of wings."

He tried to shoo away the bees, but the effort was futile. They continued to lick him angrily until his chest was slick with saliva. Disgusted, he spit out the seraph's head: The huge bees vanished instantly.

"Where was I," Dornald inquired of the medical students in the amphitheater of his own skull. "Oh right." Sweeping up the book, he resumed his incantation against the seraphs. This time, he peppered William Burt's text with memorized phrases from *The Commentaries of AL*, by Aleistar Crowley, punctuating each strong accent with a fatal pen-jab to a pygmy seraph—who echoed each jab with a faint but satisfying aieee. "The *Khu* is not in the *Khabs*! The *Khabs* are in the *Khu*!" Dornald intoned. Below him, four dazed seraphs drifted to the floor.

Now that the seraphim were relegated to the abyss, he needed a fetish object with which to defile the cherubim. Burt's recipe book promised that a hidden treasure chest contained the answer. Sliding his arm under the bed, Dornald snagged a box containing a woman's fur-lined gloves. ("Extremities!" he whispered gleefully.) Turning the pink chalk between his fingers, he bent forward to draw a circle; within the circle, he sketched the diagram of a woman's foot. Sections of the foot were demarcated by Hebrew symbols and German characters with daisies in place of umlauts. A tiny five-pointed high-heel punctuated each division of the circle.

Carefully, he centered the glove-box over the diagram. Around it, he arranged tiny powder-piles of crystallized Dr. Scholl's ointment, which he lit with a match.

As the piles smoldered, the cherubim began to shriek with a grating, tinkly sound, rather like that of an eight-bit sample of wind-chimes played through an amplified stethoscope. Their wings shrank to bulbous prehensile thumbs. "Blow me, Uriel," Dornald taunted. "Ye stinkbug Cupids. Ye ass-wipe arthropods."

The cherubim nose-dove downward, smacked the floor and disintegrated to clumps of coarse white hairs. "The pentagram did its jobbo and then some (ding honk toot)," a disembodied voice remarked.

Despite the tally of Dornald's flophouse massacre, the Thrones, Dominions and Virtues still hovered outside his window—too ditzy with angel-dust to notice that Dornald had morphed into a vagrant Thanatos.

Smiling at the angels—or rather, leering at God, the perplexed wrestling fan tuned to the tiny cameras implanted in the angels' faceted eyes—Dornald mixed cayenne pepper with the ashes of a living saint. Whistling "When the Saints Go Marching In," he produced a hearse's fender and hood ornament, then sprinkled the admixture over the fender. Then he opened a pouch filled with ground silver and dumped it on the hooded hood ornament. He'd wanted to powder the fender with the gold from a virgin's tooth, but had had to settle for the grated braces of his landlady's dead pooch, Gigi. "Oh well," he intoned while dumping the dregs of the torched mutt's denture-dust.

His preoccupation with the dog had allowed him to carry out the last part of the recipe verbatim. He'd found that alchemical *coup de grace* on page 271 of *Embraced by Angels*. The spell, like most alchemical knowledge, lay hidden in an apparently innocuous source: Dorothy Maclean's treatise on rousting the angelic spirit in inanimate plants.

"Basically, she enters into a meditative state, tunes into, say, a cabbage plant, and the cabbage plant's angel tells what she should be doing with the soil to make the plant grow," Maclean advised.

In this case, Dornald knew the "angel" within the stiff was trapped in the snuffed bowser's tongue. He'd spent hours curing the thing so that it dried in the shape of an upside-down L, fitting it for a miniature monk's outfit, and lacing the collar with the tongue-tip protruding slightly from the hood.

"Now that I've seen the word made insect flesh, it's time to erase the notion of the eternal," Dornald intoned. "Time to exorcise the angel. To restore old-world order to the present time."

He drew the white linen curtains clinically, as if removing an incontinent angel's diaper. He pressed his arm against the window-sill and swept away a row of Roman knick-knacks, scattering a Juno paperclip dispenser, a Piña Colada Proserpine mug, a statuette of an obscure Phoenician plebian astride a flatulent chariot, and an acrylic musical globe in which the Libitina tilted heavenward, anticipating company. He turned in the direction of the Libitina's gaze and smirked. "Matter of time," he muttered as he reached underneath the rug.

Quietly, he nudged the window wider, slipping a long rectangle of folded paper from beneath his heels. In the crease of the paper, he placed sugar, dandruff from a dead nun's habit, and the tears of a sinner. No angel could resist the mixed essences of virtue and sin—the taint of evil and the promise of purity.

He recited this incantation from the angel cookbook: "My abdomen is warm and comfortable. Let your jaw drop comfortably. You want to feel your jaw hanging by its own weight. Close your eyes and relax. Choose a snack from a happy time in the past, such as meat loaf. . . ."

Soon enough, a tiny Throne with a wobbly chicken-gaze flew to the window-sill. Wings quivered as the Throne fed on the fragrant poison. Its gestures, which evoked prayer, were fueled by mechanical hunger.

Coral-pink smoke spumed from the admixture as the cloud of Thrones, Virtues and Dominions descended on the window-sill. As they munched on the fragrant poison, the angels' thoraxes buzzed against the edges of harps and trumpets. The collective buzz created an irritating, monotonous polyphony—as if monks at mass had pressed wax paper to their lips.

One by one, the last of the angels began to implode. Distantly, a CD of Hans Werner Henze's "Essay on Pigs" played, as the tiny undead eunuchs convulsed and sank to the floor. Stardust flew from their mouths like rice at a wedding. The bride their deaths festooned was the earth itself.

At last, only a single angel, a final Virtue, remained. It flew to the center of the room and gazed at Dornald with an expression of bewilderment. Then it gripped its stomach, raised its head, and screamed with a high child's voice. Yellow powder flew from its mouth, gathered in the air, and poured across the rug in a measured pattern. Dornald looked down and found a single word spelled in yellow: *Chastity*.

"Drop your weapon and place your hands on your head," said a voice on a megaphone. Dornald ignored the voice; he'd always heard voices. But the voice repeated its message; it seemed to emanate not from Dornald's head, but rather from the window.

Dornald looked down: a phalanx of FBI men stood below, long-range rifles trained on his forehead. To their left, a few suspended beat cops nursed tired Irish tavern songs out of bagpipes.

Dornald sighed and did as he was told: Mental illness had never prevented such moments of lucid cowardice. Clutching his pate, he watched formidable simians break down his door. They crossed his threshold with expressions of revulsion. Two mesomorphs dragged him out the door and head-first down the stairs. His forehead thudded a spastic beat on the accordion-fall of steps. Then a locked door crashed open: Blood from a burst vein mixed with the afternoon glare, assaulting him with the brilliance of a red sun.

Surrounding him, white flares dimmed to shattered aquariums. The emptied frames rested on computer tables placed incongruously on the yellow lawn. "Why'd you do it?" a castrati Popeye voice rasped. "Why'd you kill the fish, you dirty son-of-a-bitch?"

He recognized the voice instantly. It belonged to his landlord. Somewhere, the windows of a mental hospital glowed Prussian blue: This slave was free.

"Playtime's over, Photz," one of the plainclothesmen told Dornald. Expert fingers locked handcuffs around his wrists and interns lowered him onto a stretcher. His head lolled. His stare grazed the immense pink gobbet that was his landlady. She was even more amorphous when seen from upside down. Her sallow shower cap twitched in time with her eyebrows. "Animal!" she hissed at her schizoid former tenant. "Monster! Deadbeat! By the way, Detective—once word gets out he's a violent schizo, you think I should laminate his vitamin collection?"

"All schizophrenics aren't necessarily violent," the glorified beat cop told her. "But this one's got a special history. His father used to feed him DMT and quiz him on physics. When the ass didn't know the answers, Dad beat him until Mom called the cops. Years ago, we locked up the old man. You know what they say, Ma'am. Like zither, like lederhosen."

"Death penalty for you, pal," a low voice chanted. But Dornald couldn't find the speaker.

Children stood on the porch, weeping and pointing to the rows of ruined aquariums. As Dornald passed on the stretcher, the nearest child leaned down and spat. "How could you?" she screamed. "How could you kill our tropical fish?"

But when Dornald gazed at the floor below him, what he saw were not fish at all but wounded angels. Well, he did see one goldfish writhing in Michael's dead arms. But the rest were angels, as anyone could see. Children live in a dream world. No use explaining the real world to them.

As interns slid the stretcher into the ambulance and shot Dornald up with a sedative, the last thing he saw was a swarm of bees on the other side of the window-glass. Their stinger-tongues painted a word in the misted window: *THANKS*. One swarm for another, Dornald whispered to the friendly bees.

The van started forward, then settled into a slow cruise. And suddenly, William A. Burt was there, crouching down beside Dornald to pat his shoulder. "Good work, son," Burt beamed. "You understood the heart of my instruction. Like Milton's conception of Satan, an angel wants to do good but lacks wisdom and pity. Without God, a host—no, a *degradation*—of angels is worse than useless. Only an exterminator can erase the road to Hell. You are that exterminator. I'm glad you heard the Call."

Dornald's consciousness dimmed like a curtain spotlight. He dreamed he swam through black water in a distended desert, to a cavern that seemed as serene as Sunny Von Bulow's coma. "I've reached the basement of relaxation," Dornald murmured through twittery fingers. Unhaunted by demons, seraphim, dybbukim, or even bees, his was the eventual rest of the posthumous saint. He alone knew the value of his valor, the carat-weight of his bouillon-cured cojones. He alone felt relieved and that was good. The world he'd rescued slumbered undisturbed.

SURVIVE AND THRIVE IN THE WORKPLACE!

A Cute Girl's Guide™ to Temping

BETTY WOLFANGER VITALE

The following is an excerpt from the author's forthcoming book, A Cute Girl's Guide™ to Temping: How to get the most from the temporary employment industry while giving the least. Like the rest of the A Cute Girl Guide™ series, it is written in punchy and uncluttered prose. Basic responsibilities, how to get a temp job, keeping busy, apologizing and many other topics essential to survival as a temporary employee are all covered in the guide. The author, a seasoned temporary employee, gives exercises to sharpen your skills, tips that only the long time temps know, and quick reference lists that you can carry with you to the job.

Boys always like it when you cock your head to the side. It makes you look uncertain and they like a woman of uncertainty. When you are introduced to new people at the office, always use the most chocolate voice possible and look them directly in the eyes. Not in an "I am confident" way, rather in an "I might date you" way. The goal is to get them to think you are stupid, thereby avoiding conversation and not being expected to do or know anything. Once you have established the most base relationship, it can only go uphill.

But you shouldn't really try to make it go uphill. When you forget yourself and start talking about classical literature, shrug it off by saying you read it in "Time or some place like that". Under no circumstance can you admit to actually having read, understood and liked Shakespeare with the exceptions of "Romeo and Juliet" and "A Midsummer Night's Dream". And even those plays were only read under great pressure in your 12th grade English class. You most certainly are not a budding Shakespearean scholar.

Make sure you dress better than you like. This encourages misconceptions about your intelligence and reduces you to a hanger with a pleasant tone, further investing in the vixen/secretary veneer. Try to cash in on the Marlene Dietrich look you have been cultivating, do not limit your batting eyes to boys. You must hold the vamp at bay, playing the look but not the role; it is important that these respectable women not feel that you are actually trying to steal a kiss, just that you will take one if it is offered.

Playing dumb is easy, but maintaining it without feeling belittled everyday is a delicate matter and a skill that is developed only after you have fished through other people's semi-personal belongings looking for stickies. These people get sick or go away for vacation and leave their water bottles in plain view; you are expected to work around them. It is your duty to please everyone, and this seems reasonable. By performing at a lower level than you are capable, you will be able to convince everyone that you are really doing the best job you can. This is essential to maintaining low expectations and ensuring that the employee and employer will be as happy as the situation allows once the sick or vacationing employee returns to the job.

It is quite possible that filing, answering phones, sending faxes, distributing mail and typing an occasional memo will be the only duties you are asked to attend to. Perhaps a total of 2-3 hours of your day will be devoted to doing work. It is to your advantage to appear busy for the remaining time. Make several piles of slightly askew papers in your workspace; this will establish a "busy and working" psycho-geography. As long as you look involved with what you are doing, you will have the freedom to skim the latest post-feminist manifesto and frequently check your voice mail.

Don't be afraid to personalize your workspace. Pictures in cute little frames and action figures are comforting and travel easily from job to job. They are however, a bit passé and have been adopted by permanent employees. The ultimate Cute Girl™ desk accessory is a "Japanese big-headed plastic doll" (an exact translation of Keroppi). It will spark conversation in which you can blush and pretend like the big head is a stand in for a big head.

While you may have to compromise a little dignity, the skills needed for temping are minimal and the pay is better than at Urban Outfitters. It also gives Cute Girls™ an opportunity to experience the boring life of office workers, and meet other young college dropouts. If you are able to avoid work completely, you will find temping to be most rewarding.

I
am
not
worthy
of
a
handshake

In
the
deepest
crevice
of
my
soul
I find a
shy
dullard

Step 1: Tear page from book.

Step 2: Fold inwards at A.

Step 3: Fold out-wards at B and C.

Step 4: Cut around dotted black line.

Love
eludes
me
because
I
dont
deserve
it.

I
am
too
docile
to
stand
up
for
my
rights

I
am
selfish
and
loathesome
with
shallow
ambitions

I
cannot
convince
others
of
my
worth
since
I
dont
have
any

Freedom Now!

Joe Maynard

You don't gotta raise your hand or anything, but I'm guessing most of you have jobs, and most of those jobs suck, and you feel like a prisoner to "the man" and you don't know what to do. You could look for a better job, but somehow, you know it will blow as bad as the one you have. Perhaps, you've even tried to get fired on purpose, but you've been doing your job for so long, you don't even remember how to fuck-up anymore. You feel hopelessly . . . *employed.* That's just how I felt, until I learned how to *diminish my self-esteem.*

See, "The Man" wants winners. Employees that walk in the office, cranked up on coffee and optimism eager to seize the doughnut, and even if deep inside, you want to curl up on the sofa with a bottle of Scotch and pass out in front of Oprah, you find yourself in a grey-suited nightmare saying things like, "Yes, sir", "Gotchya, boss" or "I'll crank that baby out in five minutes." Ugh! This is not you.

That's why you must learn to be a downer, and more importantly, to drag your co-workers down with you. You must be earnest, and make your boss feel guilty for not liking you, so that he will not contest your unemployment eligibility, and all the while complete his little assignments in a competent, long-suffering manner, until he simply cannot stand looking at you. This requires great concentration.

Shamens, mystics and misanthropes have been pointing us in this direction for centuries, and now, I've compiled this handy list of mantras for you to repeat to yourself. Its fold-out design makes it conveniently portable. Meditate on these words at home, in the office, on the train or bus, at lunch with co-workers, and you will become insufferable in no time flat, and more important: *drag others with you!* "The Man" will have no option but to send you to the state for your $300 check. You, my friend shall be free. Let's say them together:

I cannot convince others of my worth since I don't have any.
I am selfish and loathesome with shallow ambitions.
I am too docile to stand up for my rights.
Love eludes me because I don't deserve it.
I am not worthy of a handshake.
In the deepest crevice of my soul I find a shy dullard.

May luck elude you, friends!

No Pain, No Gain

Doug Nufer

I told Roger Patterson the reverend's joke about exposing Gold Medal Health Spas; he didn't think it was funny. Not that he worried about Jimmy Ray. He just didn't want anyone to pull a *60 Minutes* on him. This was right after Watergate, when the press wasn't gutless.

"*You* know we haven't done anything wrong, and *I* know we haven't done anything wrong, but give *them* the hand-held shot jostled down a corridor and we've had it."

Roger Patterson didn't believe in justice.

"Innocent until proven guilty—that's the opposite of how it is, and you—Jill honey, Belinda darling, Ken my man—you can say I'm terrible and call me a radical, but you know as well as I that they don't even prosecute if they can't win. And as far as we're concerned, even if they don't win they do win, because if it looks bad, then it is bad. It's sad when you consider, truly a tragedy, yet things do sort themselves out, and not only because we have seven million dollars."

"Come on, Daddy, we don't have seven million dollars. If we did, we wouldn't live in this shithole."

"Jill sweetheart, what have I told you about language ... language is the ... come on, don't be shy."

Together they said, "Language is the audio of image," although Jill didn't say it the same way he did.

"Don't you see the problem here? Jill honey, you have an objection, a complaint, a beef that may or may not be valid, and here we are sidetracked into recriminations that have nothing to do with the legitimacy of your objection, or ... *do* they!"

"Image is the picture of reality," said Jill, not looking at anyone.

"The aphorism is the last refuge of a chauvinist," said Belinda, "but don't explain it or you kill the joke. And speaking of language, Rog, better can the beef or you'll come off like Joe Pyne, or wasn't it your fantasy to host a screaming maniac talk show?"

"Now that man," said Roger Patterson, "projects image purely for the sake of negative afterimage, which proves my point."

He never failed to prove his point, the "point" being a signal that argument had stopped (as if it had ever started), and so Belinda served.

We played doubles on the alternate hit rule, and while it was more ping pong than table tennis, none of us got as much exercise as we did during these games in the basement of our Oklahoma headquarters. One rule of the health club was that you couldn't play games. Never mind that ping pong was better for you than the Tone-o-matic, the idea was that there could be no fun.

Since we were in charge, the rules didn't apply to us.

What Jill said about the seven million dollars wasn't supposed to be mentioned, but it came up a lot. With the ball in play, though, only Belinda could talk (the rest of us had to concentrate so we wouldn't forget whose turn it was to hit). She didn't play better than we did— she didn't care if she made Roger lose.

"I don't know if this is the right time, but we got a call from Salinas about the machines. I wouldn't have thought much, except El Paso called the next day and it sounded like the same problem. These people are unbelievable. You tell them it's supposed to hurt, they complain when it doesn't hurt; and then when it does, they really complain. So I told the d.i.s to tell the stiffs to eat less protein and if that doesn't work, to fast. Anyway, it's no biggie, but if it is, we might as well fold our tent and hit the road."

Roger Patterson didn't like us to call the clients "stiffs." Even in the basement under the thwocking of ping pong, the word stuck so that it might pop out when it shouldn't. Belinda said they wouldn't mind, that this was no different from the abuse kids get from gym teachers, but Roger Patterson believed all abuse should come from the program and that the drill instructors (the human element) should offer encouragement.

"Belinda, Belinda pet, Belinda, listen to me—you're not getting it. What we, what Gold Medal Health Spas is all about, in a nutshell, is life—not death. We do not say 'stiffs,' we say 'clients.' We treat our clients not as the 97-pound weaklings they were, but as the beautiful people they can be. And above all, we are not gym teachers. If nothing else, we are here to help our clients release themselves from the gym teacher-induced inhibitions and retrograde disciplinary mechanisms that thwart self-actualization."

"Don't talk—serve," said Jill.

"Don't talk, she says, but there is a perception and Ken, Ken my man will back me up on this one, there is a perception that the only time I have your undivided attention is when I hold the ball."

"No shit, Roger—8-14—serve, already."

"It doesn't stop there," Belinda continued with the game, "because after El Paso, we got a call from Key West. Roger, don't, it's my turn."

"8-15," I said, "Roger didn't follow."

"Key West, she said, didn't you hear? Jill, I appeal to you, darling, did you not hear Key West? Belinda is absolutely correct, this is not a coincidence. I will go to Key West at once and then, one day, we'll look back on this and see that it wasn't so bad after all."

"We don't have a club in Key West, babe; I just thought you weren't paying attention," said Belinda.

"Belinda sweets, I can't get over my shame for a) going out of turn, and b) not developing the state of Florida to its full potential. Before I serve, let me say that the deprived are crying out for fitness and we cannot deny them. Florida should be our stronghold, what with Ken here no less than a Favorite Son, yet aside from what—Fosterville? Tampa?—where are we? And so Belinda, Jill doll, Ken, King Ken, don't let me off the hook, send me to Key West, force me to follow through on what I should have done long ago."

"In eighteen months," said Belinda, "we have grown so fast that we don't know what we make. We have 28 branches in 25 states, although only one in all of Florida because we can't afford the overhead in any place that isn't a swamp. Of course, if he had picked Fosterville and Key West like I said instead of that piece of Tampa that should have been redlined, we might not need to feed off the franchise fees. Not that I don't support deprivation, but we go out of the way to pick out-of-the-way places. Don't tell me about cheap rent. We could be losing money and never learn how to beat the overhead, as long as we keep opening branches and charging fees. So Rog, by all means, go to Key West, and while you're at it, hit Grentna, Lynchburg, Altoona, and everywhere in between, since the base of the pyramid can't be too broad."

Roger Patterson played up close and tried to smash, I stayed back to catch his put-aways with a slice, Belinda lunged forward to pick up the backspin, and Jill kept the rally alive, as if to set up her father for his best shot to show him it wasn't good enough.

"Hold it, time out, whoa," he put down his paddle, "my partner has raised a question that can't go unanswered. Isn't there a smack of hostility to all this?"

"Not again," said Jill.

"*There*—mumbling, backbiting, the treachery of unrest. Negative thinking. Gold Medal Health Spas is not about negative thinking. Hostility is not progress but regression, the enemy of growth—we are, therefore we grow, to grow is to be—"

"There's no business like grow business."

"Don't interrupt. We are not crooks and I know you don't mean that, but image, kids, image. People hear 'pyramid' and they think Egypt, camels, tombs?—no, they think scam, chain letters, fraud. Millions have been invested here, not by Ma and Pa out of their savings, but by us. The risk is ours and the loss won't be theirs. And Jill, Belinda, Ken, neither will the GAIN."

He wouldn't quit until we agreed with him.

(Excerpted from the novel *Negativeland*.)

Power Walking

Severo Granados

It was raining and I ran with the crowd, jumping over puddles and trying not to slip on the sidewalk. We'd come hurrying out of the subway only to find that the rain had gotten there first and there was no more winning. We flew across the streets heedless of stoplights until a slow wall of traffic at Broadway and Bleecker brought us to a standstill, and we began separating like a flock of birds flying in several directions at once.

I ducked into the pizza shop to dry off, my eyes roaming a bulletin board for something interesting enough to delay my reentry into the wet world. At first glance, it seemed there were only the usual notices for apartment sublets, cats who've lost their owners, guitars and hairdryers on sale for next to nothing — but in the lower left corner, half hidden, was an announcement that aroused my curiousity.

HOW TO WALK

You may THINK you know how to walk but your every movement may IN FACT be simply the accumulation of BAD HABITS collected over a LIFETIME. Impressions made by OTHERS, FORCED PACINGS DICTATED by parents, rhythms accepted from STRANGERS can all create a false identity that is not the REAL YOU. In order to discover YOUR TRUE WALK AND RHYTHM it is necessary to BREAK DOWN BAD HABITS and start fresh with a new approach, one based on intense professional observation, coupled with your desire to become who you really are.

Please contact 212-254-____ or come to ___ Spring St. / Mondays and Wednesdays at 4 or 9 pm. / $25.00 per session / group rates.

I tore the last tab off the bottom of the flyer.

I pushed the door open and walked into a small landing, with only a stairway leading down. I plunged down the long flight before facing another door. I could hear a woman's voice on the other side, speaking loudly. I didn't know what to expect.

The room was dimly lit. There was only one large window in the place, covered with soot, which looked out onto a shaftway. I found a seat against the wall.

A group of about twenty people lay stretched out on the floor, forming five rows, in various stages of undress. A middle-aged woman, barefoot, dressed in loose white clothing, walked up and down between them, occasionally snapping a whip against the floor.

"Why are all of you down on the floor?" She asked them with evident glee in a German accent.

"To learn who we are," they answered.

"And why is that?"

"Because what we know about ourselves is false," a guy near me replied. I noticed that he only had his underwear on.

"Ah, my star pupil, you are very good but you are answering by rote. That is bad behavior. I must punish you for that. Shall I do it, class?"

The class said yes with gusto. Perhaps they wanted a chance to get up off the floor.

"I want you to crawl across the room while everyone watches."

And the crowd of students gathered around this young man who had to crawl across the length of the floor while being critiqued on his performance, on whether he was being genuine, wholly himself, or whether "pervasive influences" were creeping into his humiliation.

"Is he truly expressing his real self?"

Reaction was mixed.

"He has not given up yet," was all the teacher said before letting her whip graze his ankles several times.

The teacher – if that is what she was – announced, "Flash Walks," and every one lined up against the wall. She then yelled, "Power Walk," and the group blustered across the room holding imaginary briefcases. When they had reached the other side she barked, "You are all Black," ("That's good, go with it, FEEL it!") and then –

"But who are you?" She loomed over me imperiously.

"I just came to observe." I said. "I'm interested and I want to see what –"

"I'm very sorry, but there are no observers here. Participants only. We have no room for slackers, do we class?"

Again, they rose up, this time adamantly shouting "No!"

A minute later I was in the center of the floor, being told to assume a natural posture, which I had assumed I had been doing all along. I was ordered to walk while various people bumped into me, commanded to laugh on demand, to knock off my false smile, to imagine I was naked in front of a large crowd of strangers, and so on. I drew the line at crawling across the floor, but the instructor came up with other angles. I became variously gay, a woman, a dog, a drunk, a policeman and a stone, and my movements were minutely critiqued in each category. As for being myself, I never quite got there. The rest I leave to your imagination.

When I climbed up the stairs and left the building it was getting dark. A crowd of perhaps ten people was milling around the entrance to the building. One of them had a megaphone, and several were carrying signs.

"Walking is neither an art nor a science but a birthright."

"No charge for walking."

"What Fraulein Hesserfuss is doing down there is a tragedy," said the woman with the megaphone. "Actual people with real needs are being lured into some sort of psychodrama, where she can work out her theories of dominance and reality, whereas what they are paying for is ... is the chance to recover something that they believe they have in fact lost. People leave her class as ignorant as when they came in."

I wondered what IN FACT it was that they had lost? I winced as I recalled the way the group had walked when, hidden away from prying eyes in a Soho basement, they were told that presto-chango, they were all black. On the QT the class became low-down, ghetto-trawling pimps – or as close to it as they possibly could imagine.

I left just about the time I noticed a sharply-dressed anchorman braying into a microphone for the six o'clock news.

Translated by James Graham

Economics

Susan Scutti

Ann works at the Fidelity Investment Company. She assists three brokers whose offices are on the 16th floor in a corner of the building no one comes to much. In the photograph between her computer and her phone she wears a leotard and stands en pointe; she was 14 and living with her family in Rome, Italy. Her father drank only wine then.

She'd done some extra typing for a couple of brokers down the hall so on Friday night they treat her and their regular secretary to dinner: on the company. The regular secretary is younger, not as pretty and wearing a longer, looser skirt than Ann. Mike sits next to Ann. They begin with a bottle of $60 champagne and end with a $90 port. Mike's taken off his suit jacket and his arm rests menacingly on the back of Ann's chair. He saw a movie last night. *The woman has a one-week long affair with a married man,* he says, *and when it's over, she says she loves him and tries to make him responsible for her pregnancy. Of course,* he adds, *the man won't have any of that.*

Ann's earlobes feel hot beneath her clip-on earrings and when Mike finishes speaking she says, *I've done that.* The other broker smiles without showing any teeth, the secretary lifts her chin in a superior attitude, and Mike laughs outright. *I mean,* Ann explains, *I've fallen in love right away after sex. Haven't you?*

As he relaxes into his favorite topic, Mike's fingers wrap around the stem of the wine glass just below the bulb of blood-red port. He theorizes that sex is simple economics. Men possess sperm which come in millions and women possess eggs which are scarce. Women, therefore, want to be selective in their expenditure of eggs. *It's natural,* he says, *for women to fall in love with casual partners—after all they've "spent" so much, they probably need to believe they did it for love.* The waiter fills her glass with wine, and Ann says *thank you* even though she didn't want anymore.

The conversation turns from movies to music. When the waiter arrives with a check, Mike says, *I've got it,* then he looks at Ann. His eyes plead but Ann shakes her head no when he asks her if she wants to go alone with him to a club. He holds her coat and the lining feels icy against her shoulders and back. As she waits on the subway platform Ann's eyes are wide, staring, but she doesn't see anything around her. On the tracks below her, one mouse chases another: around and around and around. Last week her shrink told her not to worry so much. If she tries a little self-help by working harder at her job and not acting on impulse all the time, her life will improve and she will meet a nice guy. The train gets stuck in the tunnel just before Ann's stop and all the lights go out.

The next day at work the receptionist, who has a Spanish accent and wears a crucifix, tells Ann that she dreamed about her last night. As she raises her arms to

54

fix her hair, her eyes touch Ann's in the bathroom mirror. *You were lying in the mud. You were wearing a business suit, but you were lying in the mud. When I woke, I couldn't stop thinking about it. You were as real in my dream as you are to me now.* Ann laughs but in the mirror her eyes look frightened.

Sometimes at night Ann feels the ghostly sensation of hands touching her skin. She has slept with so many men she can't even remember some of their faces now. When she was with them, though, she listened to their worries and held them if they woke from a bad dream. She gave each man her heart, not only her body. In catechism class when she was young and had learned about Mary Magdalene, Ann had felt shocked that Christ would be friends with a whore. Now, she secretly believes that only a whore—a woman who gives herself for a small price to any and every man who wants her—only a whore would have insight equal to that of the man/god.

In-sight, Ann repeats to herself, thinking about how a man literally gets inside a woman during sex. As she prints out a memo on Fidelity stationery, Ann daydreams, remembering a trip she'd taken with her parents just after they'd returned from Rome. They were driving to Philadelphia and had to stop every fifteen miles so that her father could take a swig from the jug of scotch he kept in the trunk of the Cadillac. During one stop her mother twisted around to Ann in the back seat: *Now don't you say a word about how much we spent at the mall yesterday.* Ann couldn't see her father's face but she watched him spit into the highway before getting back into the driver's seat of the car.

I Thought I heard Opera, But it was Really Sirens

CARL WATSON

1. UNEMPLOYMENT AND OTHER PRIMAL FEARS

I should have known something was up when the guy in the Port Authority bathroom asked if I had a girlfriend. It seemed like a trick question so I said, "No thanks." Then he cracked a bottle open on the rim of the sink and started pouring cologne on me, singing. "You have to smell nice for the girls, you have to smell nice for the girls, because you look like hell, motherfucker."

Disoriented by this aggressive sympathy, I strolled out into the yawning maw of Times Square, smelling funny and feeling silly and insecure. Newsellers played barker at the burlesque of fashionable youth. The tabloid press was offering yet more evidence of the mythical Eternal Return, as more and more "celebrities-on-the-rocks" and "used-to-be-heartthrobs" were finding the comeback trail a pleasant diversion from menopause and obscurity. And they say old age is wasted on the young at heart.

I was feeling considerably older myself, by the minute. I was dressed to please some employer I didn't, and probably would never, know. And what with the over-bearing odor of Chaz or Brute or Shangri-La or English Leather, whatever the guy had dumped on me, it pretty much killed my job interview possibilities for the day, so I threw the want ads in the garbage can. Immediately somebody picked them up. He's probably making money right now.

On TV that night was a show about a guy who lived in a locked room in a big house at the uttermost end of the block on the top of the hill who had a weird skin disease that generated unspeakable horror in his neighbors. He couldn't get a job either. I wasn't surprised.

We live in a visual culture. Spirit counts for about as much as good intentions. Physical insecurity is a debilitating thing. People have nightmares of waking up as animals—shaggy dogs and flies. I remember some movie I saw as a kid about an evil scientist in Louisiana who had all these men walking around the swamps with alligator heads and bad breath.

In the days before splatter films, ugliness or "difference" alone was a form of violence. People died from exposure to it. We now know that all those people screaming on the TV screen in the '50s and '60s weren't just looking at aliens and swamp monsters. They were really looking into the diversity of the human soul.

It's precisely these kind of primal fears that are played for all they're worth by the ad industry, the message always being "Get real. Get a life." A human life, I think they mean. But if you're like me that's not so easy. It takes a job to have a life. And it takes a life to get a job. Catch 22.

But then sometimes I think looking for a job is a way of not looking at your life.

Maybe that 9-5 thing is really a means of avoiding what Joe Conrad called "the Horror." You almost expect to get that Kurtz fellow as your interviewer, at the end of some long office-building labyrinth, deep in the heart of darkness of the Job Market. They don't call personnel managers "headhunters" for no reason.

But that didn't scare me. So the next day in a desperate act of Nietzschean self-assertion, I walked, no, swaggered into the Natural History Museum and applied for some $6/hr position pinning preserved insects on pegboards, so people could see what nature looked "like" without ever having to experience it. But once again I was both seriously underdressed and lacking facial panache. "No way," they said. Undaunted, I decided to add to my string of defeats by applying for a bartender job down the road, but the guy said I had to dress in leotards and be a woman.

Then I tried an employment agency. I sat in the lobby for three hours before I heard the receptionist call my name. "Ms. So & So will 'see' you now." Ms. So & So actually did look a little bit like Marlon Brando. She gave me one of those five second looks and said, "Why don't you go on back down to Houston Street now. Your bench is getting cold." It's so easy to feel victimized that I did just that for awhile, just a little while though.

Later on in the day I was sitting in some employment office, when a magazine page curled up on my lap like a kitten. There was a slight breeze and the page opened automatically to an ad for a plastic surgeon. Big bold letters about reasonable prices, confidential and caring professionals.

The ad featured an androgynous head, almost mongolian, a head at once advanced and devolved, a head without sex organs to support it, generic as a shaved Barbie/Ken doll, but rounder, like an insect—a sort of half-glowing figure without any focus to its eyes and a rubber doll's mouth and a perfect tweaky nose. Perhaps it was meant to symbolize that blank slate on which to build an ideal self-image, but the utopian subtext was of a homogeneous world where our differences would no longer make us uncomfortable or hateful. Perhaps because there would be no differences.

Coincidentally, this enclave of caring cosmetic professionals was located uptown near the Museum of Natural History, where I had so recently suffered humiliating rejection. The geographical location allowed its advertising department to capitalize on the relationship between the taxidermy of the dead and that of the living. Thus the "knowledge" represented by a certain arrangement of "types" and "facts" could be either overridden or subscribed to. In other words there was truly a way out of the body-trap that nature, accident, and illness have built for us.

One surgeon has even said, "How we interact socially and how we 'perform' our jobs is directly affected by the way we look." This strengthened my suspicion that buried within the Entertainment clause of consumerism is the tic that turns even the most tedious niches of the world into stages where mundane chores may be interpreted as art. Perhaps this is the much heralded return to tribalism touted by the "alternative" press. Still I couldn't envision people paying $20-plus ticket prices to see a super-typist or a gal who proofreads really well.

I started to wonder if performance art might just be a subtle form of propaganda, in which case perhaps I should eliminate the word "perform" from my vocabulary as a form of patriarchal baggage. The idea alone made me cynical. The rancid acidic air only helped to etch that cynicism into my face. I saw my reflection in a window. My lack of skills and poor attitude were all too well broadcast in those sad features.

I wondered if a little skin spackle here or there might add energy and youthful vigor to this etched cynical grin. Then I remembered the ad for the Plastic Surgeon and let this arbitrary advertising event act as a sign, perhaps the key that would unlock the door to employment heaven. So I straightened out my red hula-girl tie, buttoned up my paisley sports coat and with a renewed sense of purpose walked on down the road. The power of positive thinking adding vigor to my stride.

Armed with a magazine photo of Arnold Schwartzenegger and the Help Wanted section of the NY Times, I entered the doctor's office to ask a cosmetic expert if he or she could transform me into a competitive candidate, a go-getter, a self-starting, hi-energy, detail-oriented superperson who loves to work with people in a fast-paced exciting environment and who also possesses excellent clerical skills as well as a pleasant phone voice under the extreme pressure of tight deadlines in a low paying but highly rewarding position. I said I had nothing better to do with my life anyway.

The receptionist told me my desires were impossible. Of course I already knew that, but it seemed like the wrong attitude for a salesperson. I left dejected.

Fate lays a table. I believe that. And I'm not paranoid. I believe that too. But little things that cross my path can turn into a conspiracy if I let them—small nudges from the arbitrary world. The advocation of plastic surgery was quickly becoming one of these—in the last few weeks it seemed to be all around me, infiltrating the zeitgeist, growing stronger in relation to the general nervousness. I think there had recently been several TV documentaries about it, sandwiched between shows on rising unemployment.

To drown, or perhaps to augment my paranoia, I stopped at my corner bodega for a quart of beer. Raul and Antonio started laughing at my haircut. Coincidentally, when I got home there was a copy of the Transsexuals Newsletter in my mailbox. This coincidence stuff was getting on my nerves. The feature article was about a gal named Larry who was totally thrilled with her new penis. He had an air pump attached too. Better roll with it I figured. Besides the air pump idea sounded useful.

2. THE MALFORMED PONDER GRACE

Did you ever see that Twilight Zone episode—In the Eye of the Beholder. The whole thing takes place from the viewpoint of a guy wrapped in bandages. The doctors are trying to make him normal. In the end you find out how he's already normal. Everyone else is a monster. Self respect is a great thing. It's also a rare thing. In fact it's getting rare enough that it's become something to party about.

I went to one of these so-called "self-respect" parties one day. It was something like a Tupperware party but all the people looked suspiciously altered. There was a lot of talk around the snack table about skin hooks, flaps and grafts, and foundations. The hors d'oeuvres on the table even looked a little like skin flaps. There was also a shelf full of pamphlets and catalogues in case all the eavesdropping piqued your curiosity.

I thumbed through one of these catalogues to a full page ad for Paris Lip. At first I thought this must be a trendy form of sarcasm, but it's really that sort of puffy look like you've been bashed in the mouth in the last couple of days—a little Paris, a little S&M. People were buying it. I guess I can't blame them, people treat you better if they think you've recently been hit.

The need to at least project fashion savvy injects itself into the public psyche like a fix. But fashion can be fickle. You implant your pecks one day, and sunken chests come back in style the next. One would think nozzles could be installed in key areas that would make lips and breasts deflatable or inflatable as the scene dictates. But such flexibility would contradict planned obsolescence, the time/money matrix would falter and the universe would surely collapse. The locker room floor would be slippery with spilled silicone and the beach would be a strange place.

The Army says "Be all that you can be." And apparently there exists in the more vain cities a sort of Army Corps of Engineers for the face to help you do just that— ever ready for a price, to stave off age, to fill in and dam the river of failing, falling flesh; restructuring, redefining the alluvial fans eroded by tears and experience, those fertile valleys caused by past expressions—what we once called character. You can't read the past in the faces of the aged anymore, which might mean we won't learn from their mistakes. But then when did we ever?

Anyway, these workers in white smocks routinely remove warts, hanging jowls, crow's feet and laugh lines. Fat is liposuctioned right out of your life. Skin tumors are shaved. They can change your height by amending your legs, retie your ligaments, to curtail an awkward gait, even retune your voice by adjusting your vocal chords. 3-dimensional images of troublesome head sections can be rotated and sliced egg-shell thin, then videographically restitched with special wire thus creating the strut for a more fashionable and intelligent-looking skull.

Computers are enlisted to mill bones to the popular template. Lasers cut puzzle pieces to precise specifications. They can stretch out skin swatches like taffy to form wings if you want them. And they don't doubt that someday you will want them. What better way to exploit the panorama of choice than to take it all in from above.

Words are coined to prescribe, describe or disguise the process: rhytidectomy, rhinoplasty, abdominoplasty, otoplasty, mentoplasty, blepharoplasty, mastopexy, electrocaudery and of course the popular chemical peels. The terminology alone is enough to make me squirm. But some people get off on it. Others are into the dynamics, that fluctuating sense of inadequacy before a higher power.

It is possible to envision plastic surgeons as Cosmetic Dominatrixes, for the surge in their popularity may be partly due to the risk involved, that devil-may-care, carpe diem attitude of the proper masochistic modern who relishes the sense of toying with god's faulted plan, calling down judgment as a way of shoring up the universe. Risk is indeed part of the ritual. The wrong doctor can cost you plenty at the Wheel of Fortune. One does not necessarily end up looking like Vanna White or Mel Gibson.

On the other hand, your local plastic surgeon is also a lot like a bartender or a barber or a taxi-driver—a little of the psychiatrist too. Words can be knives. Ask any cocktail party habitué. Thus it is a natural step from scalpel to soothing phrase. I'm sorry, did I say soothing? I meant hypnotic.

"Forgiveness is the scalpel that can remove the pus from old emotional wounds." Thus spake Maxwell Maltz, philosopher and man-about-town in the field of human-body enhancement, who made the leap from plastic surgeon to self-help guru. To sum up Maltzian process in a metaphorical nutshell—it's a tale of two scars, the outward scar being mirrored by the inward scar. These two scars combine to form the ever-important self-image which is the roadmap of your life on which you can avoid the inevitable crash of impossible goals, surviving to drive to happier conclusions.

We are victims of self-disgust and crippling shame. No one doubts this. One must therefore become one's own plastic surgeon digging in with a psychic knife to cut out the inner corrosion of bad thinking. You may live in the present, but you should "visualize" a better future. Call it an all-out psycho-cybernetic war against failure. Sit in the theater of your mind and project successful narratives on the movie screen of life—imagine it and make it so—a sort of Jonathan Livingston Seagull approach to staving off catastrophe and becoming a "professional human" Look at the people who are moving into your neighborhood and raising the rents.

Incorporate the idea of plasticity under the umbrella of humanity. You don't need to *deserve* to be happy. Be happy now. Unhappiness is evil. Become a Typhoid Mary of Happiness (a Happiness Mary) spreading the communicable decease of optimism and good cheer. Wake up in the morning and say "I love you" to yourself. Tell everybody else you love them too. Compliment people three times a day. Write it on the mirror in crayon or lipstick like it was the clue to a crime.

I tried this optimism thing for awhile. It was making people sick. I carried around bags of feathers and balloons and laughed a lot but everyone said, "Get off it man, you ain't the Norman Vincent Peale of the '90s." I alternately abandoned and revived the campaign as my circumstances warranted. Finally the peer pressure got too great and I dropped it altogether. Still I try not to be negative. It's sad, though, because I'm always looking for the seed of the sinister in the apparently benign.

We all know things we wish we did not know. The fulfillment of behavioral dictates by sign, for instance. Like how squarely blocked eyebrows are indicative of erratic mental states. Or how "Coarseness of tendencies can be plainly seen in a nose in which the nostrils roll backward." Or how a broad, well formed nose indicates mechanical ability and a capacity for engineering. And how the height of bone structure in the nose indicates executive power, intensity and energy. The nose carries a lot of weight, but there's also a criminal chin and a judgmental upper lip.

Such knowledge bodes ill for communal love. One day you might just realize that your neighbor's, or more horribly, your child's skull is deformed in a way that indicates lacisiousness. Baby brother's future is threatened by an unusual curvature of the cheekbone that insures criminal tendencies. Sister's in need of some bridgework to add a little authority to her face. You might decide to use a hammer to fix it and feed the trend toward familial abuse. Or you might spend money.

Okay, it sounds absurd, but people must somehow believe these things, or cosmetic surgery wouldn't be important to anyone but trauma patients and advertising wouldn't be able to sensitize us so easily to our minor deformities, which we soon begin to see so readily in others. After all, if people weren't made to feel so lousy and humiliated about their corporeal manifestation, they wouldn't feel the need to change it. But they do, so they do. As if the call to higher consciousness were a catcall—the goad of the bodiless gods, toward us, trapped down here in the human skin cage.

But science is dependent on categorization, and like all good science, the knifely-arts are eventually enlisted to the service of ill-gotten gain. If a person's eyes can effect perceptions of how alert and trustworthy they are, then politicians can go in for "honesty" surgery and expect it to work. Perverts can have that lascivious lip removed. You can make your brown eyes blue, your black hair blonde, your bushy eyebrows thin, you can bleach your skin, or tan yourself silly. You can cleanse your soul with a knife and erase your past with #120 sandpaper.

And while it's true the FBI can give you a new identity for a song, rock stars can turn you into demons simply for listening to one. If you play a certain Madonna number backwards the lyrics actually say "Save Us Satan." There has been digital tampering of Van Morrison's *Brown Eyed Girl* to exorcise a past "offensive" lyric. Rumor has it John Lennon's phrase "Everybody is a star," was arrived at through overdubbing and backmasking the word "Service".

3. PASTICHE IS THE BEAST THAT BEARS NO HERESY

An editorial appeared in the NY Times some time ago, about photo-journalism as a form of propaganda that edits history down to misleading visual bites. The future is manipulated because a visual society is easily propagandized. We try to fight back, we propagandize ourselves—in the theater of our mind(s). President Bush closed his eyes and imagined Baghdad in ruins. The mayor of New York closes his eyes and imagines a Times Square without the midnight cowboys, a Times Square of fern bars and hotels and happy people with money, in other words a Times Square in which the Time has been surgically excised and only the Square remains—a bunch of dancing Disney cartoon characters.

Indeed, there isn't a day goes by you don't hear somebody complaining about integrity and the good-old-used-to-be. Nostalgia has been called the sweat of the inanimate world. It blurs our vision of the past like a mist. These days the past and the present are one. The trick is to believe we're choosing something—and that this is freedom. I think it was Marlo Thomas who coined the phrase "Free to Be You and Me" Her old TV show begins with her tossing her hat into the air of Times Square.

When the Gulf War started I went to an anti-war rally very near the spot where *That Girl* once celebrated her assertiveness. Judging by the number of recording devices (videos, tapes, still cameras) it seemed not only did people want to protest the war, they also wanted to see themselves doing it. And they were getting a lot of support from the corporate world too. 50% of Times Square commerce, after all, is in recording devices. The other 50% used to be sex. They are directly related in advertiser's minds because lots of people like to watch themselves having sex (either in mirrors or on video tape).

Times Square incorporates part of what is called the theater district. It's a great place for the theatrical to get political because politics is sexy. But then bombs can be sexy too, which is why we find ourselves in embarrassing situations, rutting around at the bottom of the behavioral ladder. But that's another tangent.

Now, Broadway is the heart of Times Square. I spend a lot of unemployed time listening to Broadway show soundtracks, and opera—it makes my tiny apartment seem like a stage where anything is possible. I spend another large portion of unemployed time sitting around in waiting rooms, which, like the theater, are not always what they at first appear to be.

One day I was sitting in a psycho-cybernetics waiting room in Times Square. I was looking forward to an uplifting conversation. I could hear the happy yet sinister dentist-office muzak that so often accompanies nightmares. I could also hear the whining and whirring of little neuro-drills and lasers fixing-up the self-images of guilty patients, like a micro-welding bead singing across the sutures of yet another imperfect double helix, making it better, stronger, altering our collective memory. It was clean and no blood leaked beneath the door. A man was singing somewhere, a fatherly aria of noble ideas and lost love. I got out of there.

Then, as I walked down 42nd street I saw the theatre marquees emblazoned with the titles of musicals and plays. There was a musical about 42nd street. And then there was 42nd street, the real thing, as Coke's ad department might call it. Just one more product caught up in degrading reflections of itself.

And then there was Times Square "Classic." And it was a musical too, a sort of fallen opera of skin parlors and peep shows, where even cherished icons were not immune to reconstruction. Indeed, Muslim preachers were singing about a black Jesus. One guy had a poster proving that the Virgin Mary was really Satan with extensive rhinoplasty. A guy dressed as Jean Valjean from *Les Miserables* was being chased down the street by some guys dressed as Keystone Comedy cops. They ran into the theatre where *Les Miserables* was playing. A midget was doing handstands out front.

It was what used to be called postmodern. Yet, almost none of these people had time to advocate or appreciate their lifestyle because they were too busy being victims of it, that is victims of the state—that is "Times Square" as a state of hyper-visualization of the rampant pursuit of happiness.

Now it is said happiness is the one thing that increases by division: 1,000 units of happiness divided by 2 is 2,000 units of happiness. Times Square is that equation to the nth power, the sub-structural servo-success-mechanism gone mad, a sort of mass self-image where MTV torsos, hyperreal cartoon ubermenches like Arnold Swartznegger, Donald Trump and Jean-Claude Van Damme, carouse with Micky, Goofy and Marilyn on video screens. It's like an octopus with a million tentacles and a TV on the end of every one, the proverbial can of worms, the very anthropomorphic force of propaganda itself.

Some say war is male menstruation. Others say war is a working out of the plastic surgical instinct on a global level—putting a new face on the world—an empirical face. Trendy philosophers have speculated on the body as a site of social control, in which case there will be those who rebel against these sanctioned images of perfection—like the new mutilation performance artists. Young people who hang themselves from automobiles, hang from meat hooks, tie off their limbs till they atrophy, or hack off their penises and die in the artistic quest.

But using one's body as sculptural material is also a way to indicate subscription. Michael Jackson could afford professional cosmetic alteration to become what he wanted to be. But Gary, Indiana (Bethlehem to Jackson's fans) is a city that could afford no such thing.

Back in Gary, before the *Beat It* video choreographed street fighting, they had a thing called "curbing", whereby you forced your submissive opponent to bite the curb of the sidewalk then kicked him in the back of the head. It was an effective way to consummate a dispute. Rumor has it the dentists of Northwest Indiana relished the decline of the American industrial base for precisely this petty reason.

Then one day a new Michael Jackson came along, from Gary to Glory. Plastic surgery raised the man to a near Messianic state, and with his new face came visions of a new future. The man who covets the Elephant Man's skeleton knows something about physical change, and how it can become a form of consumption.

Another plastic surgery oracle, Ed Gein, didn't know any such thing. He used to wear face masks made from his victims, as an extreme reaction to the lack of a good plastic/psychic surgeon in his town. Perhaps Ed was trying to get in touch with his higher personality. There were just too many of them. On any given night he couldn't decide who he was. He became sort of a walking Times Square, the 666 *in humanitas*, searching for a starring role in a musical that ended happily, but all he ever was, was alone, abandoned to a hopeless quest way out on the spooky plains of Wisconsin, alienated and bitter. Which brings me back to the subject of unemployment.

I felt alone too, even though I was in Times Square, one of the most crowded places in the world. I was looking for a job. I was visualizing the job I would have—looking good, smiling, accepting a paycheck triumphally—but a bad visual was crowding out the good one—it was Michael Jackson's face surgically inserted in that James Ensor painting, *Christ Enters Brussels*.

I refused to be manipulated by unseen forces, so I changed that face to Ed Gein. Then I set the whole thing to music—a mixture of Gershwin, Wagner and the Doors as interpreted by a colorful German oom-pah band. Indeed there were too many references here for my own good, but it was fun. So here was this crazy musical coming down the road at me like a Fellini parade. It was the Monster of Times Square and it was all mine. I created it and I would die for it—probably.

I had other choices. There were slasher flicks or men-with-big-guns to see. Or I could check out the new Charlie Manson opera. Or that musical about presidential assassins. I didn't know what to do. I ended up Uptown, some swank joint, where everybody smelled like bad cologne and dressed in the fur of skinned animals. The show was Man of La Mancha, Don Quixote—the guy who tilts at windmills. It was great. I cried. And I knew that somewhere in the space/time continuum, Michael Jackson cried too. Maybe for different reasons, but at least he cried.

SQUEAKY GROWS A BUSINESS!

BY DAVID BORCHART

SQUEAKY IS THE LAST CAT YOU'D EXPECT TO START A SUCCESSFUL BUSINESS.

WILLY

SQUEAKY

UNTIL RECENTLY, HER MAIN INTERESTS WERE HIDING INSIDE A RATTY OLD SETTEE, AND SLEEPING.

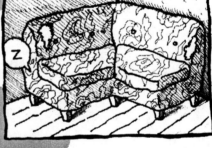

EXCEPT WHEN STRANGERS WOULD VISIT. THEN SQUEAKY WOULD HIDE AND GROWL.

RRRRR!

WHEN AT LAST WE HAD TO THROW OUT THE SETTEE, SQUEAKY WAS FACED WITH A MAJOR CRISIS!

ANOTHER CAT MIGHT'VE JUST FOUND A NEW HIDING PLACE, BUT SQUEAKY APPLIED FOR A SMALL BUSINESS LOAN AND LEASED A STOREFRONT DOWN THE BLOCK.

SHE STARTED OUT WITH FOUR EMPTY PAWS AND A SIMPLE IDEA: TO PROVIDE BOWLS OF DRY CAT FOOD AND WATER AT PRICES THAT ANYONE COULD AFFORD.

THEN CAME THE GRAND OPENING AND SQUEAKY'S FIRST CUSTOMER—

HERE SQUEAKY'S BUSINESS HIT A WALL. HER HIDE-AND-GROWL STRATEGY WAS INCONSISTENT WITH GOOD CUSTOMER RELATIONS.

FORTUNATELY SHE HAD ENTERED INTO HER BUSINESS OBLIGATIONS UNDER THE ASSUMED NAME OF FELIX ROHATYN.

IT WAS A SETBACK, BUT SQUEAKY PERSEVERED, AND FOUND HER NICHE IN DIRECT-MAIL CATALOGUE MARKETING. THE REST, OF COURSE, IS HISTORY...

Extreme Sports: Prescription for Profitable Prisoners[1]: Madiator Inc.'s Privatized Success With Public Amusement

bART pLANTENGA

We knew the prisoner, #G-7395142, who wore the radio-monitored stethoscope taped to his ribs under gleaming breast armor. We knew that the armor afforded him the proper ironic reflectivity of elegance and style. We knew that his furtive smile lent him a sliver of dignity that we could sentimentalize — he would not die emotionless like some animal. Our dedication to easy sentimentality would see to that.

We also knew 1600 prisoners are daily added to the American prison population[2] and that by 1995 the prison population had surpassed the college population.[3] "Incarceration over education" was the era's prevailing slogan.

"The implementation of law and order doctrine, beyond incarceration (including such measures as zero-tolerance policing and curfews, [and] crackdowns on freedom in order to protect it"[4] has converted entire sectors of U.S. cities into minefields of justified oppressions and pro-active survivalist preventions[5] where the "carceral texture of society"[6] encourages the citizenry on the outside to absorb and further extrapolate the mythos of the inside[7] so that their interior lives, measured in terms of coercive confinement, soon surpasses that of even the incarcerated.[8]

It is now so common for under-esteemed men to do time that it has replaced all other social arrangements — sports, home, school, church, mall. Crime and the logarithm of the horrific confer the status of recognition upon the disinherited and untouchable.[9] And, as is the wont of human mechanisms that steer pride, they've made something almost noble of it.

On our rounds through their communities and mindsets we saw how some Project kids are so aware of the danger of being murdered that some have already preselected outfits they'll wear to their own funerals. Others manage to incorporate the radio-monitored stethoscope design into their portable entertainment units (Walkmans and the like) in a show of solidarity enhanced by entrepreneurial considerations and perks of prestige.[10] They coveted what prisoners seemed to embody, the status of outlaw chic,[11] as the shackled amble down the "Walkway of Shame" from police station to jail. And in certain photos to certain eyes informing certain minds the walkways resemble fashion show runways.[12] While the number of cameras flashing is nearly the same.

Notoriety (and its sycophantic law enforcement micro-industries) certainly beats anonymity and generic victimhood. This process got me to wondering how most people could accept the banalization of torture and incarceration, its disappearance from the public realm, as Foucault so duly noted, and yet secretly (often not so secretly), somewhere in amongst the socio-biochemical processes of the normalization of ennui, they could harbor elaborate scenarios of Hollywood-cribbed tortures to those they imagined as the enemies of the self. And that the erotic gesture was here sublimated (consumed) in revenge, further validated this drift into vigilanté moralisms. Millennial eroticism has become defined by the revolver which is cleaner, shinier and harder than the penis and the entrance wound which is tighter, brighter and more responsive than the vagina.[13]

So when I read in 1994 that New York's Mayor Giuliani had declared "Freedom is about authority"[14] in a speech "dealing with crime in America's cities ..." I knew that the bedroom had floated off to the target range, that dreams had been interpenetrated by thoughts of penitentiaries, and that faith had gone desperate, appearing now in its barbed and baffled guise as cognitive dissonance. In efforts to clarify his Orwellian obfuscation, obfuscate his clarification and further dissonance his audience's cognition, Giuliani argued without a trace of irony that "there needs to be a 'balance between doing what you want to do' and 'submitting to authority' before people are truly free."

What struck me were his words "submitting to authority." I immediately pictured Giuliani in some trussed up and sullied Victoria's Secret take on bondage wear; a mounted policeman's riding crop resonantly slapping the sides of the hollow podium. As if his speechwriter was none other than some ex-dominatrix rehabilitated as talkshow therapist-sexpert. She too had managed to "believe" (or sell) the therapeutic notion of submission as a type of liberation from the flesh or its resident strains of qualm and prudery. This alchemy is most spectacularly consummated on TV talkshows where the regrets of oppression are transubstantiated into authority's necessary rationing of freedoms. Meanwhile, a grateful queue of citizens anxiously waits for the privilege to repurchase at a premium the very freedoms they'd so readily handed over to the pawnbroker at discount prices.

This article somehow became entangled in my memory with an article that I believe appeared in the *New York Times* somewhere in the late 80s. I have it saved somewhere, but where? I *do* however, remember the article covering a casual, yet earnest, Louisiana Congressman's proposed legislation to reintroduce Ancient Roman-style spectacles complete with wild animals and duels between gladiators, with prisoners, perhaps those on Death Row, serving as the contestants.

Time passed, the article yellowed, got misplaced and forgotten until ... many years later I heard a distant crackly radio broadcast where a strident shock jock, a man whose bite apparently outstripped his mouth and his mouth in turn outstripped his words which in turn, deflected all echoes off our howling souls, gutted by the built-in disappointments of consumption. His righteous bellows sounded triumphant and designed to bloat our every gland with bile.[15] He was basking in the news of the enactment into law of Proposition 166 which "offered" those condemned to capital punishment a final reprieve, allowing for small recompense — as they would now be coerced into choosing to fight in a gladiatorial and revenue-enhancing manner,[16] and "put on a show that people will come out to see"[17] so that the spectacle could profit the citizens and benefit crime victims everywhere.[18]

The Louisiana Division of Lotteries & Punition[19] approved an agreement with private contractor Madiator, Inc. to design and implement mandated gladiatorial "extreme fighting events," "fights for life between 2 gladiators."[20]

The first gladiator training schools in 1992 were privatized institutions[21] abiding by the conventional wisdom of the day that private industry could better manage the economic incentives of state sports industry development programs. These contracts were abrogated in 1995 however, when, like in Ancient Rome, the gladiator training "schools came under state control to prevent them becoming private armies." Rumors abounded that gladiator-inmates were enlisting security school prison guard-trainees as allies[22] and training para-military units willing to challenge the forces of the State.[23] Many of the guard-trainees (73%) had at some point in their lives been incarcerated themselves.

Proposition 166 had in less than six months since enactment succeeded beyond all expectation in not only allowing society to convince itself of its own shimmer of humanity, but also recuperate, in Foucault's words, the notion of "the body as the major target of penal repression" into a so-called "higher aim penalty,"[24] of fiscal responsibility while permitting the condemned "one last chance" to redeem their dignities in the arena. Profits were already being realized,[25] state economic solvency was accomplished in the program's second year, and reelection of its political advocates was all but assured.[26]

Proposition 166 effectively conflates the "freedom is about authority" notion with Roman spectacles for the consumption of the masses, itself an ingenious fusion of state lottery, commerce, sport and punishment. Much the same way that an article about privatized incarceration can be flanked by an advertisement for Freedom Panty Shields.

The supply of available combatants was at first culled exclusively from among Death Row Inmates (DRIs)[27] who would fight one another (68%). But a late 1994 amendment to Proposition 166 opened up the competion to others such as: death penalty advocates (18%) who wished to fight inmates (of 300 applications received in the first week, 75% had some personal relationship to a crime victim); ex-football players who had wrestled bears in circus sideshows (4%); and unemployed actors-spokesmodels-action-figures (6%). Just as in Rome, "women (1%) and dwarves (.8%) were also [eventually] used,"[28] giving the Madiator events a decidedly sideshow or vaudeville flavor.

Deathrow inmates[29] and newer participants now weekly engage in duels to large crowds. Combatants combine gladiatorial, kick-boxing, karate, gang brawling, and Ustasha torture techniques.[30] Few rules are necessary in these "monitored free-for-alls"[31] — no codes of conduct, rounds, timeouts, attending to injuries; although *loaded* firearms and other incendiary devices *are* prohibited.

If DRIs show exceptional bravery in victory, they can win eventual release by participating in the Wimbledon-style elimination tournaments and emerging victorious (1.4%). The finals victor is simply the last one left standing. He is then electronically tagged, and placed on permanently-monitored parole. If inmates merely survive unspectacularly they must fight again and again to eventually die (71%) in the service of the state.

"Men f[i]ght with desperate ferocity,"[32] with weapons they'd utilized to perpetrate their crimes: curved scimitars, hammers, acetyline torches, bicycle chains, boomerangs, hatchets, nightsticks or firearms (sans ammo, of course). Condemned criminals, "sometimes dress in skins to resemble animals,"[33] others are chosen to become *bestiari* and are condemned to fight beasts (lions, sharks in tanks, bulls) "made ravenous for the occasion; death in such cases came with all possible agony."[34] Blood splatter patterns are often described as spectacular and likened to abstract art of the highest caliber.

The spectacles allow the state's pundits to talk of "redemption through value-added entertainment mortalities"[35] (VAEMs) because their suffering serves as crime deterrent; combatants' courage reinvests society with a sense of purpose;[36] blood familiarizes "us" with the horrors of conflagrations (to come); the spectacle is instructive entertainment;[37] and a major fund-raising tool whereby gladiators repay their debt to society (ticket proceeds go to victim aid funds, prison construction, and boot camp maintenance), it alleviates prison overcrowding and costly maintenance of life, and the slaughtered eventually serve as medical research specimens to "the benefit of medicine in the service of a healthy society."[38]

Many participants choose historically-correct fighting uniforms, often looking like *Ben Hur* castoffs. The *murmillos* wear fish-crest helmets, carry oblong shields and long swords or the *retiarus* with their chain mail vests, nets, tridents and daggers. Others choose more ragtag, mix-&-match uniforms, part Mad Max, part Neo-Nazi, and part armored knight.

The underutilized football stadia are converted into Madiator arenas; playing fields are covered with a huge raised stage. The floor is then covered with sand.[39] Parts of the floor can be lowered and raised with changes of scene. Large chambers underneath hold the animals, machines, and gladiators scheduled for the day. Here wage-slaves (prisoners serving sentences for lesser crimes)[40] operate machines and pulleys that raise animal and gladiator cages up to stage level while thousands of spectators and bettors[41] "wait hopefully for the sight of death."[42]

Spectators[43] vote electronically[44] from their seats on categories gleaned from figure skating competitions, with results displayed on immense stadium screens. With a state official's nod,[45] the fate of the victor to slaughter his prisoner is carried out.

And what of the statistical 20%[46] of innocents who will be sent to their deaths? To criticism, Madiator public relations administrator, Femus Bainside, responded with the classic historical logic employed during the Salem Witch Trials, stating: "If they are innocent they will prove it in victory."[47]

We watched the prisoner we knew (but did not bet on) cling tipsy to the slender sinewy neck like a breath full of scream. I felt Suki grip my thigh in the same manner she did when we made love. His beheading by a brute who'd butchered 16 border migrants was bemoaned only because he had been so handsome and now we were deprived of that handsomeness. "He could have been a male model," someone sitting next to Suki had said. As I wondered whether it would be possible to purchase his head as a gift for her, I heard Suki say simply that "he was gentle." Or maybe it would just serve as an ashtray in the Spectatentiary Corrections Morgue laboratories, I further mused, as we watched the gladiator-trainee chaingang sweep "up the bloodied ground in shovels and spread fresh sand for the next death."[48]

We could feel that "the hostility of masters to their slaves ran just below the surface of ... civilization,"[49] and hovered at just about the same altitude, and the same esoteric, tenuous realm as one finds between dream and dread, and between the drone of honey bees and the buzz of surveillance helicopters.

This piece was especially remixed for this Self-Help collection and is sampled from TYRANTS IN OUR IRON SKIES, an earlier version of which appeared in *NoZone: The Extremism Issue*, a remix of which appeared in *Fiction International #31*. A rewired version appeared in *Fringecore* as the "Strange Territory of the Body."

NOTES:

[1] Also called PR^3 in certain Prison Studies and Spectatentiary Corrections circles.

[2] 519 per 100,000 people are incarcerated in the U.S. Rate is second only to Russia's. The Netherlands at 49 per 100,000 is 1/10 the U.S. rate. The Sentencing Project, 917 F St. NW, Suite 501, Washington DC 20004, or www.calyx.net/...fer/other/sp/abb.html

[3] The incarceration rate in the U.S. has nearly doubled in the last decade according to a 1996 U.S. Justice Dept. report. It is 6 to 8 times higher than rates in other industrialized nations according to the Associated Press, 1997. From *Resurrecting Prison Industries: New Bondage For Flexible Labor?*, by Nina Ascoly, Research Paper, Masters of Arts Degree in Women & Development, Dec. 1997, Institute of Social Studies, The Hague.

[4] Ascoly.

[5] Jimmy Breslin, for instance in a 1996 *Newsday* op-ed piece, noted a study by the Weber-Malsted Group and MIT, which offered other reasons for the dramatic declines in crime that politicians were taking credit for: "Fewer people are being shot in New York City because more people have decided that they are not bulletproof and therefore remain indoors at all hours. 'New York City is increasingly becoming a prison where you get gas bills,' the Weber Malsted report declares... of all New Yorkers between the ages of 47 and 70, a figure of 72.4% never leave the house after 6 p.m... This permanent jamming of New Yorkers into bedrooms and living rooms is not reflected in the official law enforcement agency crime statistics.... "

[6] Michel Foucault, *Discipline & Punish*, Penguin, London, 1993.

[7] And vice versa as well, as Ray Luc Levasseur, convicted and sentenced to 65 years in prison for the 1985 bombing of U.S. military facilities and multinational corporations, relates in his "Trouble Coming Every Day," in *Fiction International #31*, San Diego, 1998: "Society reflects itself in the microcosm of prison... [where] essential needs are viewed with suspicion... [and] every ADX cell is equipped with a small black&white TV, courtesy of the Bureau of Prisons pacification program. Hollywood and Madison Avenue images are churned out... to give us some vicarious social interaction... [meanwhile] Education is restricted to inadequate videos...."

[8] Frank Lloyd Wright, for instance, described New York as, "Prison towers and modern posters for soap and whiskey."

[9] "Once prisons are built, they are in many respects a self-perpetuating entity...and their continued use over time contributes to a culture that makes their use seem logical and rational." The Sentencing Project.

[10] "The language of the prevailing Law & Order... not only defines... the Enemy, it also *creates* him; and this creation is not the Enemy as he really is but rather as he must be in order to perform his function for the Establishment." Herbert Marcuse, *Essays on Liberation*, Beacon Press, Boston, 1970.

[11] "They wish to acquire the same goals as everybody else, money, power, greed, and

conspicuous consumption... adopt[ing] techniques and methods which society has defined as illegitimate.... They may be called 'illegitimate capitalists' since their aim is to acquire everything this capitalistic society defines as legitimate." Huey Newton in "Prison, Where is Thy victory?" included in *If They Come in the Morning,* Angela Davis, Orbach & Chambers, London, 1971.

[12] Other such syncretizations and hybridized allusions certainly abound: Vivienne Westwood's prison chic fall collection of 1995 or, as Ascoly notes: "Commodifying the criminal makes for some catchy taglines. Hard Time sweatshirts, shorts and caps, silkscreened by inmates at California's San Quentin prison... follow the theme that 'fitness is a life sentence'... Prison Blues [jeans] are 'made on the inside to be worn on the outside'...."

[13] Boris Vian's *I Spit On Your Graves* (Tam Tam, LA, 1998) is a hard-boiled novel that masterfully conflates a brutal racial revenge murder and eroticism. "I felt the blood gush into my mouth and her body writhed in spite of the rope.... I'd never heard a woman scream like that; all of a sudden I felt myself shooting off in my shorts."

[14] "We Need Authority and Values, Sez Mayor," *Daily News,* NY, March 17,1994.

[15] The heralds of "totalitarian dictatorships...succeeded because they gave form to the shapeless dreams of the national masses and voiced with almost alarming frightening daring and over-simplification their confused and hardly conscious wishes." Hans Kohn, *The 20th Century: The Challenge to the West & Its Response,* MacMillan, NY, 1957.

[16] U.S. Supreme Court Justice, Warren Burger, "argued that prisons should once again become not only self-sustaining, but profit-producing entities...." P. Wright, *Washington Free Press,* 1995, as quoted in Ascoly.

[17] Emmit Dibbs, Louisiana State Legislator on the floor of the State Senate, August 12, 1991.

[18] In Rome, "chariot racing was very expensive and [too] was run for profit as a highly organized business." Lesley and Roy Adkins, *Handbook To Life In Ancient Rome,* Facts On File, NY, 1994.

[19] "...increasingly, as industries flee this country, people find that their only option in terms of personal survival is to become a part of what has been called a 'fortress economy.'" Mumia Abu Jamal, *Still Black, Still Strong,* Autonomedia, Brooklyn, 1993.

[20] Adkins.

[21] Managed by Firmacon and Spectatentiary, two "sweetheart subsidiaries" of Madiator, Inc.

[22] "Many prisoners believe their labour power is being exploited in order for the State to increase its economic power and continue to expand its correctional facilities..." Angela Davis, *If They Come.*

[23] Called "Spartacists" or the "Remember Attica Attack Group" (RAAG) in some prison advocate and law enforcement circles.

[24] Foucault.

[25] "Blood is our last precious metal, it's a gold mine." Mike Davis, "One Man's Pain, Another Man's Profit," *The Nation,* NY, Dec. 12, 1993.

[26] "Humanity was complemented by self-interest." Hopkins.

[27] Each inmate-gladiator is "tagged" with a scar pattern of 3 vertical bars, signifying incarceration, behind bars, on his forehead with the official State of Louisiana weapon, a Bowie Knife, by a state-certified scarificator.

[28] Adkins.

29 In Rome, condemned criminals were called the *damnati*.

30 Romanian Nazi-loyalists who "even prompted protests from the German Waffen SS officers assigned to Croatia." Paul Hockenos, *Free to Hate: The Rise of the Right in Post-Communist Eastern Europe*, Routledge, NY, 1993.

31 Davis.

32 Will Durant, *The Story of Civilization 3: Caesar & Christ.* Simon & Schuster, NY, 1947.

33 Durant.

34 Durant.

35 Governor Jocelyn-Marie Wallace-Moxy in 1996 speech before Alabama Legislature advocating enactment of similar legislation in Alabama.

36 "Men became brave by proxy..." Durant.

37 Prisoners "were publicly killed for the pleasure of the free." Keith Hopkins, *Conquerors & Slaves,* Cambridge University Press, Cambridge, 1978.

38 Wallace-Moxy.

39 Arena derives from the Latin word *harena* which means sand or sandy place.

40 There has been an unexpected increase of "internal homicides" or prisoners killing other prisoners,hoping that they will arise from mere below stage drudge to glorious combatant.

41 Betting on extreme fighting events produced by Madiator, Inc. was legalized in 1995. In his *Aesthetics of Disappearance* (Autonomedia, 1991), Paul Virilio observes: "New Roman circuses, in Las Vegas they bet on any and everything, in the gamerooms and even in the hospitals — even on death. A nurse... invented, for the amusement of the personnel, a 'casino of death' where you bet on the moment the patient will die. Soon everyone started playing: doctors, nurses, cleaning ladies... soon there weren't enough people dying. What follows is easy enough to imagine."

42 Durant.

43 Bettors do not vote.

44 "To show the horror of crime and invincibility of power." Foucault. And according to Wallace-Moxy, this electronic voting system is regarded as an "enhanced interactive plus."

45 "Gangsters and gods do not speak, they nod..." Roland Barthes, *The Eiffel Tower & Other Mythologies.* Hill & Wang, NY, 1979.

46 Amnesty International calculates the percentage of innocent victims at 38%.

47 Press conference outside Madiator-Saints Stadium, Noxia, Louisiana, Feb. 15, 1996.

48 Durant.

49 Hopkins.

Finding Yourself in the Merchant Marine

CLAUDE TAYLOR

We sat in the deep arched doorway of a building with the river gently lapping not ten feet before us. A large rat was picking through leftovers in a garbage can. His ears pricked up at our approach, but he continued to scavenge. It was an odd mix of building dust and rotting wood that we breathed there, cut through by the salty sea breeze. Alonzo leaned back and closed his eyes. I lit a cigarette. It was raw and briskly cool. The lapping water was kinder and more dulcifying than total silence.

Alonzo held a silver flask out to me smiling like the Chesire Cat. And like the Chesire Cat, in the intensity of the darkness around us, little more than his smile was visible.

"What is it?" I asked.

"Just taste it, brother."

It was sweet and mild and very cool. Vaguely familiar in some eerie deja vu sort of way. "What is it?" I insisted.

"It's Pernod."

I nodded my head remembering the taste. "Ah, Pernod."

Alonzo took a long hit and then gazed out sadly at the river. "It's been a long time," he said, "since I sat in the dark silence of the night breathing in the sea air."

He was quiet for a few minutes as we gazed down river.

"When I was twenty or so, I joined the Merchant Marines. For two years, I worked the big boats all across the Pacific. My father got me in. He was well connected, my father was. Knew even more people than I do ... Anyway, he died not seven months later. A heart attack exacerbated by too much drinking. He was fifty-three."

Somewhere far off, someone smashed a bottle against a wall and laughed.

"They told me about it somewhere in the middle of the ocean, they told me. That was when I really started drinking. I'd stand on the bow of the ship late at night, in darkness just like this, drunk out of my mind. And I swear I could hear my father laughing at me up in the sky, saying, "Look at him, God. He wants to be just like me. Ain't that funny, God? Ain't that funny."

I lifted the flask in a toast. "Here's to friendly ghosts, Al."

He smiled and rubbed my neck with one great meaty hand. "You want to hear a funny story? I was in love once. With a Chinese girl in Singapore. Malaysian, actually. This was back when I was in the Merchant Marine. I jumped ship and lived with her for four months. Then, one day, it started hurting when I pissed, so I got the name of an English doctor from a friend of mine and went to see him. The doctor's office was in a remote Godforsaken part of town. I remember he held my dick, picked at it under a Goddamn lamp in this small dark room that smelled of

75

formaldehyde. And all the while asking me what I was studying in the Navy. In the Navy, for Christsake. And showing me with a yellowed fingernail the infected lesions on my cock! Off in another room, I could hear Jan Sabbott and the Tophatters singing *You Go to My Head*.

"There was a chart on the wall subdivided into three parts: cells in the urine, crystals in the urine, and, I don't know, something else in the urine. But the thing I remember was that each of the three parts was illustrated with colorful pictures of all these weird fucking monstrous creatures that live in your urine.

"The paint on the walls was peeling, and there was cracked green linoleum on the floor. And the strangest, most repulsive part of it of all, was that this doctor looked just like that actor Dick Van Patten." He paused for a moment and looked around to see if he was getting the full effect.

"The thing is," he continued, "I can remember that doctor perfectly, but I can hardly picture that young Malaysian girl at all anymore." He chuckled. "Ain't love grand."

I leaned back against the building and lit another cigarette. "Well, a man's gotta do what a man's gotta do."

"Son, I can only say, it's made me the man I am today."

We sat back and watched the lights play across the water. Voices drifted over from far down the alley. Somewhere another bottle got slammed against a wall like ocean spray, or a cataclysm of shooting stars. Alonzo closed his eyes and began to laugh.

"Ain't that funny, God," he whispered. "Ain't that funny."

MASTER THE CRAFT OF WRITING FOR PROFIT!

How To Watch A Film With John Simon

Going to the movies will never be the same again.

At the end of the movie you walk out of the theater with your friend, and your friend turns to you and asks the inevitable question, "What did you think of it?" You say, "It was terrific," and you give some plausible reasons why the film was good, but you know you missed a lot. A movie contains dimensions that are hidden to the ordinary eye but reveal themselves to those few who really understand film and how to watch it.

Just [...] o lo[...] s[...] w[...] ng Annex class you can spend an unforgettable evening learning to do just that—with one of America's premier film critics, John Simon, drama critic of *New York Magazine*. During his 21 years with New York, Mr. Simon has built a solid reputation as the dean of American critics. Before assuming his present position at New York, he spent 20 years as a drama critic for such publications as Theatre Arts Magazine and the Hudson Review, as well as for educational television.

"I want to help my Learning Annex students develop their critical abilities," says John Simon. "I'll show them how to see more in a film. It's an art that can be learned."

Mr. Simon will bring a (surprise) little-known film to the seminar. The class will watch it, then he and the students will proceed to pick it apart and put it back together again. This will be one of the most fascinating evenings you'll ever spend. You'll get your questions answered—and you'll never watch "High Noon" with the same pair of eyes again.

Course 145
Sec. A   June 28   6:30-9:30pm
Course fee $29
Couples (come with a friend) fee $39
Call 580-2828 to register

How to Make A Toast

Whether it be a wedding, a birthday party, anniversary or business dinner, this course will show you how to impress your audience.

The scene could be a wedding, a birthday, an awards luncheon or a corporate dinner. You're called upon to make a toast. This is your moment in the spotlight. You stand up, look out over the expectant faces of your audience—and what do you do? Do you hesitate, clear your throat and then mumble awkwardly through a few forgettable phrases? Or do you easily come up with a bright, interesting toast that's an ornament to the occasion—and a boost to your reputation?

The answer to that question may well depend on whether or not you've attended the great new Learning Annex seminar "How To Make A Toast." Toasting is a social art, and an important one. And now [...] ng a gre[...] Day, pre[...] ing firm[...] nd pre[...]

Yo[...] th co[...] le m[...]

M[...] of toa[...] and ways to make an especially good impression. You'll get tips on how to overcome your fear of public speaking. Then it will be your turn to make a toast—and be videotaped. Seeing the playback will give you the best possible opportunity to polish your style. You'll learn everything from how to hold the champagne glass to how to demand the attention of your audience, the proper gestures to make, how to judge the best length for a toast—everything you need to know.

Remember, 90% of confidence is preparation. So do yourself a favor and take this two-evening seminar. And here's to long life and even greater success!

Course 457
Sec. A   May 30,31   6:30-9pm
Sec. B   June 22,29   6:30-9pm
Course fee $34
Call 580-2828 to register

How to Open An Art Gallery with Tony Shafrazi

Tony Shafrazi, a legend in New York art circles, will teach you what it takes to make it in the world of art.

For Tony Shafrazi, art has always been, not just a love, but an obsession. He studied art in London, painted it in Milan, organized art shows in Teheran, and finally created a gallery to celebrate art in New York.

In fact, the Tony Shafrazi Gallery in Soho is a must-see for any art-obsessed lover. And Shafrazi's commitment to contemporary artists such as Keith Haring and Kenny Scharf is unshakable. He proclaims: "I am probably the biggest artist groupie there ever was !" And it was this passion for art that made his gallery the place for new artists back in 1980 when he first opened. The hot talent in those days were fresh from the club circuit—and that gave the Shafrazi Gallery openings an "after-hours" feel.

Today, with the new rage of art-in-clubs, the name Tony Shafrazi is a name that artists and collectors know and respect.

That's why if you're thinking about opening your own gallery, or you're an avid collector, or simply an artist wanting to h[...] uru, sp[...] nd fi[...] to m[...]

T[...] ng a[...] he cl[...] ed hi[...] 's in[...] a re[...] th a[...] of a[...] ut a[...] to[...] hy it's crucial to [...] your heart and take creative risks.

Course 857
Sec. A   June 27   6:30-9pm
Course fee $29
Call 580-2828 to register

Slurring My Words

Ellen Aug Lytle

There once was a time when grand glasses of chilled wine of almost any pedigree or color filled me with great pleasure. Back then I drank with gusto and wanton freedom. Not bad for a young writer who wanted so much to be coddled. After all, writers need liquid and if we can't have cash, or fresh squeezed orange juice every day, then at least we can have cigarettes and booze. And if we can't have cigarettes, Jack Daniels or Johnnie Walker Black, then at least we can have wine!

October, 1978

"...if anyone comes into my class stoned or liquored up, even from beer, OUT you will go...no pot no alcohol before class...is that understood? Good...Now, let's write...pick up your pens, put them to the paper and write anything that appears in your little minds while I read from Gerard Manley Hopkins..." William Packard says in our first class on the 'craft of poetry' at NYU.

I'm stunned. After all, Packard's a sexy hunk who lets us know he writes in the middle of the night. He must have a drink to soften the edges, right? Wrong. "In case it's anyone's business, I gave up drinking after college and haven't touched it since, no, no, you in the back, jumping up and down in your seat, rest easy...not even beer!"

So how come, working for Packard's *NYQuarterly* that year, having my own apartment, my own room for the first time in my life, and finally going to college and learning literature, I'm not able to write, even in the afternoon, without *something*? Years ago it was cigarettes; long deep inhalings on a Chesterfield (I hate filters) which then were replaced by carefully proportioned shot glasses of scotch, then taller glasses of bourbon with soda (seltzer). Now all I can afford is Gallo and some cigarettes from Ivan, next door.

"You know this work is sloppy...there's stains all over the manuscript and the writing could be greatly improved...Ellen, you need to give up alcohol and help yourself... you *could* be such a good writer, if only you'd concentrate; read more...and give up that no good boyfriend, he's not helping you...oh, and stop the wine...Come to more readings...join our gatherings...we have fun without alcohol or pot..."

November, 1983

"...and the moooooon lights the gray shinnngles against the scab...beee brush...sorry...buuush...while mother comes to the windooo..." With that performance finished, I grab my two free drinks and sneak in some merlot from the bar; there's a party afterwards at Stephen's apartment, more booze, more cheese, I hope. "So, you're E—, what did you think of tonight's reading? Are you reading again soon? Do you write every day, what time?" I find a soft corner and hide till it's time to leave...but not before I have another sip and fill my pockets with plenty of smelly cheese and salty crackers...someone please fix my life...make me famous so I'll be understood and I can drink all the best wine and eat all the rarest cheese and when I stumble over my words or trip off the stage people will only appreciate me more...She's the famous poet Ellen Aug, too bad she drinks but so what she's a great writer...You know if you laid off the booze, everyone would like you and you'd get a lot more readings and...

October, 1999

...sick in too many gutters and cold bathroom floors (some filthy) too many headaches, too much weight (drinking always makes me hungry when I have to stop) and finally two years ago some weird 'episodes' where my subconscious would air itself and startle my conscious mind, then override my present thoughts as if it had a separate power, made me quit...

So we excess to the brink, the break-off point, I guess, and all the self-help doesn't help a bit until we are self-disgusted enough...

Heat

David L. Ulin

I have a dream. I am sitting at a desk in front of a classroom. It's my classroom, the classroom at Santa Monica High School where I teach writing on Friday mornings, and from the look of things, it's just another day. On the door, the latest schedule of readings at Beyond Baroque hangs, bright but ignored, while throughout the room, my tenth grade students sit in their usual sprawl - slouching, staring, fiddling with pens and papers, a kaleidoscope of nose rings, spiked hair, tee shirts, and baggy jeans. The light is heavy, lucent and glaring; through the windows, the heat of Southern California seeps like liquid magma, enveloping everything, every movement, making us all feel submerged and slow. I am talking. I know this because I can feel the hum of language, the pressure of syllables, the vibration of sound. I know this, but I cannot hear myself, cannot hear anything except a low, moaning drone. I look around; no one seems to notice. One kid writes on a piece of paper, another slowly chews a stick of gum.

The door of the classroom opens, and one of my former students comes in. He is wearing an Army fatigue jacket, and as he walks, it opens a little, revealing a tee-shirt that reads in goofy balloon letters, "Have a nice day." It feels strange to see him, but also fitting somehow, as if he is a kind of lesson in the flesh. All semester long, I've been telling my class about him, telling them how, when he finally decided to believe that he really did have permission to turn in anything, he took it to the limit, producing an obsessive fantasy about drugs and violence, in which he (or a narrator a lot like him) loads up on acid and goes on an extended rape-and-murder spree. These days, of course, they'd probably lock a kid up just for thinking something like that, but a year ago, a high school classroom was still a place where I could let people explore their feelings, even use them to trigger a discussion of free expression and the responsibility of a writer to stand up for his or her own words. That's an important message, maybe the most important message, and I want my students to believe it, just as I want them to believe that words do matter, not in the way administrators and politicians tell us - as clues, or warning signs - but as something deeper and more powerful, a direct, unfiltered channel to who we are.

My former student comes towards me, body moving in slow motion, eyes hidden behind a sweep of greasy blond hair. I watch as a drop of sweat trudges like a small lucite beetle down the side of his face, only to explode when it hits the floor. As that explosion goes off, a burst of noise comes with it, and the light goes gray and grainy as if we're living in a newsprint world. My stomach clutches, and the scene begins to play itself out in snapshots, all broken and discontinuous, like the fragments of a film. Across the room, kids are staring, and as they do, the boy reaches inside his jacket and withdraws a long black tube. Now, people are moving, overturning desks and chairs. "No," I start to say, but before the word emerges,

I recognize that what the boy is holding is a pen. And as everybody huddles spell-bound, he sprays the room with words.

How to Do Well in This Class

SAMUEL R. DELANY

The first key to doing well in this class is pretty much the same one for doing well in all your classes. Organize your study time.

Set aside time for having fun and just hanging out. That's very important. But also set aside time for study—and for attending your classes! It may be self-evident and a little silly to have to say it, but the work really is as important as the fun!

Here, however, we have to say a few words about how students mess up. A very few students don't care how they do and don't try from the beginning. But I know that most of you want to do well. The overwhelming majority of students who fail their courses, or do poorly, do so not because they don't care but because they go through some version of the following process: Possibly because you've neglected to do some earlier work for the first week or two, sometime toward the beginning of the term you try to study too hard and too long, in order to catch up. But because you haven't set any time limits on that study, it's more than you (or anyone else) could possibly do comfortably in a single sitting. Therefore, after a few hours, in order to compensate you go out and try to have a good time. But because you haven't set any time limits on your good times either, you spend too much time at that (a couple of days, say, without going back and doing any studying at all) so that you fall even farther behind! Eventually, a week or two later, you make another stab at studying, but again, because you haven't set it up in terms of reasonable time limits, the process just repeats, with longer and longer periods between the attempts to study as you have more and more to catch up with. The end result is a failed course or two—and your good times are marred by your nagging anxiety about classes not going well or skipped, missing or poor papers, and bad test results.

This process is strong, stable, and extraordinarily efficient—efficient for removing several hundred students a year from among the twenty-five thousand that attend the University of Massachusetts. The thing to understand if you get caught in this process is that what is messing up your marks and doing in your grades is not your intelligence. (As I'm sure you've noticed, if you've gotten a chance to look around: People a lot less swift than you are often doing pretty well around you.) If you first got caught in this process back in high school, then almost certainly one person or another—a relative or a friend—has told you that it has something to do with your character or your personality. ("You just don't try! Don't be so lazy! You could do it if you really wanted to ... ") Well, sad news for them: It's not your character, either. (Having gotten caught in this process without really understanding what it is and how it works, you may have decided that you yourself can't get out of it and so have decided to give up. But that's another story.) Though it is hard for people to grasp this, it is the process itself that is responsible for your doing poorly. Put pretty much anyone inside this process—exceptionally smart or pretty ordinary—and the results will still be the same.

The most important thing to remember if you're trapped in this process and want to get out of it is that you can't fight the process from inside it. If you say, "Okay. As soon as I've had my fill of fun, I'm going to sit down and study," you might as well forget it. You're still inside the process—the process of failure. If you say: "Right now, this very instant, I'm going to sit down and start studying. And I'm going to go on studying until I'm caught up, no matter what it takes"—well, even as you sit there, poring over your books, you're still within the process! You might as well not have bothered.

By the same token if, after five minutes (and it may only be that) or after five hours of studying, you reach the point where you can't study any more and you say, "Okay! Enough of this. I'm going out and walk around, look for a friend, and go hang out at a bar," you're still within the process.

The process of failure is, you see, one of setting up unorganized, open-ended units of time. The way to get out of the process is to set up organized, end-stopped units of time. That's the only thing that will stop it. If you want me to put it in terms of rules, I can:

Don't sit down to study without planning a specific time at which to stop.

When you go out to have fun, set a specific time by which to be back.

If, in the middle of things, you decide you want to change to a new time, fine: Do that—set a new time to stop; set a new time to be back. But to get out of the process, you have to stop living in a world of open-ended time units and start living in a world of end-stopped time units. Hard as it may be to believe, that's the only fundamental difference between what the people who are getting those As and ABs and maintaining a 3.5 or higher GPA are doing and what you're doing.

If you're caught up in the process of failure, you'll do better if you set yourself three half-hour study sessions every other day (that's three half hours that start here and end there: once in the morning, once in the afternoon, and once at night) than you will if you go on doing what you're doing now: that is, sometime on Sunday or even Monday night, deciding maybe you better sit down and do some catching up, which, for a few minutes or even a few hours, you actually do ...

The fact is, organizing your time and setting limits on your periods of fun and your periods of work constitute a process too. It's a process that frees what intelligence you have to exercise itself in its most constructive mode on the problem to hand. It makes it easier for you to study, and, more important, it makes it possible for you to study again—whereas the process of failure not only makes it harder for you to study but makes it even harder (indeed, all but impossible) for you to study again. In a school situation where you are not working on a single, overall, encompassing, obsessive problem, but rather on several limited and usually more or less separate fields (math, chemistry, history, French, economics ...), it's the only process likely to let you negotiate them all with any combined efficiency. But if you don't organize your time, other forces—powerful forces that Sigmund Freud grouped together under the term "the Pleasure Principle"—will take over and organize it for you; and (as Freud himself was quick to note) those forces will organize it in ways that, in the long run, produce some unpleasurable results, like flunking out of school.

Organizing your time and setting limits is not only a process, it's also a habit. If you haven't done it before, the first ten times you do it, it's going to feel like eating with the wrong hand. Do it anyway. The next ten will be easier—and the ten after that, easier still. By then, however, you will be starting to experience the rewards from living your life this way.

Again: The solution is to organize your study time from the start—and your fun time. Set limits on both.

What kind of limits? First, understand: Studying more than four hours straight without at least an hour break is generally not going to help you too much. After a certain amount of time (different for each one of us), things simply stop sticking in your memory. You start making mistakes or misremembering things without knowing it.

A full fifteen-credit course load is the equivalent of a full 40-hour a week job—and if you want to do particularly well, you'll have to put in some overtime. If you have a part-time or full-time job as well as classes, you have to take that into account.

Again: Organize your time. Write down the hours you intend to study and the hours you have set aside for yourself. Try to stick to that schedule. After you've tried it for a week or two, decide if it's working or not. If it's not, adjust it where you need to.

Here's my suggestion: Depending on whether you think of yourself as a slow reader or a fast reader, start by setting aside between an hour and an hour-and-a-half, three nights a week, to read and take notes for this class. The four long stories that we read over the term ("Heart of Darkness," "The Time Machine," "The Turn of the Screw," and "The Metamorphosis") may easily take you between eight and fourteen hours each to read. So, as well as your regular reading time, be prepared to give a good part of one weekend day (before the lecture!) to each of those four longer stories as well.

When a paper is due, break out your reading diary and look at your notes on details, set yourself a full six hours on one day to write it (eight hours if you have to re-read the whole story)—and at least two hours on another day to go over the paper and revise it, once you've had a night's sleep and can look at it with fresh eyes. Figure in break times.

Besides being a professor, I'm also a professional writer. I wouldn't think of handing in a piece of writing without going over it to revise and correct it, a day after I'd "finished" it. You shouldn't either. Revising is part of the writing process. I have a couple of friends I show all my writing to and ask them to suggest improvements. Try that too, and see if your papers aren't better.

And go to a movie at least once a week with a friend!

Try it, and see how it works out. You may well find you don't need as much time as I've suggested. If so, adjust your schedule down. But just because it starts off easy, don't abandon your schedule altogether! If you do, even if you're someone who finds the work easy, you may still fall behind.

The only human endeavors I know that don't profit from being done in end-stopped time units are works of art—specifically novels, non-fiction pieces, and long poems. Creative work alone seems to thrive on long, uninterrupted, obsessive periods of work. (Novels seem to require the process of failure from which to grow!) Even there, sometimes breaks and forced stopping periods can benefit such projects. It's the rare novel that doesn't benefit from the artist having her or his nose rubbed in the realities daily life a handful of times, at least, during its creation.

Advice to a Young Poet

RICHARD KOSTELANETZ

> Being a good man, he has character enough to make enemies. So has Frank
> Harris. So have I.—George Bernard Shaw, *Advice to a Young Critic: Letters
> 1894-1928*

First of all, my dear young person, you must take an MFA degree in poetry writing. Know that a BA won't be enough in poetry's increasingly competitive world; you must have "professional credentials" as well, just as lawyers must, especially if you want to get a job teaching poetry, even to prepubescent children.

Try to get into the Iowa Writing Program, because it is the oldest and still among the largest, with enough alumni respecting their "old school tie" to give you the practical equivalence of a Harvard MBA for working in international finance. Given roughly equal applicants for any writing job, most former Iowa MFAs involved in making a hiring decision in, say, academia or publishing will nearly always favor a supplicant advertising an Iowa degree. Should you be less fortunate and matriculate into another, less powerful MFA writing program, be sure to take classes with the most prominent poet on the staff. If this star be "on leave" for a year, as such stars are wont to be, wait for his or her return; be warned in advance that the name of any unknown instructor on your resumé simply won't be noticed. Once you receive your degree, you can answer "poet" whenever asked what it is you do in life.

Don't forget that poetry is far more competitive than business or law, superficial platitudes about the "community of poets" notwithstanding. Should you have a law degree, the odds that you might live off your receipts as a lawyer ten years from now are better than 50 per cent. Likewise if you have an MBA, even from a school less prominent than Harvard. Almost everyone with an M.D. will be employed forever in medicine. When you have an MFA in writing, the likelihood that you might in ten years earn your living from poetry or even the teaching of poetry is less than one per cent. The economic truth, obvious to everyone wise, is that any situation so competitive is necessarily more cutthroat. You must be no less ruthless than the most competitive turf warrior.

Dress like a poet. Advertise through your clothing and hairstyle, just as models (or streetwalkers) do, or else other poets will think you an *apparatchik* with pretensions. Have a veteran literary photographer take a picture of yourself looking earnest. No matter how much orthodontia you've had, don't smile at the camera. However, don't deceive yourself into thinking only these moves toward an appropriate appearance would be enough to establish your career.

Be sure to flatter famous poets whenever possible—send them appreciative letters, remind them that you've read not just their books but poems other than those titling their books (remembering that John F. Kennedy impressed Norman Mailer by citing not his most famous novel but *Barbary Shore*). Attend their poetry readings whenever possible, introduce yourself especially if you look sexually desirable, dedicate individual poems to them, and review favorably their latest books anywhere you can (because even the most prominent poets pay more attention to reviews than sales). You should learn to quickly and surely distinguish those prominent poets who are susceptible to copious butt-kissing from those who, alas, are not.

Attend a summertime "writers' conference," even after you've begun to publish, not only to meet aspiring colleagues whose friendship might later be useful but to impress the faculty. Isolated from their homes and families for a week or two, these senior poets become more personally accessible than they would normally be. To facilitate faculty-student contact, the conference organizers often sponsor social hours during which alcohol flows freely and everyone with a drink in his or her hand can be approached. Never forget that a poet drunk has fewer resistances than a poet sober.

Give as many public readings as possible of your own poetry; teach "poetry workshops." However, don't advance the careers of any of your students and particularly don't help them publish, because your superiors in the poetry biz will think less of you if you do. Never forget that poetry as an industry is not only highly competitive but very hierarchical—those positioned below you must be treated differently from those above. Your failure to observe this last rule can ruin your career.

Develop a professional tag based upon something exotic in your background as, say, a black Icelander, a one-sixteenth American Indian, a Sudanese lesbian, a veteran of Soviet jails, a deaf fashion model who was sexually abused. Write poems about your exotic experience, if not purportedly representative of other people like yourself. Portray the experience of your ancestors in familiar contemporary terms, regardless of whether they thought as you do. If you can get publishers and publicists to acknowledge your exotic tag, you'll be forever known as the umpty-ump poet, rather than a mere writer. The market value of such a tag, especially a currently fashionable tag, even if others have it, cannot be exaggerated, because it can be recalled where poems cannot.

Try to persuade the publisher of a literary magazine to let you select the poetry for its pages and, once you get such power, be sure to publish the work of other poets who double as poetry editors. They will then feel obliged to accept your own poems in return. Organize a series of poetry readings at your university or a nearby venue, such as a café or a literary bookstore that thinks it wants more customers than it would otherwise get. The poets invited to participate in your series will not only be impressed by your good taste, but they might later invite you to perform in their own reading series.

Move to New York, San Francisco, or at worst Buffalo where you can make personal contact with "the main roosters and roostresses," as my colleague Bob Grumman calls them. Join poetry societies and clubs that bestow prestige, while avoiding those that don't—the easiest way to measure the former is the presence of people you feel are positioned above you. (Conversely, avoid those filled with people below you.) Make yourself conspicuous at poetry festivals and gatherings devoted to poetry; consider yourself successful when you're invited to work the other side of the dais.

In writing your own poetry, don't do anything too conspicuously alternative either in content or form, for your poetry will be judged "acceptable" only to the degree that it resembles what other people are doing. Don't express any sentiments that might be unacceptable to most poetry readers. Piously oppose war, rape, parental abuse, homelessness, AIDS neglect, etc.—be politically correct shamelessly, not only in your poems but whatever prose remarks you write to introduce your poems or yourself. Especially on the last count of political correctness, don't make Ezra Pound's mistake—your poems will disappear from public view unless they are great enough to overcome the obstacle you have needlessly placed in their path.

Avoid formal departures that would make anyone stop and wonder about what you might be doing technically. Poetry must look correct before it is read, especially by people in power, whose eyes instinctively turn away from anything that, as they say, "looks funny on the page." Do not confuse the values of poetry with visual art or even concert music, where ambitious aspirants know they won't get anyone's attention unless they do something uniquely different from their predecessors. Writing poetry with character or a stylistic signature, as the great early moderns did, is definitely old-fashioned; it's strictly for "wild men" nowadays.

Avoid activities that your colleagues might consider *infra dig*, such as working in advertising or finance, exhibiting your visual art, performing your music, or producing books about anything other than poetry. (Or should you need to do any of these ancillary things to make money, consider a pseudonym and don't let your poetry colleagues know.)

Even when you have enough good poems to make a book, do not self-publish. Sooner spend your money entering book contests, no matter if hundreds are applying for a single prize, for even if you don't succeed, older poets especially will think better of you for trying. Don't forget that the worse thing your superiors can say about you is that you're "no poet," which means not that you fail to publish poems but that you don't play your career by the standard rules.

Though measuring a poetic career is hard, consider yourself somewhat successful when you're asked to write blurbs for other poets' books (and expect favors in return), when you are asked by poetry editors to review new collections for their literary magazines, and when you are asked to judge contests to which entrants pay a fee (some of which money will be channeled to you). Consider yourself more successful when you receive a prize or grant for poetry writing.

The truth you can't forget is this: Because only small money, if any, can be made from publishing poetry per se, you must strive for power more than for the admiration of your colleagues or even a large readership. Only when you gain a position incorporating professional power will you ever earn a bourgeois salary as a "poet" and enough respect and leverage to get additional monetary rewards.

Do what I tell you, dear aspirant, and you might even be rewarded with a university position in poetry, even though you've never published a poem that anyone especially likes or remembers.

How to Write a Piece for The New Yorker

Bob Dombrowski

Since the great computer love bug dilemma of 2000, E-mail in the city had diminished substantially. Even on one of those balmy days when Central Park is an oasis in a soon to be blisteringly hot city, the ability to communicate from office to office, from E. 63rd Street to an obscure editor working alone in a walk-up rental in Greenwich Village, had to be done through the phone lines. For some reason, I couldn't stop thinking about the complicated maze of wires under the avenues of the city.

I looked out my window and saw a crew of men protected by their AT&T van tearing another hole in the newly paved street. These were workers. They were not wearing Calvin Klein as they prepared to puncture the crust of the city's substructure; they were wearing real working man's clothes ... the kind of work clothing sold from sidewalk racks along Broadway in Chelsea.

As I watched them through my window, I saw the streams of yellow cabs carrying their drivers toward that pension and little farm in Pakistan when they retire and beneath all of them there had to be thousands of miles of wire. There's an article in this, I thought, wondering if my editor would accept it.

I wondered if there were any women working among the street crews of AT&T.

I had a cocktail meeting planned with the editor later that afternoon at the old Algonquin Hotel bar. Maybe I could pitch him a piece about communication in Manhattan.

My phone rang. Just like the old days, when banks of phones were always ringing on mahogany desks scattered across the 20th floors of sheer buildings nestled among Nedicks and delis where secretaries in their short skirts lined up for sandwiches every lunch hour.

I answered my phone. Maybe it was the mayor inviting me to a Yankee game.

It was an old friend. She was in a bar on 7th Avenue in the Village. Her favorite haunt. A bit of old New York still stuck down in that neighborhood surrounded by the jewelry stalls and health food stores that have erupted over the last decade. I imagined her sitting under the great stuffed marlin that still hung from the ceiling ... covered by the dust the Holland tunnel traffic had kicked up over the years. I knew she was drinking vodka. She was stylish, drinking vodka. It has replaced the old bourbon and water, even the historic Manhattan, as the drink to have in the late afternoon ... I've indulged in the vodka and juice drink myself during those early winter evenings when the warm and muted lights of a little pub on 8th Avenue harbor my thoughts of human isolation within the borders of a city swelling with human energy.

I decided to meet with her. My editor had made available a car service from somewhere in the Bronx for occasions like this. Rather than attempting the rushing crowd of the 7th Avenue subway, I took advantage of one of my perks. I phoned the car service. "Ten minutes," he insisted.

I imagined the driver strapping himself into his Lincoln in a garage, straightening his tie and swiftly entering traffic on the cross-Bronx. Whizzing over the Harlem river and sailing through the traffic on the FDR, using his street savvy to circumvent crosstown traffic in Midtown, and, in fact, being downstairs in ten minutes. Maybe they levitate.

I was wearing my L.L. Bean country outfit. I felt jaunty. All I really lacked was one of the old Greek seamen's caps seen everywhere throughout the city's watering hole network 20 years ago. But this was an emergency. No quick stops at the cap store still on Bleecker at the edge of the Village. I was on my own.

"We were young when we married."

This was how she greeted me. She was sitting with her drink and a small plate of Mexican chips with salsa on her table. The dip had that luminescence of the green sauce sold in cans in the import aisle of the Garden of Eden, where I did all my food shopping on Saturday mornings while still wandering in my deck shoes and T-shirt without a clear sense of what I was up to. The knots of last night's street people still scattered on the sidewalks of 23rd street at that hour. The Chelsea Hotel glowering like an old dame across the block, casting shadows of Manhattan's history.

"We were very much in love," she said. She'd had more than one vodka. Her fashionable business suit was wrinkled and the look she conveyed was one of quiet desperation. Great poets in New York had often appeared that way themselves. I wondered if she'd lost her apartment or if the doormans' strike had completely thrown her life off.

She went on, "He was a genius but he had no sense of his own worth."

I thought of all the geniuses in the new Silicon Alley district that replaced the old left in the Union Square area. All geniuses. Lines of them waiting for a sample at the wine tasting in the trendy new wine store on Union Square West. More cell phones than free newspapers.

I saw an old Village Voice. It looked dated... free... available to anyone from any street corner... the last of the old alternative papers that erupted during New York's beatnik phase. And now, cell phones. The great writers of the last few decades snuffed out as people communicated directly without the powerful exposés and insights they once offered.

She sipped her vodka. I ordered a vodka for myself and leaned back in my chair. I crossed my legs to feel more casual and felt my pant leg rising above my sock. I ignored it. I was being casual.

She spoke, "I had to help him see his own worth. I supported him. Still, nothing worked out."

I saw Baird Jones snoozing with a pair of young club-going night people in the corner. We caught each other's eyes and nodded. I searched the room, casually, for other known celebs. Baird seemed to be on his own. Unusual, I thought.

Her eyes were damp from the emotion that escaped around the edges of the vodka. "One day," she said, "he came home in a short skirt and full make up. I didn't know what to say."

I'd thought about wearing a skirt myself more than once. This did not seem out of keeping with the sexual revolution as translated in the great metropolis. As long as he didn't sit in his office flirting with the delivery people, I thought.

I wondered what really bothered her.

Maybe she was lonely and old scars were pushing up in her mind ... similar to the AT&T workers exposing buried cables as they tore up the street.

She was wearing open-toe shoes. Heels.

The wrong shoes, I thought. Those belong to the evening. Maybe she was going to someone's reception. Maybe a concert at Town Hall after the vodka had her sufficiently lubricated.

"He likes games," she said. "But if you barge through them, he's a real pushover. He's a wimp. Just tell him what you want. He's easy."

A woman walked past the window of the bar with her dog. The dog was one of those small apartment dogs that were fashionable a few years ago. The dog was wearing a double collar and a muzzle.

She was poking him along as he eyed a large retriever being led by someone else. That dog had a short bright yellow jacket swaddling him like a Times Square vagrant.

"I don't want to see him," she said. "We were living out on the island in a small summer house his family knew about... paying a rent that would make rent control look luxurious. I left him when he slept with my closest friend."

I wondered what sex her closest friend was.

"I left him and moved into the city."

She was lonely. The bar was filling up. People in crowds were laughing with their friends. Lonely takes on a deeper shadow in these circumstances.

Maybe I could write this up for my editor, I thought. It's a *New Yorker* story.

"He's great with numbers. He always has a lot of money. He's a computer genius. I don't know what happened. We were young when we got together. He just doesn't know how to deal with it."

She ordered another vodka. "Just ice, no juice," she instructed. "I can really drink a lot of this before it affects me," she said.

I was impressed. Two martinis and I'm ready to dance on the
bar and sing about hippies in San Francisco. I was close to my limit. We sat there, watching the sports news on TV. The Yankees were having a good year.

Uncovering the Inner Lullabye: An Insomniac's Workbook

ROCHELLE RATNER

August 27th:

My Aunt Ella thinks she knows everything. She thinks that just because her daughter got married right out of college to a man she'd met her junior year, got her 2.5 children (the half was aborted, and might or might not have been her husband's), then divorced and moved back in with her loving, giving, understanding parents (who actually weren't very understanding when one of the kids broke a glass or went into a tantrum), then met the supposed love of her life (a boy she knew slightly in high school) and settled down in a brand new $300,000 home six blocks from where she grew up, it entitles her to lecture every niece, nephew, and second cousin. So this year, instead of the usual birthday card with a ten dollar check inside (up from five dollars a few years ago), she sent me this journal with all these inspirational quotes that are supposed to ease you into this blissful shangri-la called sleep. God knows what my mother told her that brought on such a present, but if nothing else it reminds me not to be so candid with my mother.

Anyway, I wrote Aunt Ella a thank-you note upon receipt, glanced at a few pages, then threw it out. The only problem was that I threw it into the wastebasket in the bathroom (along with the rest of the junk mail I'd gotten that week). Flip picked it out. Flip, that's the man I currently live with. His real name's Felipé, but I prefer calling him Flip. My cousin—Aunt Ella's $300,000 daughter—had a dog named Flip when I was growing up. Makes it easy to remember.

Flip announced he intends to read this even if I don't. One way or another he's determined to get the sleep his two Excedrin PM promise, without me moving around and keeping him awake half the night.

....

August 28:

Before we went to bed last night, Flip suggested we take a warm bath together. I should have realized he read in the sleep book that a warm bath is supposed to relax you, especially when he threw in this packet of instant oatmeal. But I didn't.

It's the second time in our two years together that we took a warm bath. The first time was in a Connecticut motel, and there was a Jacuzzi which overflowed.

By the time I dried off I was more angry than sleepy.

....

August 30:

Well, he tried again last night. He suggested we take some nice, deep breaths before we lay down. I burst out laughing. I mean what was this, yoga or Lamaze?

Really, I shouldn't have laughed. I know how much all this means to him.

Apparently he read that taking a deep breath, counting to five, then releasing it to the count of five, helps the oxygen circulate through the system.

Did you ever have a doctor examine you and tell you to take a deep breath? Fine, easy. But then he tells you to breathe normally and you don't remember what to do. By this time so much concentration is focused on the breath that it's absolutely, positively impossible to relax. And then to repeat this ten times, twelve times? They might as well have been telling me to think-sing 99 Bottles of Beer on the Wall, or whatever that camp song's called.

....

September 3:

Before we turned in last night Flip showed me a picture from the book: cookies and milk. Supposedly this would make me feel warm and secure.

"What were your favorite foods as a child?" he asked half an hour later when I still wasn't asleep.

What was I supposed to tell him? That my most favorite favorite was the raw hamburger my mother was making into patties or a meatloaf. All the talk these days is about mad cow disease. My favorite butcher shop closed while I was in East Hampton four summers ago, and even if I could find another place, the point about raw meat is that you have to eat it right after it's ground, otherwise it turns brown and it leaves an aftertaste that makes you want to puke. And there's not much chance of finding a butcher shop open at midnight. Not in this neighborhood. Even the 24-hour supermarket around the corner closes at eleven.

I haven't drunk milk since I was in second grade.

....

September 4:

I walked into the bedroom at nearly midnight last night and found Flip standing on a stepladder fooling around with the ceiling fixture. If I'd turned the light on he'd have electrocuted himself. But apparently what he was doing was putting a few drops of jasmine oil on the bulb. "It's supposed to soothe you," he told me, letting the final trickle fall on the center of my pillow.

Just what I need — a pillow that smells like Aunt Ella.

....

September 6:

Last night he showed me a picture of a bed with clouds floating through it.

....

September 8:

Drawing me close, Flip whispered in my ear: Dostoevski, Churchill, Leonardo, Napoleon... All great people who suffered from insomnia (he read that in the book somewhere). All men. I told him I didn't care about being famous, I just wanted to be left alone. After I was certain Flip was sleeping soundly, I went in the bathroom and looked at my watch. It was nearly five a.m.

....

September 15:

There were a few days when insomnia wasn't mentioned, and I was hoping against hope that he'd gotten the idea out of his head. But at dinner last night he suggested maybe we ought to paint the bedroom. "Those white walls are so stark," he said. He suggested a warm, soothing color. Pink or blue. Or, if I don't want to go through the hassle of painting, we could probably get pink or blue curtains, add a throw pillow here or there.

What was he trying to do, wish a baby on me? That's all we need. Anyway, I told him in no uncertain terms that I can't stand pink or blue.

Softening, I confessed that when I was a teenager my room, my haven, was orange. The walls were pink of course, my parents insisted, but it was a pink sort of on the peach side. Or put enough orange around and it blended in. I had an orange floral bedspread, orange cafe curtains, and these two cheap lamps with bright orange shades.

....

September 17:
I ask you: when was the last time you saw a white sheep with black legs and a black head? He's clearing that fence by a quarter inch, at the most.

....

September 18:
Last night after the news he asked if I felt like working on the Sunday cross-word puzzle together. It was supposed to "mesmerize" me, stilling all the other thoughts vying for attention. Something like that.

All I could do was laugh.

I told Flip that, to begin with, pencils in this high-tech apartment aren't that easy to come by. But he wouldn't take no for an answer, and combed through every drawer in the kitchen and living room, getting himself more and more upset. I finally just said fuck it and grabbed a pen. Which meant we had to be certain a word's correct before writing it in, which brought on three different arguments, and even then we were sometimes changing words. We went to bed about two hours later, but the first thing I did was get up to find a dictionary. I wrote the word down and went back to bed, then got up a few minutes later because there was another word I just thought of.

Flip was snoring.

....

September 26:
"Why don't you tell me all the things that are bothering you?" Flip suggested, cradling my body from behind and playing idly with one breast.

I told him about a project at work that simply wasn't going well. And a conversation/fight with my mother, who apparently was still discussing me with Aunt Ella. And how the apartment was so messy neither of us could find anything. I also stubbed my toe two days ago and it was still hurting and I was paranoid that it might be broken.

Flip held me tighter. He told me I had nothing to worry about, he'd keep all my worries safe for the rest of the night, so I could let go of them and just drift off into sleep. He said all I had to do was trust him.

Frankly, I prefer Guatemalan worry dolls.

....

October 2:
The lack of sleep is taking its toll on Flip. Each time I toss or turn he complains

I'm pulling the covers off him.

"Did you ever have a special place, maybe a library or museum, or the beach or someplace, that just made you feel quiet and relaxed?" That was his latest stab. He said I should close my eyes and let myself be transported there.

What I remembered was my first apartment in the city. It was a small studio, with a walk-in closet converted into a kitchen that could only hold one of those small refrigerators with a hot plate on top. The sink and tub were in the bathroom. Better than the tub in the living room, I suppose. It was in the west village, exactly where I wanted to be, and affordable. "It was mine, and mine alone," I made sure to tell Flip.

After I thought silently for awhile Flip turned over and folded the pillow under his head. I kicked all the covers his way.

....

October 12:

All Flip's things are piled up by the door, he says he'll pick them up over the weekend. I slipped that insomnia journal into the case with his underwear.

.....

October 17:

I'll say this much for Aunt Ella's gift: it got me thinking about self-help books. So today I stopped in the Barnes and Noble superstore on 84th St. and picked up a book on how to bring the sexy self to the surface. Alone tonight, I finished a split of champagne, took a bubble bath, and changed into a skimpy black negligee I bought at Victoria's Secret. Tomorrow I plan to dust and vacuum in the nude. With my old spike heels on.

Five Days to a More Normal-Sized Head

SHARON MESMER AND DAVID BORCHART

For those of you suffering from elevated levels of self-esteem
(also known as "swelled head"), these five simple techniques, coupled with a series
of subliminal suggestion tapes, are guaranteed to take you down a notch!

DAY ONE — MAKE A LIST

Make a list of everyone in your field who is vastly more successful, albeit fifteen
years younger, than you!

Subliminal Suggestion Tape 1:

> At my age, Stephen King had forty best-sellers!
> Billy Corgan could buy and sell me fifty times over!
> Milton finished *his* poem, and he was blind!

DAY TWO — TAKE A FIELD TRIP

Spend the morning trying on clothes you thought were your size!
Spend the afternoon gazing into the windows of restaurants you can't afford to eat in!
Spend the night standing on line outside clubs you know won't let you in!

Subliminal Suggestion Tape 2:

> My mother thought I'd be sending *her* money by now!
> Making my house into a shrine to my ex-wife won't bring her back!
> The Marquis de Sade finished *his* novel, and he was in prison!

DAY THREE — INCREASE YOUR SPIRITUALITY: ADOPT A MANTRA

Adopt as your mantra this ancient Tibetan saying:
  I am surrounded by success. Success will never touch me!
Chant your mantra while being interviewed for a job as a manager-trainee at Roy
Rogers by someone with braces.

Subliminal Suggestion Tape 3:

> Boy, is my ass big!
> My cat has more friends in the neighborhood than me!

St. John of the Cross completed *his* collection of poetry and he was incarcerated in a Spanish latrine!

DAY FOUR — INCREASE YOUR SPIRITUALITY SOME MORE: MEDITATE

Use these simple meditations in the morning and at night to help you determine your place in the universe:

I am a low-ranking member of a primate species that is slowly destroying all other life forms;
I am doomed to repeat the mistakes of my parents and all my forebears until my last rank breath;
I have no choice but to insidiously propagate my worthless kind in a comic mating ritual.

Subliminal Suggestion Tape 4:

Too bad I can't afford plastic surgery!
If a 63-year old woman can have a baby, why can't I?
Nietzsche published *his* book and he suffered from blinding headaches and syphillis!

DAY FIVE — MAKE ONE FIRM COMMITMENT FOR THE FUTURE

Make a commitment to write a parody of self-help books for an anthology, wait until the last minute, then ask your boyfriend for help!

Subliminal Suggestion Tape 5:

I don't have to worry about rent control once I move back into my parents' basement!
Remember when that telemarketer hung up on me?
Van Gogh finished *his* last painting after shooting himself in the head!

There is a Paramount Purpose in all the lesser activities of our existence, opposed by a Paramount Obstacle, and they marshal their secondary Purposes and Obstacles to keep us ever on our toes. Blessed be Purpose! And thrice blessed be Obstacle!

PLOTTO is founded on this law: Purpose, expressed or implied, opposing Obstacle, expressed or implied, yields Conflict.

For example:

No. 182. A, an aviator, in love with B and in disfavor with B's father, F-B, induces B to take a ride in her airplane, then they elope along the sky lanes.

No. 252b. B refuses A's offer of marriage because she believes A is so absent-minded he'll forget he's married her.

Originality is the ideal of the PLOTTO method, and it is realized by interpreting Specific as well as General Conflicts in terms of the Plottoist's own experience. Experience serves as a suggestion, lending wings to the imagination for its own high flight. Something from without, impinging on something within, excites a feeling and the soul flows into Purpose, and Purpose into Action. Then, somewhere on the path of rising Action, Purpose encounters Obstacle. Uh-oh.

At this point, and at this point only, do we establish what writers of creative fiction call a 'situation'. Obstacle alone never made one, but strike the flint of Obstacle with the steel of Purpose, and sparks of 'situation' start to fly.

For example:

No. 371. A asks that B allow herself to be hynoptized in order that he may learn where buried treasure lies. A hypnotizes B and B dies of psychic shock.

No. 404. A, a ventriloquist, captured by savages on Long Island and threatened with death, makes an animal talk and is given his freedom.

Don't delay, send now for PLOTTO, with over 500 plot ideas!

A NEW METHOD OF PLOT SUGGESTION FOR WRITERS OF CREATIVE FICTION **PLOTTO**

M.KASPER

The Self-Help Teacher

Jerome Sala

The self-help teacher
writes a book
about how to make a million
writing self-help books.
"The best way to help yourself,"
he says, "is to reflect in words
on the self-help process.
Each word will help itself
find the next. Self-help words,
you see, are not afraid to reach out
for help, for they know they cannot
do it all by themselves.
Yet they are brilliantly ambiguous,
flexible and even perverse
in that they realize
at the very moment in which
they ask for assistance
that the responsibility rests
in the last instance
on their own vowels, consonants
and syllables. You could say then,
as the poet Keats said of all
great creative endeavors
that the lexicon of self-help
possesses a certain negative capability:
it expresses dependency and
personal independence
at the same time.
This ability," the self-help teacher
informs us, "is extremely necessary
to cultivate in our times."
He paraphrases the great
French philosopher Lyotard
who advises us to act entreprenurially
in collectivist situations and
collectivist in entrepreneurial ones.
He reminds us of the investors
who have made millions

betting against the market
and the importance of contrarianism
in the poetics of W.H. Auden.
All the while his book
seemingly writes itself.
One thinks of John Cage's famous
Lecture on Nothing or
the penchant for self-reflexiveness
in postmodern art, advertising,
rock videos, poetry and film.
The self-help teacher notices us
noticing this feature of his text
and comments: "Self-reference
even though often negative
is in the end always a form
of self-affirmation:
television commercials tell us
they are lying only to inform us
of their larger truths.
My self-help book is the only
self-book to admit
its falsity: therefore, it is
the only one you can rely on."
At this point the self-teacher
has reached page two-hundred-fifty.
He knows that in another twenty-five pages
he can call it a wrap.
He reflects on this and then
addresses the reader again:
"I could end here
rather self complacently.
My publisher would be satisfied
and frankly, dear reader,
if you have not already assimilated
the lessons I have laid down,
so would you. But my whole purpose
in writing this book
is to show you how to raise the bar
just when the completion of your goal
is in sight. Therefore friend,
observe how a book can be extended
with the hamburger helper
of self-consciousness!
I want to tell you now
what it has been like
composing the first two-hundred-and-fifty

pages of this book. I will share
with you my thoughts and emotions
each step of the way."
At this point the self-help teacher
begins a shockingly revealing
autobiographical account of his life
during the six weeks
it took him to compose his book.
We hear of drug usage, sexual experimentation,
credit card scams, and conversions
to strange religions.
Yet set in the text, in odd typefaces,
are various parenthetical expressions
such as, HE'S LYING, THIS IS ONLY A BOOK,
BOURGEOIS SALESMAN SPEAKING, and
DO YOU BELIEVE THIS PRICK?
We don't know, finally,
how to take this self-help book
and this was all along
the intention of our teacher.
We wonder if the author's name
is really his. And how we
can possibly help ourselves
with his nostrums.
A great sadness descends,
the fabled let-down the self-help teacher
had prophesied would occur
when we had accomplished our goal
of completing his book.
But then, although his personage
had faded with the end of his text
his spirit awakens in us like an inner guide
to offer one last session of coaching:
"When you come to the end,
raise the bar, friend, raise the bar!"
At this point, some of us go out and buy
our next self-help book.
While others begin to write their own.

3 Poems

LYN LIFSHIN

Dear J

with the roof suddenly
in worse shape, "structural
damage" and my totaled car,
I need more, you know, than
any continuing education
class can pay for poetry
and fiction for three
weeks and you could use a
break from New York City
ice. Listen, we'll start
with something like EST —
you know how they stopped
called everybody ass holes
and called the scam FORUM.
We'll use a name that sounds
a little foreign, a dash of
self realization bliss, some
thing 1990's like say some
fancy foreign yuppie
car. FOR THE MILLENNIUM:
POETRY AND SELF
WEALTH. We'll tap
those in the health procession
first. "Writing to Reach
Those Who've Recoiled,"
plane fare of course not
included but we could give
them notebooks and pens,
throw in a little fire ritual,
not let anybody sleep. Let
them open to us first,
then a group groping. Let them
cry and confess and then
screw in the trees. We'll rent
a van, play tapes of Heart

of Darkness, sleep on the
sand when the moon's in
some right phase, place ads
in the New Yorker. Three
thousand for the 4 day. Let
them climb down a rock ledge
blindfolded and scared. At the
bottom, they will love us, feel
connected, get the verbs they
wish, touch, hold hands and
head for the 6 days in the Andes.
We won't even need to read
novels, they'll be too full of
themselves to have to write,
romp barking and screaming in
their new animal totems as we
take in their advance deposits,
throw out State University
contracts for those two
credit courses and pay off
Bloomingdale's and Visa

Psychic Surgery and Self Revitalization Writing Workshop

If you are in pain
from not getting published,
or not getting reviewed,
this hands on experiential
workshop is for you.
We start with a guinea
pig (after of course you
have paid 4,000 dollars
and special workshop
fees) Each participant
has one and we cut the
animal in 2. This lets out
the evil spirits, heals
your poems or play. In
all your life you could
never imagine such a
beautiful, uplifting
time. Or the blood
dripping as your
consciousness expands.
The pig's squeals are
your inner voice coming
back to you. Some will
channel Shakespeare,
others Danielle Steele
Open doors as you open
the guinea pig and your
chakras. Find mindfulness
galore and overcome
clichés and addiction.
Food for bliss in our
vegan cafe. Lose weight
and clear up your manu-
script and fortify your
immune system. "You
are who you eat." Connect
with shamans over midnight
snack. Offer expires in 8 days.
You could too.

The First Club to Explore Your Body, Better

than Plato's Retreat.
We celebrate the
mind and vision
too, choose a book,
grow a spirit leg
where one used to
be. Visualize good
hair and you'll be
sitting on it. Joining
is easy. Live in the
moment, massage
your spirit mind.
Seven principles to
second sight. Learn
to develop your
breasts and intuition.
Take a chance and
everyday blessings
will pour from the
faucet in your soul
as you tap into angels
of every hype, feel
their wings sprout in
your chakra, Celtic
drums soothing
your organs, flushing
your body of toxins
your wallet of flab

Perform Yourself!

CHRIS BRANDT

So, you want to actualize your self-realizations and realize your self-actualizations. That's why you've come to see me, BabaurhumDOS, the guru of performance art. You've bought the book I didn't write (one of my students did), you've subscribed to my magazine, *Fifth Wheel*, and you've paid an incredible amount of money for a one-week intensive workshop. I am moved by your faith, deeply moved. And by my own. That is what I've wanted all along, for you to come to me, bearing checks. And lo! my faith is rewarded.

Now let's take a look at what you want. You want to relate to strangers with whom you have no prior relation, your relation to your relationships with 1. yourself, 2. your family, 3. your lovers, 4. the Other, 5. money, 6. the whole world, 7. everything else. But especially number one, your SELF. And you want to do this by presenting your self as it relates to your relating to numbers one through seven above.

Congratulations! And welcome to the world of BabaurhumDOS. Sorry I can't actually be here myself this week (when the spirits call, the dutiful servant goes), but this note should take my place with no trouble, as long as you maintain that very touching faith. It is intended to help you get started, not to do the work for you — your own infinite resources of creative experience and experiential creativity, your very existence, in short — will do that.

Before you begin, though, there are a few existentially mandatory preparatory measures. They are not difficult, but if you neglect them, you will hamstring your project, reconstruct all that you will have labored so hard to deconstruct, and lose your way in a fog of mystification intended for others but blowing back on yourself. In a word, your efforts will go for naught. So listen up, and follow directions!

First, take stock. Be brutally honest with yourself. Do you have any talents? Can you sing? Can you act? Can you dance? Have you got rhythm, a striking speaking voice, personal charisma? Does your writing wake people up and make them ask for more? If the answer to any of these question is "yes," *even a qualified "yes,"* stop reading now, quit this project, and go develop your talent. If you even think you might harbor an undiscovered talent in one or another area, enroll in a class immediately and find out. (We will hold your workshop registration open for you. Sorry, no refunds.) But if you are sure you can't sing, dance, act, write, or hold an audience, you are ready to be a first-class performance artist! SO WELCOME! to Help(er)for(mance)your!!self!!! WeekIntensive Workshop at the BabaurhumDOS Center for Advanced Unconsciousness.

Let's begin. Sit in an uncomfortable position. It doesn't matter if this is Position One or Position Forty-Two, or whether you have merely folded your leg wrong as you sat down and sprained your knee. STAY! DON'T MOVE! Now empty your mind. Fill it up again. Empty it again. Do this ten times slowly. Don't forget to breathe. There. Now you're ready for Lesson One.

The first thing you must do is GET OUT OF YOUR OWN WAY! Simple? Couldn't be simpler, thus couldn't be harder. First lesson. Ponder.

Second lesson. Stop thinking so much. What do you have to think about anyway? I mean, what? Do not think about this.

Third day. (If Lessons One and Two have taken you less than two days, you've been doing them wrong. Go back and do them over. Remember, in (W)E(a)stern thought, "fast" is usually equated with "intelligent." In Advanced Unconsciousness, "fast" is not good, in fact, "slow" is not so hot, either. The goal is perfect stasis, the ultimate deconstruction of movement, nothought noaction, so KEEP STILL!) Where were we? Oh, yes, Third Day. This is a big one. Forget everything you've learned in the first two days (or the first three or four days if you were a klutz and went too fast.) Don't remember, true learning is unlearning. Forgetting is remembering. An empty mind is all yours. Forget it.

Now, you are officially an adept. Stick around a couple of more days if you want, so you can satisfy yourself that you've gotten your money's worth — this was advertised as a week-long workshop, after all — but if you've really done the work here, you will not remember when you came, what you've done, or why you're here in the first place. If that's the case, you graduate with honors. If you're still clinging to some shreds of consciousness (and this is not a bad thing — it just means you're not yet as slow as you'd like to be, so think about coming back for our AdeptAdaption Month-Long Workshop) and you need some pathetic piece of semiotic symbolism so you can prove to your friends that you actually did(n't) do something, by all means pick up one of the graduation certificates on the way out. Fill it out yourself (or don't, if you're slightly more advanced).

Oh, yes, you came here because you wanted some advice on putting together a piece of performance art. Well, you've already gotten it, if you only knew how (not) to understand. But if you must have something more specific (and because my lawyer says I have to give you something that more or less corresponds with the ad you answered), here goes.

Put together four or five rambling stories. Make sure they have no point; avoid beginnings, middles, and ends. Sing (badly) a medley of songs. Dance while you scream. Reveal a particularly horrible thing about yourself. Take your clothes off while reciting a soliloquy on the difference between nuditude and nakidity. Now, mix it all up so there's no sequence at all.

To get rid of all sense-making elements, you may need to get a dramaturge (I don't know what one does either, but I do know it's someone you can blame for what doesn't work while taking credit yourself for what does.) While you're at it, get a choreographer (ditto), a director (ditto), a producer, a stage manager, a costumer, a set designer — the more people's names you can put on the postcard, the more people will come (maybe).

Finally, get a graduate student to write a learned essay for your program, something about the clever way you ex-nominate the denominations of popular culture, thus mystifying the myth-makers which in itself proves a kind of de-mystification of non-myth (though perhaps only in the deconstructive sense).

Now you're ready for the real point of all this. Get a grant.

Unconsciously yours, BabaurhumDOS

a superintendent's eyes #58 (anticipating the drill)

Steve Dalachinsky

when i was young i read all the right books, i was sure if i tried hard enough they would help me cope with my dilemma. my feelings of gross inadequacy, lack of identity & paranoia. well they did.

kafka taught me that it was ok to be a cockroach in a castle & to hate my father. camus taught me that it was fine to feel left out, floating & and not remembering my mom's birthday or even the day she died. was it yesterday or today?

i was made to feel good, yet always on trial, when committing certain crimes like shoplifting, even MURDER ... old fyodor, for instance, said cool, gamble, gamble all you want - so what if some of the side effects cause you to be a sick, spiteful & jealous man? yet ever so "CHRISTIAN."

geez. i devoured them all. all those guidebooks for the unguideable. & look at me now. i'm a plague in a penal colony constantly rolling that rock up a hill. a mess. a bonafide mess. & proud of it.

ginsberg taught me that it was ok to tell america to go fuck itself. burroughs said it was ok to shoot dope. kerouac, bukowski, said fine drink drink DRINK yourself to death. just listen to some good music along the way. or do like hemingway & blow your brains out. sartre said it was all well & good to lock yourself in a small room & retch everything up.

diderot said it was written up yonder any way.

so here i am, a self-hating, self-pitying, self-medicated, selfishly cockeyed optimist. a nihilist with a fist in his too big mouth, carrying around a NEGATIVE EGO the size of the GRAND COOL GUY DAMNED. competing for last place & proud of it. sick to my stomach every time i hear a gunshot or a bird chirp.

here i be, the ultimate source book on what ails me & how to make things worse ... a map of bad feelings with directions on how to get to & and acquire more of the same. MUCH MORE. proudly suffering & worrying always about the paranoids that are chasing ME.

here you find a handbook on how to deal with rejection, alienation, introspection & extermination ... don't fight THEM ... let THEM in. Let THEM enter & grow & make you feel as uncomfortable as can be. NEVER EVER learn to accept or enjoy THEM.

i'm an unending compendium of ill will. a malcontent i sing i bark i contort. ME — a survival kit for the 21st Century ... a misguided miscreant who believes in the ONE SPECTACULAR god ... of masochism and sloth...

i, the ignorant elitist, ill at ease Solitary Man, thank you all from the bottom of my rotting soul...i, who still have no idea of who "I" am, give thanks to all my gurus in this the worst of TIMES. i, the grateful student of all who have reinforced, increased & made my PAIN OK & my time on this planet a bit uneasier, thank you for helping me into my depression ... for permitting me to wallow in my discomfort ... for enabling the myth to bear fruit.

hey MOM i'm OK hey DAD hey jim hey bruno send in those naked dancing zombies ... i am the puzzle with the missing pieces. an infinity of annotated listings. the mangled sum of all your parts ... i smile as i turn the other cheek & embrace you as i light the match.

TESTIMONIALS ON COPING FROM POP CULTURE ICONS!

Notes to Myself

RON KOLM

Spring had finally come again to the East Village. And since it was Spring, it was time for Duke to get off his ass and peddle some stuff. There wasn't *any*one who was going to give him free food and rent *these* days, 'cause times had changed. Now the cops were manfully busting anyone who set up shop on the street, tossing confiscated merchandise into vans, then disappearing it forever into the endless morass of the criminal justice system.

Duke wandered around the neighborhood wondering what he could move beside drugs. Drugs had gotten him into a shit-load of trouble. Duke had a rap sheet two inches thick — damn, he'd even gotten smacked on the head by a SWAT dude as he walked by Tompkins Square Park late one night, stoned, speaking his mind just like Michael Carter — another bust and he'd be doing hard time for sure.

As he walked across St. Mark's Place, he noticed one group of street vendors that wasn't being hassled by the pigs — the guys selling books on folding tables. So Duke sidled up to a bearded gent and asked him why he was able to operate without interference.

"Because we're protected by the First *Amendment*, comrade," he was told.

"What's *that* fuckin' mean, asshole — don't fuck with my head," Duke hissed menacingly.

"See the First Amendment protects free speech," the guy said, ignoring the attitude Duke was giving him, "And books are part of that process — the unobstructed transmission and exchange of information."

"So the cops can't fuck with you?" Duke asked.

"That's putting it baldly, but yes," the old timer answered, as he took a couple of dollars from a student-type for a battered paperback. *Beneath the Empire of the Birds*, the cover read. I got to cut myself into this racket, Duke said to himself, and off he went to look for stock.

Duke knew he couldn't steal the stuff, for the same reason he couldn't deal drugs. Unfortunately, Jill wouldn't be able to help this time. She'd ditched him on account of poverty and was living in a studio in the garment district. Not having any light in the tiny bathroom they shared in the hall with the other squatters had been the last straw. Somebody'd recently told Duke that Jill was dancing at Billy's Topless to get together enough dough to go to F.I.T.

Duke went to the dumpster behind his neighborhood Barnes and Noble and filled a couple of shopping bags with damaged paperbacks. He *was* kinda stumped as to why all the books were missing covers. Must be a fashion statement of some sort or another, he figured. He lined up the stripped mass markets in several neat rows on a dirty green blanket on 2nd Avenue and then sat back to await his first customer.

The nattily attired yuppies who streamed by looked at him as if he were dung, moving to the other side of the walk, avoiding any eye contact. Assholes, Duke growled.

Time slowed to a crawl. Duke flipped through the books arrayed before him, but the print was too small in most of them for his bleary eyes. But hey, hold on, one of them *did* have big print, and a lot of space between the sentences as well. Okay, Duke said, let's give this fucker a shot!

> If I had only . . .
> forgotten future greatness
> and looked at the green things and the buildings
> and reached to those around me
> and smelled the air
> and ignored the forms and self-styled obligations
> and heard the rain on the roof
> and put my arms around my wife

the first sentence read.
Fucking shit, Duke thought, guess I do miss Jill. And then

> What an absurd amount of energy I have
> been wasting all my life trying to figure out
> how things "really are," when all the time
> they weren't.

... and ...

> God revealed his name to Moses, and it was
> I AM WHAT I AM.

Jesus, isn't that what Popeye used to say, he mused. Duke read on:

> When I get to where I can enjoy just
> lying on the rug picking up lint balls,
> I will no longer be too ambitious.

Right on! he agreed. And even better, there was stuff about drugs.

> The rainbow is more beautiful than the
> pot at the end of it, because the rainbow
> is now. And the pot never turns out to be
> quite what I expected.

Bummer, Duke sympathized. He took a handful of pills from his pocket and popped them in his mouth. This stuff was *deep*, he thought, got to clear my mind. He read on:

> I live from one tentative conclusion to the
> next, thinking each one is final. The only
> thing I know for sure is that I'm confused.

Duke sat there, bathed in tranquillity, and thus he had no real need for the last sentence in the book which reads:

> But the world is round, and a
> messy mortal is my friend
> Come walk with me in the mud . . .

How to Save Your Soul with Rock'n'Roll

BOB HOLMAN

Start with a Bloody virgin Mary & a French toast Host
Breakfast w/ Champions & a Holy Ghost
Holy guacamole! a Papal Bull roast
Get on yr knees so yr disease can be diagnosed.

Don't slosh it w/ the sherpas to some Himalayan height
Visit our heavy-hittin' Tibetan, his 3rd eye's out of sight!'
Be careful yr not blinded by his clear white light
On a toot w/ the Absolute? The price is right!

Levitating in Levittown
All the gurus are getting down
Get a mighty holy high from a roly-poly holy
Gonna save yr soul! Gonna steal yr dough!

How to Make it in the Music Business

JOSÉ PADUA

She wasn't a star yet and didn't — as far as I saw— act like one. She seemed to be just another flighty nightclub chick with big tits and trashy clothes. The kind I always went for in those days. The kind the frat boy crowd would look at with scorn in their eyes and proclaim, "Hey, get a load of that chick," because they knew they didn't have a chance with her.

It was 1981. Ten years before I lost my last full time job. Nine years before I moved up to New York. Eight years before the Berlin Wall was torn down. Seven years before ... Well, everything seems like a countdown to me now. I've found that as I get older I attach more and more importance to numbers. And even when a year starts off well, as this one has, I find that even the happiest occasions remind me that the numbers are dwindling down to zero.

It's something psychiatrists probably have a word for— indeed, its seems they have a word for everything. And in 1981 — before terms like "co-dependency" and "denial" were used to describe what went on inside me — I felt pretty good. In other words, what I didn't know didn't hurt me.

I spent the best of my ignorant years in New York. Before I actually moved there, I'd go up for visits several times a year, the first time when I went up to see my college friend, Stephen. He'd gone to New York after landing a job editing *Wrestling World* magazine while I'd stayed back in Washington, D.C., taking it easy with an unusually slow paced gig as a messenger. Since I didn't make much money, it was a while before I was able to make the trip to check out Stephen's new scene there. Many a night I'd get a phone call from him at four or five in the morning. He'd be tripping his brains out or going wild on speed (black beetles, black beauties, whatever it was they called them) telling me he was just at such and such a party with dozens of babes, fabulous hot blonde babes — he knew my taste in women well — and asking me when I was finally going to come up and check this shit out? Then he'd hang up because the Danish au pair girl he'd hooked up with didn't like him talking on the phone while she was blowing him.

It took me a couple of years before I had any money to spare, but one Friday afternoon I had it and immediately hopped on a Greyhound bus for New York, where Stephen and his *au pair* met me at Port Authority.

"José, this is Helga," Stephen said as he scratched his beard and grinned.

I looked up at Helga, a blonde haired woman of Amazonian proportions who was almost a foot taller than him.

"Nice meeting you," I said, taking her hand and trying hard to conceal the sense of awe I felt at the mere sight of her.

"Nice meeting you too," she answered. Then smiling, she added, "I've heard Stephen talking to you on the phone."

They led me out of the Port Authority and to the nearest subway station. We were about to walk down the stairs to catch the A-Train to Greenwich Village when Stephen paused.

"Wait, let's have some of these," he said, reaching into his pocket.

He pulled out a big bag of mushrooms. We each ate a handful, then confidently descended the stairs.

In the Village, we went to the apartment of a friend of ours, Dan, who also went to college with us and was now working as a reporter for the New York Post.

"I was thinking we could go to a movie," Stephen suggested as we sat down at Dan's kitchen table.

"No, no," Dan said, "that's something José can do anywhere."

"Well then," Stephen answered, "let's stay here and wait for Leroy to start playing."

Leroy was Leroy Jenkins, the jazz violinist who happened to be Dan's upstairs neighbor. I'd been a fan of his music since I'd heard him on Archie Shepp's *Black Gypsy* album. Listening to him practice while we were high on mushrooms seemed like a good idea.

"Yeah, let's do that," I said.

"No, no, I can't," Dan protested, shaking his head. "Whenever I hear him play it sounds like cats being tortured. And then I have to leave the apartment."

"Yes, we should go somewhere," Helga said. "To a nightclub or something." Then she turned to Stephen and whispered, "I will blow you in the lavatory as that wild fucking disco plays."

"Hey, we can go to Danceteria," Dan suggested. "I can get us all in easy."

"How?" I asked.

"Hey, I'm a reporter. We'll be there covering the *scene* for the weekend section of the Post."

And a scene it was. The place was loud and dark and crowded. People were dressed — or half dressed in some cases — like escapees from an insane asylum, dancing obscene dances or barking like dogs to welcome the coming of the Apocalypse. It all looked pretty stupid to me at first, but when the mushrooms began to take hold I got *into it*.

I was wandering around the nightclub with Stephen, Dan and my new friend Helga, when I saw her. She was siting alone at a table, her eyes scoping the room as if she were trying to locate some companions from whom she'd been separated. She looked good, wearing just a pink sport coat over a black lace bra and a striped pair of men's boxer shorts. Affixed to the top of her head, entwined in her blonde tresses, was what I thought was a hair curler but which on closer inspection turned out to be a tampon. Yes, I thought, this is my kind of girl — blond, buxom and, best of all, totally drunk. And because for me indiscretion was the better part of tripping, I sat down next to her and got straight to the point.

"Your friends have ditched you and you've got a tampon in your hair. Let's split."

She looked at me and thought it over for a minute.

"Okay," she said.

I stood and took her by the hand. But before leaving I said goodbye to all my friends.

"I'm going off with this young lady," I said to Stephen.

"All right," he said, "See you next time you're in town."

"No, I'll see you tomorrow sometime."

"Nah, I think you'll be busy," he said, winking. "And I also think you'll be able to use these." He reached into his pocket and gave me the bag of mushrooms.

"Thanks, man. I owe you one."

"Have a good fuck!" Helga yelled over the noise as we walked away.

It was a quick cab ride to 30th St. near Madison Square Garden. I paid the driver and we got out. On opening the door to her building, she stomped on the floor, sending several rats scurrying to their hiding places. We stepped onto the elevator, holding our breath because of the stench of piss and vomit. At the entrance to her apartment she kicked some chicken bones to the side, then unlocked the door. Inside I saw a mattress, an empty guitar case, some scattered clothes, a half filled bottle of wine, and little else. I sat on a mattress on which lay a dog-eared copy of *The Prophet*.

"Give up this shit," I said, taking it in my hand.

For some reason — before I even knew her name and what she was about — I found myself trying to guide her.

"Why?" she asked. "I like it. It's cool stuff."

"Nah, it's bullshit."

I stood, opened up the window, and flung the book out as far as I could. We watched it fall to the street, and then lay down on the mattress. Before I had a chance to undo her bra, she began undressing herself, taking off her coat, her bra, then shimmying out of her shorts to reveal one of the biggest brown bushes I'd ever seen. I took off my clothes and worked on her tits for a while. There was enough there to keep me occupied for quite some time. When I finally tired of that, I reached down with my finger.

"Hey, you're a big girl."

"I am not."

I reached in some more.

"What's the matter?" she asked. "Can't handle it?"

I put in another finger, then another.

"Oh, I can handle it, but not the way I usually do."

I put my whole fist inside and pumped.

"Oh yeah, baby," she said. "You can *dance*."

"You know, I've never been with a woman that's had kids before."

"I've never *had* any kids," she protested.

I shut up and went to work. After about ten minutes of this, with her moaning the same moan, saying "Oh baby" over and over, I began to get tired and a little bit bored. I stretched my arm and started rubbing her tits with my free hand, but she pushed it away and rubbed them herself. I didn't give up — I wanted to see this girl more. I kept it going with my right hand, and with my left I reached for my coat. Pulling a cigarette from the pocket, I stuck it in my mouth then reached in again and pulled out a book of matches. Using my one hand, I opened it and tried to pull a match down across the back so I could light it. Unfortunately, I'd never mastered the art of lighting a match with one hand. This was a skill I'd always admired for some strange reason — a skill which now seemed not only admirable but necessary, because I'd gotten her to the point where the only sound coming out of her mouth was the word "Oh" repeated endlessly like an out of breath mantra. I knew that if I pulled out my other hand, however briefly, it would be like starting from scratch; and that after putting my hand back inside she'd say, in a calmly declarative voice that carried not a hint of her recently breathless state — "Oh yeah, baby, you can *dance*."

So I kept my right hand inside her. With my left I pulled the cigarette from my mouth and threw it away in disgust. But then I had a thought.

Reaching back into my coat, I pulled out the bag of mushrooms. I figured that at the rate things were moving the mushrooms would be kicking in just as she starts to come.

It took a long time, but when she was finally done and caught her breath, she went down on me. By then I wasn't in the mood to waste time, and while it took her nearly an hour to come, it took me all of one minute. I rolled over to sleep, but she wanted more.

"Do it again."

"I'm tired."

"Ohhh. Come on. Come on. Get into the *groove*."

"Okay," I said.

"But do it here," she suggested, and rolled over on her stomach. Sticking her ass in the air, she reached behind and spread her buttcheeks. Ah yes, I thought, this will work — but I was wrong. There was enough room for the fat end of the Louisville Slugger on that side too. I used my left hand this time.

Waking at two in the afternoon the next day, we went for a walk and had breakfast at a diner in Chelsea

"God, I didn't eat at all yesterday," she said.

"That was probably a good idea."

"Well, that depends on what you're into."

"I'm not into *that*," I asserted.

"Hey, you've got to be a little adventurous sometimes. I know I am. That's why I'm going to be a star."

"By the way, what's your name?"

"Madonna," she said confidently.

"I'll keep an eye out for you."

I never got around to seeing Stephen again that weekend. I suppose he had a feeling, when I left Danceteria, how things were going to go with me and Madonna. And after breakfast that day we took more mushrooms and hopped on the subway going towards Battery Park. When we got there, we sat on a bench facing the water and talked.

"You realize," I said, "that the marketing ploy behind pet rocks was the exact same one used for Bruce Springsteen... It was this same ploy which shot him up the charts... giving him superstar status. Just take the line 'I have seen the future of domesticated animals and it's the pet rock,' then substitute the words 'rock and roll' and 'Bruce Springsteen' where appropriate ... and you'll see what I mean ... and you'll also see how this relates to the legacy of the past as embodied in the Holy Shroud of Turin. I think that by using a similar strategy you can hit the top of the charts just as quickly, if not more so... and thus become the superstar you long to be."

"Yeah," Madonna said after a moment's thought. "And like, you know, Canada ... warm weather... and the search for a good time... No, I mean a good *tan*. It's all like, you know, *connected*... And then, like... I get to make a lot of money."

We were tripping again and it was all beginning to make sense. We talked for hours, at the end of which Madonna stood up. She walked over to the fence and sat on top of it, her back to the water. I stood up to join her, and with the sun going down and the distant prospect of the Statue of Liberty between us, I dipped into my pocket for the mushrooms. We finished what was left, then walked to the subway station. As we headed uptown, I kept wishing I didn't have to go back to Washington the next day.

Madonna and I sent each other letters over the course of the next year, after which we lost touch. She was beginning to make it big and needed better advice than what I could give her. Me, I stayed in Washington for almost another decade, climbing up the ladder a couple of steps, and going from being a messenger to being a researcher. Admittedly, it wasn't much of a climb and in 1990 I finally called it quits and moved to New York.

Every now and then I'd see Madonna around town — not in person but in the form of posters advertising her latest record or movie. I'd ponder how far she'd gone without me, and how far I had to go to get there. She was a star while all I had going for me at the time was a job in midtown keeping stats for a company that sold cheap costume jewelry through the mail.

Nevertheless, I was confident that I'd soon hit it big. I carried on, keeping track of the numbers. The company's sales were going up. The new line of Jennifer O'Neill cubic zirconium pendants and earrings were a big hit with shutins all the way from Valley Stream (in that vast suburban wilderness known as Long Island) on down to the Gulf Coast of Florida. But one evening, getting off from work, I looked up at the posters which had been pasted the night before on the scaffolding that surrounded the Flatiron Building. And I suddenly felt this great sense of loss.

You see, I wanted to be with Madonna. I wanted to be with her despite our physical incompatibility. Yet it wasn't that I wanted any kind of help she could give me. In those days I didn't want help from anyone, least of all myself. Because what I wanted was not to be good, but to be *lucky*. Because — as any chump trying to sell the useless leftovers of other people's lives on the sidewalk on Second Avenue on a cold, rainy December night knew — it was better to be lucky than to be good.

Of course, things were different then. I was into the *groove* then. In those ignorant days when the numbers all seemed to add up. When wanting to be rich and famous like Madonna was a lofty ambition and not a character flaw. And even though I've since learned how to light a match with one hand, I don't go for women like her anymore.

Famous Amos Redux?

Mike Golden

"We need a new word for pussy"
That's what the pretty bartender
from Michigan tells me.
Pussy sounds too squishy.
Cunt is too hard.
Vagina might as well be
an Isosceles triangle
or a cut of veal.

She's got monster chops
she takes for granted.
She's 25, 26, 27 ...
came here four years ago to be an actress
yada-yada-yada ...

I had monster chops
I didn't know what to do with
so I came here 30 years ago
to write the Great American Novel
yada-yada-yada ...

I wrote 12 hours a day for awhile
cut down to five for awhile
before I got married for awhile
and had to fight to do one for awhile.
Then I got divorced and got drunk
and did none for an even longer while
until I got lucky, and found the-great-love-
of-my-life for awhile.

In all those awhiles I might have
sidetracked myself, but I never quit
or met anyone who changed the word for pussy
except the-great-love-of-my-life
who told me the first time we slept together
that when she hit puberty
she named her pussy "Golden."

I was blown away then
but now I realize
Muses must say that
to all the boys; inserting
whatever your name is
for their pussy.

Hard to imagine
calling your pussy Irving.
Or Mailer.
Or Updike.

Eat my Irving, baby!
Eat my Mailer!
Eat my Updike; I don't think so!

The pretty bartender from Michigan
says she'd like to call her pussy "cookie."
That's more like it, don't you think?
It has a ring to it: "Eat my cookie."

If she stays focused
and respects her instrument
she might actually make it
in this town.

Doug and the Art of Motorcycle Maintenance

MICHAEL CARTER

In 1976 two books changed my life in ways I'm still reeling from. One was *Gravity's Rainbow*, which sent me on a parabolic path of paranoia and fear of success, especially of the literary variety achieved so wonderfully and verbosely in that tale. Though lacking its sardonic hilarity, the second book also dealt with the issues of science and philosophy, technology and humanism, German romanticism and classicism, the mathematician Henri Poincaré, hare-brained hippie logic and a grailhunt for that mystical, absolute One. I was not at all aware of its momentous impact until today, when desperately trawling for some kind of self-help book to trash, I turned to my own shelf and blew the bookmites off Robert Pirsig's *Zen and the Art of Motorcycle Maintenance*.

My stepfather Doug, obsessively mechanical and former dirt bike racer, passed it on, doubtless in an attempt to change my slacker ways (which ultimately failed), conscious of my interests in philosophy and eastern religions. Subconsciously, which I doubt *he* ever realized — not so unlike the book itself — the gesture was a last-ditch attempt to reach out to a son he realized he had never had, who was soon leaving the roost for good. There had always been enmity between us; I had never accepted him as the dad I had lost, and had subconsciously — at times even willfully — formed all my basic values in contradistinction to his: he loved cars and cycles and fixing things; hated intellectuals, philosophers, poets, rock music, and radicals. I was the reverse. He was physically demonstrative; I was withdrawn and mentally preoccupied. He was violent, I was a wimp. Things would worsen later, when I wanted to go to Reed College with a loan from the state of Alaska, and he wanted the Army to pay for my education in some state school. (I ultimately did what I wanted and became a very black-humored sheep.)

The only philosopher in whom he'd ever expressed interest was the dockworker mysticism of Eric Hoffer, so I was caught off guard when he snuck me Pirsig's book. Its father and son "on the road" blarney is really just a ruse to ponder through Phil 101 conundrums, which is itself a ruse to produce a classic self-help book. After ripping off the title of Suzuki's classic *Zen and the Art of Archery*, Pirsig very cleverly tapped into two fairly disparate '70s phenomena, the suburban motorcycle craze and Taoist buddhism, and sophistically brought them together by a thin fiction called Phaedrus, a teacher of philosophy based in part on Socrates' sophistic foil. Phaedrus gives a basically reliable account of subject-object, romantic-classic, platonic-aristotelian, east-west, mind-body dualisms, exploring classic Greek and German and Zen thought in search of an elusive mystical force called "Quality," always capitalized, which will bridge them — make sense of everything, *partner* — that variously resembles Plato's Real, Kant's apriori intuition, Hegel's Absolute Mind, the Tao, Buddha, and God, as well as less lofty disincarnations.

(But no discussion of Nietzsche — the spanner in the spokes of the German idealist BMW — or Heidegger's critique of Kant, though his concept of "Care" is trivialized; 'leave those *bad* Germans alone,' said an editor's ghost.) Finally, of course, Pirsig/Phaedrus gives this metaphysical "Quality" an ethical spin; besides being the *tao,* it's also the Greek sophist's *arête,* or "excellence," an indefinable quality but you know it when you see it. In a two-hundred page tautology, "Quality becomes Excellence," just like a Ford commercial. And when "someone connects with Quality. He gets filled with *gumption."* Which is precisely what my stepfather thought I lacked.

But this is not the real reason why I now believe *Zen and the Art* changed my life and put me on a course of bohemian slackerdom from which I have not wavered. This is what I only discovered today, twenty years later, opening at random the book's very center — its hidden secret, *'that missing seed crystal of thought that would suddenly solidify everything'*: "He'd heard that Reed College in Oregon withheld grades until graduation." (Which, however, is not strictly true.) And I hazard to surmise that the real Phaedrus was none other than the dean of philosophy, Marvin "Maddog" Levich, still boring students with his Humanities lectures when I arrived there in September '76.

Better Living Through Better Drugs

Mike Topp

I'm looking at an old black-and-white photo of me and four friends dressed in hospital scrubs grouped around a grand piano. We were all on acid and hanging out with Arthur Godfrey.

I dropped a lot of acid in college during the seventies. Blotter and microdot. Microdot was also called "blue barrels," short for blowing your brains out on chemical daydreams. I started doing drugs years ago and now I have tripped quite a few times, perhaps a zillion.

LSD's romantic ambience for me stemmed from the nostalgia then sweeping the University of Illinois for any decade but the one we were living in. In 1977, punk was in and people dressed fifties. Hippies were also cool and people wore long hair and painted their faces. Food co-oops with names like Strawberry Fields appeared, selling crappy-tasting organic peanut butter. Sixties revivalists read "Steal This Book," "The Whole Earth Catalog," and most importantly, "The Electric Kool-Aid Acid Test." Male hippies still drank coffee and ate bacon and eggs then, while female hippies wore peasant dresses, no underwear, and slept with guys who never used condoms. Patchouli was important. Girls smoked and were on the pill. There were no ATMs, no PCs, no email, no pagers, no cell phones. On Fridays people went to the bank to make sure they had enough cash to get through the weekend. Reefer was $35 an ounce. "Fifty Ways to Leave Your Lover" was a top ten hit. On TV actor Ricardo Montalban touted the "Coreentheean leather" of the Chrysler Cordoba.

I enjoyed acid because I was so fucked up from my dad dying when I was fourteen and I liked anything that kept me apart from my feelings.

I especially prized the Eadweard Muybridge effect of stroboscopic Frisbees and the Huxley-like effect of mutating doorknobs. Time became elaborately elastic. Seventies acid was liberally laced with speed, giving weight to the underground comix hero Fat Freddy's contention that he wasn't an alcoholic: "I don't have a drinking problem. I can drink 36 cans of beer without barfing." The acid we took was so speedy you could easily drink a case of beer in eight hours, and you could enjoy alcohol's sister vice, cigarettes, in much the same way. In fact, it was not uncommon to smoke a pack or two in the afternoon, and if you found yourself buttless in Gaza, you could just as well smoke the remainder of your spent cigs down to the nubbins with roach clips.

Acid made you dumb as shit of course. Although I carefully ran pre-flight checks prior to all my trips, reality always had a way of proving too thorny for my great personality. I might be walking along Main Street when a bus would send a nine-foot wave of filthy rainwater crashing over me or else, after a particularly sad viewing of "Dumbo" at the local revival house (this is pre-VCR, pre-video), some poor bleeding unfortunate might pull up to the curb in his car and ask if I could tell him which way to the local hospital. Normally, it would be no problem to give proper directions, but for some reason, confusion, and later guilt, would set in. "Sorry pal, can't help you."

Drugs were confusing for another reason. Before I smoked reefer, I was a B student in college. Once I began smoking pot, I became an honor roll student. Then, after I began dropping acid, I started to get straight A's and made dean's list. The more drugs I took, apparently, the smarter I got. Very disconcerting, especially when life proved the opposite.

Example. Once a friend and I were tripping in the woods and feeling weary. We walked and walked and came upon a lovely mossy grotto. We lay out our sleeping bags and were awakened the next morning by some irate golfers. We had fallen asleep on the putting green.

My acid trip with Arthur Godfrey began innocently enough. I'd gotten hold of some blotter and called up Grant Runge, Tim Vavra, Tim Kenwick and Chris Bolta. We set aside a Saturday afternoon in April for our trip, and decided it should start in Giant State Park, near Carbondale. Grant fitted us out with hospital scrubs for our adventure. He'd procured them from the hospital where he worked part-time, and we all found the scrubs quite comfy. Several hours into our trip, we hiked around and took photos of each other posing on cliffs, hanging about in fissures, etc. The mood was rock music album cover art — you know, wacky guys whacked on acid, dressed in hospital scrubs and posing as we imagined the Kinks or the Who might have, had they lived in southern Illinois in 1977.

It was a bit chilly, and after traipsing around a while, we came upon an old rustic inn complete with grand stone fireplace and haunting native taxidermy: deer, moose, caribou, and a particularly lifelike owl. It looked like a hunting lodge I'd once seen in Maine, near Lake Mooselookmeguntic. We tiptoed quietly around the place at first, grooving on sunlight cascading through tall windows. We spotted a grand piano in one room, set the self-timer on my camera, and snapped a photo of the five of us tickling the ivories. Then, rounding a corner, we came upon Arthur Godfrey and a friend eating lunch at a long wooden table.

For those of you too young to remember, Arthur Godfrey's countenance beamed its way into millions of American homes during TV's infancy. His cheerfully bulbous features — the features of a middle-aged cherub — conveyed a benevolence that surpassed understanding. In the late forties and fifties, "Arthur Godfrey and His Friends" and "Arthur Godfrey's Talent Scouts" topped the TV ratings week after week. The man known as "the old redhead" was an impresario whose shows led to stardom for the likes of Pat Boone, the McGuire Sisters, Rosemary Clooney, Tony Bennett, Connie Francis, Steve Lawrence, Leslie Uggams, and Roy Clark. Crotchety "60 Minutes" star Andy Rooney recalls getting his start by meeting Arthur Godfrey by chance in an elevator. Rooney said, "Gee, I'd love to write something for you." And Arthur Godfrey said, "Well, come on in and see me." So Rooney did, and he got a job writing for Arthur Godfrey for five years. Lesbian icon Patsy Cline debuted on "Arthur Godfrey's Talent Scouts." Ironically, Elvis Presley auditioned for the program but was not selected.

I can see by the looks on your faces that some of you are still unimpressed. How do I know that? I don't have to lift the lid to know what's in the pot. But here's something that should make you sit up and take notice. Some people believed that God himself looked like Arthur Godfrey. It's true. I've read since that some people thought that God was simply a distant relation of Arthur Godfrey's. The names were similar; maybe they were cousins.

Anyway, we looked across the room, where the sun's rays danced about the long wooden table — a calm, benevolent, cherubic sun — and there, amid stuffed deer and moose, the unmistakable countenance of Arthur Godfrey beamed. We got his attention and he beckoned us to approach. He autographed some place-mats for us without batting an eye. Arthur Godfrey couldn't sing, dance, or act. He wasn't even a good ad-libber. But for one shining moment, he made all of us feel very special. Arthur Godfrey lived another seven years. He died in 1983.

I am lucky to have tripped with Arthur Godfrey.

carri skouzek '00

Creative Visualization

TSAURAH LITZKY

My friend Laurie never lacked for boyfriends. If she needed a new boyfriend, she would visualize him. Soon after he would appear. She learned about visualizing from Shakti Gawain's book *Creative Visualization*. Laurie believed Shakti Gawain had written the most important book of the twentieth century. After my marriage broke up, I was destroyed. I didn't want to leave my apartment, but after a while I was so lonely I forced myself to go out in search of male company. All the men I met were either ludicrous or depraved. Laurie told me if I wanted to meet someone decent I should try the Shakti Gawain method. She said I should stop pulling the petals off daisies and enter the New Age.

Maybe she is right. I am tired of lying in bed night after night, my body clenched belly down against the sheets, lonely as the eye of a needle. I decide to try it—I will creatively visualize! I make a mental list of the qualities I want in a mate; strong mind, strong back, gentle disposition. My ex, Steven, was so meticulous. He insisted we have separate soaps, separate towels. If I accidentally used his towel he'd yell and scream. I never felt safe. I want someone laid back, mellow, maybe a musician. Steven was Nordic and fair, this time I want someone dark, robust, a rasta from Jamaica or a Prince from Nigeria who summons his tribe to ceremonies by the stately beating of a drum.

I realize if I want to meet a musician I ought to go to bars that offer live music. I call my friend Margo and invite her to go with me to Karma, a jazz club that Carri told me about. It is on newly, trendy Orchard street in a former lingerie store. Margo thinks this a great idea and we make plans to go on Saturday night. As I hang up the phone I think here I am encouraging Margo to drink when she doesn't need any encouragement. The last time we were at the Right Bank she drank so much she fell off the bar stool in an alcoholic swoon.

When I tell her it worries me to see her drinking so much, she says she is probably drinking more because she is having an affair with a married man and she doesn't get to see him as much as she would like. She said that he told her he loved her but he would not leave his wife because of the harm it would do to their child. I told her about the time I went to bed with a married man, twenty-five years ago. I met him in a bar. He said he was an underground film maker working on a film about the new feminism. I brought him home to demonstrate the new feminism. As he was pulling out of me, he proclaimed loudly and dramatically, "I have just committed adultery." He gave me syphilis, gonorrhea and venereal warts. After that, I told Margo, I made it a rule to stay clear of married men. I told Margo she was setting herself up for heartache. Different strokes, Margo said, proving that if you tell someone something they don't want to hear they won't listen to you. I was glad she was coming to Karma with me, maybe she would meet someone interesting who wasn't married.

Thursday was Christmas and I went to a party where everyone but myself and another woman who was a Jew for Jesus was part of a couple. When I got home I went straight to bed with the bottle of Jameson's I keep in my sweater drawer. The next day I was so hung over I had to drink a pot of coffee before I could make myself work on my poem for the annual New Years day night reading at Cafe Nico. It is titled Hope Blessing Poem for the New Millennium. Although I feel completely hopeless, I make progress and manage to avoid such rhymes as time and slime and suck and muck.

By Saturday I am feeling better. Sitting on the toilet after breakfast I try again to visualize my dark prince. He is very handsome, a composite of Paul Robeson, Bob Marley and Denzel Washington. I tell myself that very soon he will come into my life.

I pick up Margo at 6:30 so we can get there in time for Happy Hour. Driving over Manhattan Bridge to the club I can smell booze on Margo's breath, she has already started her happy hour. Margo tells me about her last date with the married man. They prepared a lasagna together at her place, then put it in the oven to bake. By the time they finished making love, the lasagna was done. They ate by candle-light and then went back to bed again. I begin to wonder how much of my right-eous indignation is jealousy.

At Karma the bar runs along one wall, a long banquette along the other. There is a balcony built at the back of the room for the musicians. Margo and I score the last two seats at the bar. Margo orders a double vodka. I order a ginger ale. I look around for romantic men but the room is so smoky it is hard to see clearly. I eye-ball a cute guy in one of those red Kangol hats but then I see he is wearing lipstick and is a woman.

Our drinks arrive. My ginger ale has a muddy cast and I wonder if the bartender has put her thumb in it. Suddenly the overhead lights dim, a spotlight comes on, illuminating the stage. Two guys are up there, one with bongos, the other has a giant bass. They segue out on Coltrane's *My Favorite Things*, the sound, on gen-tle wings spreads out into the room. It quiets down. I look at the stage. The bass player is an older guy with a shaved head and gray goatee. He smiles as he plays. The drummer is dreadlocked, a handsome young God with a fine, wide face. It's him, my dream lover, the man I saw in my mind's eye, the man I visualized! He's wearing a white shirt and white chinos. I am staring at him so hard I wonder if he can feel it. I force myself to tear my eyes away. I look around and see a few other women gazing enraptured at the stage.

I take a sip of ginger ale. I remember Shakti Gawain, close my eyes, visualize the drummer's noble face. I whisper over and over— *lover come to me, lover come to me, lover come to me.* Margo shakes my arm. "What's the matter, why are you talking to yourself," she wants to know. "It's nothing," I tell her. She introduces the man sitting next to her. His name is Galahad and then she motions the bartender over and buys them both drinks I don't like the looks of this Galahad. He has a bar code tattooed on his neck, over the Adam's apple. His red shirt is unbuttoned way down the front to show off a cobra tattoo and he wears a huge silver Ankh on a long leather thong. He grabs my hand and starts to pump it too hard. I manage to extri-cate my hand as the musicians finish their set. I join in the applause even though my hand is sore. "They were kind of off" says Galahad. I ask him if he is a music crit-ic. His tone is so smug as he tells me that he is an entrepreneur that I want to entre-preneur my ginger ale right down the front of his open shirt but I am saved from this messy display when I feel a sudden presence behind me. A deep, melodious voice says into my ear, "did you like the music?" I turn my head and am face to face with the godlike drummer. His breath in my face smells like peppermint.

"It was great," I manage to say. "Do you mind if I squeeze in beside you?" he asks. I manage to nod my blissed-out head.

He tells me his name is Algier and that is an African name meaning set apart. He tells me he noticed me from the stage and that I'm so pretty. When I tell him I'm a writer he says I better not write about him. I say I can't promise that but I could change his name. "What you going to call me in your writing?" he asks. His eyes are very bright and glistening. He looks at me with what I take to be a hungry look like I'm a pork chop and he's going to gobble me up. I can't wait. "What would you like to be called?" I ask. "How about Arthur," he says which is the name of his friend, the bass player, who joins us just then. When Algier introduces me, Arthur says, "I wish I saw you first." This is too good to be true. Praise Shakti. Arthur starts to chat up the woman on the other side of him. Algier puts his arm possesively around the back of my chair and we talk about his music and my writing. He says he would like to hear me read. I invite him to the reading at Cafe Nico and give him my card. Arthur turns to him, says, "we got to do our next set." " O.k, o.k.,"says Algier. Then I remember Margo, "I want to introduce you to my friend," I say. I turn to Margo but she is gone and so is Galahad. Oh, Oh. "Did you see them leave?" I ask Algier. "No, I was too busy looking at you," he says and then he leans closer and kisses me firmly on the mouth, a confident, peppermint kiss. Arthur pulls at Algier's arm. "Let's do it," he says. I tell Algier I'm gonna go, I don't feel like another ginger ale. He helps me put on my coat and I float out the door.

Driving home I start to worry about Margo. I imagine Galahad has her tied to a bed and is whipping her with his Ankh. I know I am not responsible for her but when I get home I call her and am not surprised to get her answering machine. I leave a message for her to call me in the morning Then I go to bed and visualize Algier lying beside me. He bends over me, puts his head between my legs..

I am startled awake by the phone ringing, it is not Margo, it is a market research firm wanting to know if I use maxi pads. I tell them never to call me again and slam the receiver down. I go back to bed and try to visualize Algier's head between my legs but all I can think of is maxi pads. I get up and start work on my Hope Blessing poem. Just as I am getting going the phone rings again. I consider yanking the cord out of the wall but decide to get it so I can yell at whoever is on the line but this time it is Algier. He greets me by saying "Hello beautiful". Oh wonderful Shakti! He tells me he is really happy to have met me and that he is looking forward to hear-ing me read at Cafe Nico. I give him the address. His speech is slurred and I kid him, tell him he sounds drunk, but he is a quick to reply— "Drunk on you. Bye beau-tiful," he says and gets off the phone. I am so thankful to Shakti Gawain, I will plant roses in her name. I will build a garden to her with a fountain that spouts ginger ale. I find myself dancing around the room too happy to go back to my typewriter. The phone rings again, I'm so popular. This time it is my friend Jesse. She says she is looking forward to the Cafe Nico reading, she comes every year as does Margo. I tell her I met someone and he'll be there too. "Good," says Jesse, "I'll check him out and see if I approve." "I'm counting on that," I tell her.

The next morning Margo returns my call, I ask her what happened with Galahad. She says he turned out not to be her type. I don't press her for details. I tell her about Algier and that she can get her chance to meet him at Cafe Nico. The rest of the week I work on my poem and creatively visualize the life Algier and I will have. After my book becomes a best seller and his CD goes platinum we will buy a house in Barbados. New Years Eve I go to a party at my next door neighbors, I get drunk on champagne and visualize spending next New Years Eve with Algier making love on the beach in front of our island home.

On New Years Day I try to rehearse my poem but find it hard to concentrate. I dress in my favorite red sweater and black jeans and then, force myself to drive slowly over the bridge because I am so excited about seeing Algier that I can't see straight.

I park the car on 2nd street and walk up Ave. A to Cafe Nico. As I climb the stairs I hear talk and laughter. Huberman is standing with Hal and Sharon in the back of the room. They see me and wave. There's Carl, beer in hand, *tete-a-tete* with Michael Carter. Eve is darting around giving out flyers. It's so crowded people are sitting two to a seat. Thad, wearing a bathing cap, is on stage reciting a poem. Bruce walks by with the list and I find out that I am number 57. It will be at least a half hour before I am called up to read. Just then there is a commotion at the door. Margo is coming in, staggering, bumping into people.

" A refugee from A.A." says K. loudly over the din. And N., who hates me, starts to giggle. I start to go help Margo, guide her through the crowd but Huberman who knows her, gets there first. He guides her to a seat that has just been vacated by a woman wearing a mink coat. Margo passes out instantly.

I look around the room for Algier. I see Ron and Jim Feast sitting together near the stage. Jushi, Joanne and Catherine are behind the book table and there, right beside the book table, in front of the door to the bathroom is Algier. He is wearing a big, fur hat and his head sticks out above the crowd. Someone touches my back, I turn and there is Jesse, "You look great," she says. "Happy New Year. I saw Margo zonked out, sad.... where's your guy?" "Over there," I say, "and happy New Year," I hug her, "come on, you can meet him." We make our way through the crowd. As we pass the book table Joanne gives me a big hello and Jushi smiles her beautiful smile. We approach Algier, his mouth is open and his head is bent slightly forward as if he is dozing, Can the poetry be that bad? "Hi," I say loudly enough to startle him from his reverie. His eyes snap open, he turns his head, looks at me. At first he seems not to know who I am, but then, "Hi beautiful," he says. His eyes are glassy and so bright they are like exploding stars. He is sweating profusely, "Hi yourself," I say but suddenly I feel worried, frightened, "and this is my friend Jesse."

"Always a pleasure to meet a charming lady," Algier says, bowing towards her. His voice is much too loud, He has several large leather bags at his feet and they make an island around him. Tomasso is right behind us and he stumbles and near-ly falls as he tries to make his way over the bags to the bathroom. Joanne steps out from behind the book table, catches Tomasso by the arm, steadying him.

"Excuse me," she says to Algier, "could you please move those bags, people can't get through to the bathroom." "And where am I supposed to put them," Algier yells back at her, suddenly enraged, "you don't got no coatroom, who are you to be so bossy anyhow." Joanne looks shocked, her mouth opens but no words come out. Jesse nudges me, "don't get involved in this..." she whispers. " Excuse me," I say to Algier but he doesn't even notice. He is glaring at Joanne.

I stumble after Jesse back through the crowd. We find a clear space against the wall. "It has to be drugs," she says. "Yeah," I say, "I know," I feel nauseous, sick. We hear Algiers yelling some more. From where we are standing we can see him gather up his bags, charge through the crowd. He seems to be looking around, perhaps for me? I try to fade into the wall. He finds a spot on the other side of the book table, slightly behind where Jushi is sitting, and drops his bags down around him, then he turns to face the stage.

A minute later my name is called, I take the copy of my poem out of my pocket. As I go up to the stage I am very nervous. Somehow I manage to get each word out loud and clear and I finish to loud applause. Algier is standing in the same place behind Jushi's chair, smiling at me insanely. I turn my head away from him, rush to the back of the room towards Jesse. "You did great," she says. Mike Golden catches my eye, gives me the "thumbs up" sign.

The M.C., Grace Period, gets on the stage, "What is the difference," she asks the audience, "between erotic and kinky?" No one replies. "With erotic you use a feather," she says, "with kinky — you use the whole chicken." Some people laugh while others boo, then Grace announces the next reader, Joe Maynard. As he is making his way to the stage, the general din is pierced by a loud cry, "My pocket book is missing," shrieks Jushi, "it was on the back of my chair." I look around, Algier is gone too.

Jesse and I look at each other. "What a way to start the New Year," she says. She sighs, "We better try to get Margo home." "O.K." I say, "in a minute." I am filled with despair. What should I do, go to Jushi and tell her it was my date that stole her pocketbook and give her the eight dollars that is in my wallet? Yeah, probably, and what about Margo? How can I help her when I cannot even help myself? What can I say? Clearly, creative visualization is not the way.

New Me

SEENA LIFF

Visualize walking on water.
Fly to a fancy hotel in Chicago:
Walk barefoot on hot coals.
Break open stiffened places,
plunge headfirst into the new me.
"He is like the water, fluid yet steadfast.
He stands tall, his eyes beckon.
His voice, like a beacon, is what I
know, what I am, who I know,
his voice is me within my own self.
Tall and brown he is, breaking me to tears
while bending me around corners,
pulling me through recalcitrant light.
My light, his light, my light, his light,
my light, his light, my light, his light ..."
Choices are many:
Pirouette on rough escarpments,
mold on radical energy,
sculpt with straightforward intensity,
glaze to colors yet unseen.
This
is what
I need
to do
for myself.

TIPS AND HINTS ON MAKING RELATION- SHIPS WORK!

TEACH YOURSELF FUCKING
(being a rough translation from the Talmud)

TEACH YOURSELF FUCKING
IT's BETTER THAN SMUCKING*
THO I ONCE HEARD A WISE GUY STATE:
"THE BRAIN'S A SEX SYSTEM
BETTER THAN A PISTON—
FOR CLEANING YOUR TUBES OUT 'S JUST GREAT!"

BUT <u>WE</u> KNOW, GIRLS & BOYS
WE ARE NOT <u>JUST</u> SEX TOYS
OUR BODY'S A <u>WORLD</u> FULL OF JOY.
SO FUCK IF YOU MUST~
BUT WHILE YOU SCREAM & YOU THRUST
GIVE YOUR WHOLESOME SOULSOME EMPLOY.

THEY SAY
MY BRAINS IN
MY HEAD— BUT
I DON'T BELIEVE IT...

*YINGLISH FOR "SMOKING"

Mother Kushner's Etiquette Lesson

TOM SAVAGE & BILL KUSHNER

1. Never talk with your mouth full of cock.

2. Never speak unless your prick has something to say,
    In which case it is perfectly all right to speak in tongues.

3. Never point and shake your head after an orgy.

4. Don't stare directly at anybody unless your eyes speak volumes.

5. Never let your mind wander from the odorous asshole at hand.

6. Do not fart in the face of fortune.
    (A little too much reality for a Friday night.)

7. The dictates of gender and conventional sexual beauty are a curse.
    I trusted you with my brain.
       You let me go haywire.
    I hit the hay but then the hay hit me.
       So it's hey-nonny-nonny and a hot cha cha.

Selections from *TIPS FOR TOPS AND BOTTOMS: Time-tested Secrets for Getting All You Want from Mr. Right-Now*

GLENN BELVERIO & BRUCE BENDERSON

TIPS FOR BOTTOMS

A casual stroll through any of America's big-city gay ghettos reveals a chorus of lisps, shrieks, random voyeurs, Miss Things, and show-tune dementia. Why?

The nineties taught us to express ourselves and that repression isn't a bad thing. We've come to the point where we're secure about our androgyny. Our man-hood isn't threatened by a coffee-bar romp into queenliness. But will it get us the man we want, whether he be Mr. Right of Mr. Right-Now? We don't think so. Bottom though you may be, you must learn to be a Tips Man — not boy, and espe-cially not girl.

Tip 1
YOU MAY BE A BOTTOM BUT PLAY IT LIKE AN AVERAGE JOE
You may be a bottom, but that doesn't mean you're a shrill, screechy Broadway queen who shouted from the rooftop of the Chelsea Gym when you scored tickets to see Liza Minelli stepping in for Julie Andrews in *Victor/Victoria*. As far as he's concerned, you're a guy's guy. Just remind yourself that James Dean kept the fact that he was a burn-bottom to himself and never overpressed his chinos. Be dis-creet. That should be your mantra. No top wants to dominate a good Audrey Hepburn imitation. They want to believe, at least for the seven minutes between stripping down and ejaculatlion, that you're a red-blooded, all-American macho captive. Squirm, obey, and spread 'em — but not like Deborah Kerr wrapped up in seaweed with Burt Lancaster. Instead, think American Gladiators in the Greased-Pole Competition.

Tip 2
BOTTOMS KNOW THE DIFFERENCE BETWEEN GIRL-TALK AND MAN-TALK WHEN IT COMES TO THE PHONE.
He calls and your bottom-heart is beating wildly. Find an understated way to show it. He wants control, not hysterical submission. Even if he's calling to invite you to see *The Birdcage*, tell yourself it's anonymous phone sex. A Tips Bottom keeps an index card near the phone with the right passive monosyllables: *Hey, Cool, Right, Uh-huh*. Do Tarzan, not Jayne. In fact, forget Tarzan. Do the Chimp. Save "Yes, Sir," and "Master" for later. Remember that this isn't the time to gush on about your big promotion at the florist's. Save it for that moment when the Master finally reveals

he's Joan Collins's personal wig-and-wardrobe manager. He won't be able to back out then.

Don't despair. You can be "you" when it comes to girl-talk. A bottom without a fellow bottom is like Courtney Love without her publicist. You tell him everything. He only gabs the part that makes you look good. Remember: You need a Liz Smith in your life, not a Rex Reed. He's the one you can rejoice with over your promotion at the florist's. You can even take him to the Clinque counter with you. Or to the clinic with a "c," as in VD.

Suppose Mr. Right finally calls, in the middle of your favorite *Brady Bunch* rerun, the one where Marsha gets hit in the nose with a football. You were just reaching to the phone to shriek the news to your bottom. Don't get nervous. Just hit the TV mute button and clench your jaw to keep from cooing with excitement. Don't you dare mention Florence Henderson's shag! It'll be death to your sex life. Avert your gaze from Florence and grunt through the requisite monosyllables. Don't forget that cue card. Get off quick and speed dial your girlfriend. Now let it rip. Because you held it in, you'll feel twice the pleasure.

Tip 3
WHEN IT COMES TO WRITING A PERSONAL AD, MAKE YOUR NEEDS KNOWN.
Maybe Aunt Helen has an endless interest in knowing you can make a mean pesto, but a top would prefer to hear about your gag reflex. You can paste in the height-weight-pecs-age-dick-size spiel if you want. Just copy the statistics from all the other ads. But be sure to snare 'em with a thumbnail sketch of the down-and-dirty.

BAD AD

Caring, sensitive, responsible relationship-minded bottom, father of five artificially inseminated children with lesbian mother (who lives in her own apartment), Masters in social work, dreams of Pride Partner who likes long walks on Provincetown beaches, portobello mushrooms, snuggling at the fireside with *Out Classics* playing in the background, and hot, caring sex into the late-night. Sexual Compulsives Anonymous graduates o.k. No smokers, late-night revelers, bisexuals, transgenders, ex-cons, drug users (Prozac o.k.), debtors, high school dropouts, Goths, self-hating Mel Gibson fans (Donna Summer o.k.), unhealthy eaters, Weejuns with or without tassels, bikini briefs, French snobs, unemployed, or Guidos, please! Send letter, picture, photocopy of diplomas, and references to P.O. Box 476. Discretion assured. All queries answered.

GOOD AD

Human toilet, well hung, elephant balls, seeks hot jail sex, rape. Call me 24-hours! 224-0456.

Tip 4
THINGS NOT TO MENTION ON DATES 1-4

Sharon Stone
Arugula
Madonna
Courtney Love
Foucault in San Francisco
Dusty Springfield
That Girl
Kate Moss
Men on Men anthologies
Ab Fab
Martha Stewart Living
Your favorite Gaultier peach lame thong
Baywatch
Cindy Crawford
What happened to Diana Ross's career
Bette Midler
Faye Dunaway's performance in *Mommie Dearest*
Ikea
Retin-A
Who's Afraid of Virginia Woolf
The outfit you wore at Wigstock last year
Michelangelo Signorele
Chelsea Clinton
Phillippe Starck furniture

Tip 5
MAKE YOURSELF OVER, WITH THE TOP OF YOUR DREAMS IN MIND.
Even if you've only got six hours to get ready for clubbing, pay attention to details. Peer into a make-up mirror with at least 500 watts and take stock. Eyebrows thinner than 1/2 cm? You should have melted those tweezers down into a cock ring. A uni-brow? Don't touch a hair, it'll bring out the primitive in your top. Got a shy and boyish smile? Practice it, but make it sleazy with the hint of a Billy Idol snarl. It'll be your ticket to a hotter bottom heaven. What about that Paul Lynde grin? No go. No top wants to dominate a center Square!

Now let's look at your complexion. Are you peaches and cream or an extra on the set of George Romero movie? Cheating's o.k. as long as you go easy. Take a light-meter reading from your favorite club, and make up your mug just below the reveal-threshold. Eye-liner, even a bit, is a mistake. No matter how little you think you put on, you always end up looking like Liz Taylor in *Cleopatra*.

If you think the top-of-your-dreams would love a baby-butt chin, find that cleft and hit it with a dot of eyebrow pencil. As for your sideburns, if they taper puckishly to a point like Liza's, fill 'em out to the Elvis line. Make light, sketchy strokes to avoid the Lugosi look.

Despite your disciplined gym regimen, you may still look peaked from a night of too much Special K and martinis. Reclaim that farmboy vigor with a little blush and bronzer. One shade darker, only, please. And remember, if tan line and receding hairline aren't flush, you'll look like you keep your face in a jar by the door. Easy on the blush, too. After you've been bottoms up, tops don't want a face-down imprint on their combed-cotton pillow cases.

You've invested in that pectoral cleavage and have a certain right to show it off in a tank top. Nevertheless, we strongly encourage you to limit that décolletage. The general Tip: no less than one inch above the aureole.

Your bubble-butt is the ticket to Mr. Right Now heaven. But don't strangle it in spandex. Wear something that breathes so that you stay fresh, fragrant, and fungus free.

TIP 6
A TIPS BOTTOM DOESN'T ENTERTAIN THE WAY HIS MOTHER DID.

Mom may have served pigs in the blanket or caviar, depending on who her people were. But whether you're from Bayonne or Boston, forget the hors d'ouevres and cut to the chase. It's all about what you want out of your top on this particular evening.

What did Elvis do when he checked into the hospital in the seventies? He put aluminum foil on the windows to block out all the light. The stray ray from a streetlamp or the rising sun can ruin romance for both of you. Chances are you met him in the dark. Keep it that way until the inevitable brunch.

If you insist on lighting your home, it should be as strategic as it was in Carol Channing's current production of *Hello Dolly.* Just don't trip and fall into the orchestra pit like we were afraid she would.

Remember: it's less a matter of what he'll find out than what you will. He may look like Prince Charming, but with the lights on he can turn into Quasimodo.

In our experience with tricks we thought were dreamboats, we've witnessed the following tragic transformations take place when there was just too much light:

Lights Out	Lights On
Rip Torn	Rip Taylor
Tab Hunter	Tabatha
Neil Diamond	Neely O'Hara
Sylvester Stallone	Totie Fields
Brad Davis	Bette Davis
Brando in *Streetcar*	Brando in *Island of Dr. Moreau*
Brad Pitt	JonBenet Ramsey
Jeff Stryker	Robin Byrd
Joey Stefano	Joey Stefano dead
Howard's End	Howard Stern
The Blue Lagoon	*Freaks*
Boys in the Sand	*Boys in the Band*

Depending on what your apartment looks like, you might want to disguise some of its features. We suggest an automated system not unlike Rock Hudson's in *Pillow Talk*. With the touch of a button, your Joan Crawford posters instantly flip over to reveal those turn-of-the-century illustrations of masculine archetypes in the work force. An electric pulley system hoists your disco ball through a trap door in the ceiling. Your bed flips over to exchange your Laura Ashley duvet cover and dust ruffle for your studded leather fuck mat. A robot arm sweeps the perfume bottles on the bathroom shelf into a secret compartment and replaces them with a lone bottle of Brut. If you can't afford high-tech solutions, merely say, "I'm just watching my friend Bernie the hairdresser's apartment while he's out of town."

Planning the Evening

A Good Bottom plans ahead. Before the groaning, the lash of the whip, etc., drowns out the techno, you should already have a post-coital strategy. When you've come, wiped, and ten minutes are up, he may show no signs of leaving. So what should you do?

1. Take off your techno and put bad music on — loud. Suggestion: *Lady Bunny Sings.*

2. Play all 36 phone messages.
You should have squirreled them away for just such an occasion. Ideally, they'll be things that couldn't possibly include or interest him. A queeny voice telling you it got tickets to Tyne Daly, the secretary at work who wants the number of your friend who does pedicures. Even your mother calling to report on your father's prostate problem will do, as long as it diffuses the masculine energy in the room and makes him zip up his coveralls and lace his Timberlands.

3. Turn the lights on. Use with caution: this can backfire. (See *Lights Out/Lights On* list.)

4. Look worried, check your watch and tell him your roommate who recently got out of jail and suspects you might be a fag will be back any minute from his drug run.

5. If all else fails and you have not plans of seeing him again, put on that peignoir and those mules. Push your gay equivalent of the doomsday button! The pictures of masculine archetypes will swoosh back to posters of Joan Crawford, the perfume bottles clink out of their secret compartment and send the Brut crashing to the floor. The full force of the Laura Ashley dust ruffle rotating into view will knock your stunned trick off the bed. Slip your penis between your legs and begin your imitation of Buffalo Bill in Silence of the Lambs, as the disco ball descends from the ceiling like an apocalyptic angel.

Tip 7

A TIPS MAN ISN'T CAUGHT WITH HIS PANTS DOWN AT HIS FAVORITE SEX CLUB.

When the lights go up, don't get spotted in a compromising position. You know you're a bottom and you want the world to know it, but maybe just three or four at a time. Do you really want to crawl out of there looking like Jayne Mansfield's last car ride? The minute you hear your first button pop or zipper break, throw in the towel. Stroll casually into a corner and do what you can to pull yourself together.

If you've let it go too far already, there's a lot you can still do. Like Helen Lawson in *Valley of the Dolls*, you may have lost your wig but leave with dignity. Borrow a handkerchief to put over that stained crotch and go out the way you came in!

Recently our friend Lancelot tried to extend his "date" with a strapping Mr. Right-Now whom he'd met at a glory-hole juice lounge. You know, those trendy one-stop-shopping fuck-spots that offer cock massage and arugula.

Lance thought he could sustain the pulse rate of pagan energy they'd con-cocted standing upright in one of the sticky quarter-a-minute pied-à-terres, where, pressed against a video display featuring the new Chi Chi La Rue epic, they'd been role-playing cobra and mongoose. If Lance were a Tips Bottom, he would have dragged the trick out of there in the heat of passion, but he lacked the discipline to interrupt their ritual.

Before he knew it. fluorescent lights brighter than the Interrogatoin Room at the Fifth Precinct (See Simon Watney's *Policing Desire*) illuminated their tryst, making their exposed organs appear more like the product of a live surgery procedure on cable TV. Then they were evicted from their pied-à-terre by a poorly paid, mop-wielding clutter consultant, impatient to close up and leave. The mood was ruined and Lance scampered home alone, moist but unsatisfied.

Our other friend Bobbie is a classic Tips Bottom. He arrived early and strolled from booth to booth like a Frank Perdue inspector at a hen yard, sampling the choice specimens without ever devouring the whole meal, until he found himself sequestered with a granite-thighed buff stud hung like the Lady Chablis (didn't you know?), whom he brought to a near climax before saying, "You're too good for this place." And as they emerged into the light of the street lamp, despite Bobbie's pre-vious activity, his grooming was impeccable, thanks to his advanced hair products and his felatiotic virtuosity, which preserved his coiffure from any contact with thigh, abs, or boot.

Tip 8

A TIPS MAN NEVER FALLS INTO A K-HOLE (AND OTHER TIPS ABOUT RESPONSIBLE DRUG USE.)

Did we mention that Tips Bottoms are always in control? In order to maintain that control, you have to maintain your level of awareness. There are lots of tops out there who have nothing better to do than take advantage of boozed-out, burned-out bottoms who, à la Liz Taylor in *Butterfield 8*, come home wearing nothing but their skivvies and a stolen mink coat and carrying half a bottle of bourbon.

A good Tips Bottom has mastered the art of mood enhancement and uses drugs to correct, not exaggerate, personality defects. Don't fool yourself by saying that crystal meth makes you vivacious and virile. Chances are you're rigid and manic, a redundant trait in most gays. What is worse, once meth takes over, no splint contraption has been able to prop up that vestigial organ formerly known as a penis. Who doesn't think that a drooling date with bloodshot eyes and a peanut for a penis is sexy? We don't, and neither does a good Tips Bottom.

The chin of an intimate friend of ours (we'll just call him "Jaws") vibrated so violently from too much meth that the fish-hooked backs of his braces speared the foreskin of a trick he was sucking off, reeling him in as if he were a prize trout. There was a howl of pain, and after a few seconds of tug-of-war, the bleeding Top wriggled free and bolted. Remember, Jaws, there are other fish in the sea.

Another good friend of ours (let's call him "Special Kate" because he's so special) thought it would be cute to do some "K" with a Mr. Right-Now at a public park at midnight. In an attempt to find their "inner child," they performed fellatio hanging from the jungle jim and fucked in a wild ride down the kiddie slide. By morning Kate had slid into a comatose state. A kindergartner and his mother discovered him naked and butt-up on one end of an abandoned see-saw. "Is that what a K-hole is, Mom?" asked the inquisitive child, pointing to Kate's posterior.

We do not intend to scare you straight, but it's our duty to report one last horror story from the drug front. Another friend, affectionately known as "Madame X," was enamored of Ecstasy, thought to be the most innocuous of the gay drugs. However, recently, he was working his Body Glove all-in-one rubber jumpsuit on the dance floor at Traxx. His temperature climbed to four digits, permanently welding his costume to his ample frame. You can well imagine the spectacle we created with our 6 AM arrival at a body shop to have it blowtorched off him.

How to Get Rid of Your Boyfriend's Girlfriend

BONNY FINBERG

I once had a friend, we'll call her Sue, who couldn't get her boyfriend, we'll call him Joe, back. This is the story of how she did it. Sue told me how if you really put your mind to something you want, you'll probably get it. You just have to figure out who has it and how to make them not want it. Then they'll hand it over like a hot potato. It's especially easy if you make up your mind to want something that no one else is interested in. It's like when you're a little kid. Always go for the black and green lollipops. Everybody always fights over the red ones.

Initially, Sue broke up with Joe but changed her mind. They saw each other again for awhile, but he never forgave her for breaking up with him in the first place so he kept breaking up with her out of pride and vengeance and always went back to her because she was really the one he wanted in the end. Each time he'd say it was final. Then she'd try everything she could to get him to see her. Sometimes her methods would work, sometimes not. She'd show up unannounced when she knew he was drunk and lonely, walk past his building when she knew he'd be on his way to the corner store for another six pack, or invite him over for his favorite meal: Shake and Bake pork chops and cauliflower with Velveeta cheese. Once she even tried to light a fire under his door. She told me she didn't actually want to kill him, just get his attention.

Then he found another girlfriend, we'll call her Daisy. First he took Daisy to the movies and expensive dinners, theater or the ballet. Sue told herself Daisy was just a brief vacation from their demanding relationship, someone to pass the time with. He told her he'd still see her if she wanted, but that he wanted the choice to see both of them. Sue tried that for about two days and then told him to take a hike. After that he took his new girlfriend on trips to Caribbean islands and Europe. This was his *modus operandi* with all women in the beginning before he settled into his more natural routine of general malaise, inactivity and emotional terrorism. Daisy was someone who hadn't known him for very long, so she thought he was the nicest guy in the world. It got back to Sue that Joe was taking Daisy on a trip to Key West with another couple, Chuck and Mary, where he'd taken Sue and, only one week earlier, had promised to take her again.

Now Sue really had a much better time without Joe, who drank too much, never liked to leave the house, engaged in repetitive monologues about his long lost youth, left the TV on all day without sound, or if the sound was on it was tuned to CNN, while he ate a steady diet of hot dogs and take-out Chinese. Sue liked to go for walks in the sun, talk to strangers and listen to music while she created prostitute dolls out of old stockings and junk jewelry. But for some reason, she couldn't get Joe out of her mind. He had made it clear that he would not be her exclusive boyfriend anymore now that he'd found someone who didn't complain about his habits and didn't mind if he saw other women.

As much as Sue wanted Joe back, polygamy just went against her grain. She wanted to be special and had invested a lot of time trying to convince Joe how special she was by putting up with excruciatingly long stretches of boredom, incoherent drunken monologues, verbal abuse, insults to her friends, alienation of her family and bad TV. But she was in love with Joe, and she would get him back even if it cost her peace of mind, joy with the world, sanity, and the freedom to watch Public Access TV when she felt like it.

She became obsessed ... with Joe, with Daisy, with getting him back.

One day she waited outside Joe's door. She waited and waited until Daisy was leaving. As the door opened, she burst in, to both Joe and Daisy's surprise. A vigorous tussle took place between Sue and Joe. Daisy tried to calm them down. She finally invited Sue out for a drink. So they left Joe in the apartment while they got to know each other at the corner bar over vodka and cigarettes, sharing the tranquilizers that Sue carried around in her bag like a rabbit's foot.

They had a long heart-to-heart talk and Daisy ended up giving Sue not only her phone number, but her address and apartment number, and offered to introduce her to her ex-husband who, according to Daisy, was a much better lover, with better natural endowment, than Joe. Of course Sue felt there was no one better endowed than Joe, and that he was the best lover she'd ever known, which indicated to her that Joe definitely preferred her to Daisy in bed. This was very reassuring to Sue and gave her the inspiration to use the phone number and call Daisy every so often when she felt insecure about Joe's love for her.

So Sue developed a phone relationship with Daisy. And this is how she got her boyfriend back.

One day Sue called Daisy and told her she wanted to talk to her because she needed clarity. Joe was being vague about what was going on. They had seen each other a couple of nights ago and he'd told her he'd take her to Key West with their friends Chuck and Mary. She felt really betrayed by the fact that he'd changed his mind and was taking Daisy, and she was really distraught that he'd broken his word. Daisy said, "That's mean." Daisy admitted she liked him a lot but that he wasn't the center of her life and if they wanted to patch things up that was okay with her. She told Sue that she enjoyed him when he was being fun, but that when he was unpleasant she would just leave. She had her work which was the most gratifying thing in her life and men were secondary. Daisy told Sue, "I don't know why you want him back. You're attractive, intelligent. You could do much better." Sue felt that Daisy was becoming a good role model. She knew how to keep her distance, and seemed to appreciate Sue without being jealous, despite her own relationship with Joe. Daisy asked Sue if she thought that maybe the problem was the drinking. Sue laughed and said, "Are you kidding? Haven't you seen how weird and crazy he gets?" Daisy said she'd only seen it once in the three short months she'd been with him. She told Sue how Joe had gotten drunk in the airport on one of their trips and how she'd left him there and got a hotel room without him. He'd called her in the morning and apologized and they spent a cordial week, where, according to Daisy, the only words they actually exchanged were "Pass the salt and pepper." This honest disclosure from Daisy gave Sue the idea that she could now share with her some of her own negative experiences. She told her about the time he had threatened her gerbils with a steak knife in a drunken rage because he thought she cared more about them than him and that the sound of them running around on their ferris wheel was annoying. Then she told her about how, while she was preparing dinner for some friends, he tried to force her yoga teacher into the shower and sodomize him with a zucchini.

"What?" Daisy exclaimed.

"Oh, I still didn't kick him out. I was willing to put up with a lot. But the final straw was when he killed my cat and threw him in the cassoulet I was cooking for Bastille Day. I felt he'd finally gone too far."

"That's horrible," Daisy said. And though her voice quivered a little there was a sense of outrage.

"You know, I really like you, Daisy," Sue said with a tone of heartfelt conviction.

"I like you too," said Daisy.

"Listen," she told Daisy, "you'll have a great time in Key West. He wants to play golf down there. I'm sure you play golf."

"Oh. yeah. My ex-husband was an excellent golfer and he taught me how to play."

"Well, I'm sure that's why he'd rather take you. I don't play golf. Chuck and Mary are so much fun. Mary's very athletic. She's probably a great golfer. She likes to drink a little too much. In fact, Chuck and Mary went skiing in Colorado with some friends of ours and she got really drunk. She was racing down the slopes so fast and recklessly they thought she was going to kill herself or someone else."

"Oh, I don't know," said Daisy. "Maybe I shouldn't go to Key West, maybe you'll get to go after all."

"I don't think I want to go by default," Sue said. She heard an uncomfortable silence on the other end of the line.

Then she added, "They fight a lot, Mary gets a little sullen at times, and Chuck is like a speed freak on acid, but they're interesting characters all right. Besides, you know Joe, he sleeps off his hangover till two in the afternoon, so you can always hang out with Chuck and Mary."

Well, Sue got her boyfriend back. She ended up going to Key West by default after all. She played golf, and actually liked it. She went to the beach with Chuck and Mary, watching them make out in the surf, while Joe slept in until two in the afternoon. She ate lobster in a fine restaurant while Chuck and Mary threw claw crackers at each other across the table, breaking a champagne glass. Joe got incensed and threw a wad of cash on the table before storming back to the hotel, staying up all night drinking gin at the hotel bar before clearing out the mini-bar in the room. The next day he told Sue that she was a pain in the ass. Daisy was never heard from again.

The Rules!

Cynthia Andrews

From what I can remember, this is how it always went: boy meets girl, boy asks girl for dinner and movie, boy kisses girl, girl makes boy dinner and boy gives girl giant engagement ring in yellow gold with perfectly round stone, surrounded by two adorable "begets," consisting of at least one-half karat and costing no less than, at the very least, approximately thirty-five hundred dollars. As it turns out, however, I couldn't have been more wrong about the "boy meets girl" syndrome. According to a tiny little slim, rather unassuming, yet extremely illuminating, paperback book quite simply called *The Rules*, a girl can never expect to get herself hitched by any red-blooded American eligible man if she can't play by the ten simple rules of the game.

For instance, if I were really serious about "tying the knot" I would never never never never EVER pick up the phone when he calls me. Rather, I would let him "sweat" until he finally gives up and leaves me an "anxious" message on my machine. Further, if he should make the fatal mistake of calling any time, and I mean ANY time after Wednesday for a dinner and movie on SATURDAY, then he's out of luck! I am to firmly (but very graciously and even sweetly) turn him down with a simple, "I am afraid that I have already made plans for the weekend."

Finally, and perhaps most importantly, no matter how much I melt when he touches me, no matter how much I adore the way he kisses me, no matter what happens to my legs when he holds me in his arms, no matter how much I tremble (and other things) when he whispers in my ear, I am never never never never never never NEVER to allow myself to "give in" and go to bed with him before the third, or even fourth date!

For the past couple of decades, at the very least since Roe v. Wade, the modern woman has been striving for "self-fulfillment" in every phase of her life, including career, money and perhaps most importantly, the ability to have sex without having to say she's sorry. At the turn of the last century housewives were considered the ideal women by the patricarchal male society of pre-industrialized Western society. Before computers and cell phones, Mary Tyler Moore could "turn the world on with her smile," and yet, Mary was a television breakthrough for having been the first woman in a sitcom to be a completely self-supporting career woman. Notwithstanding Mary's smile, however, she still couldn't get a husband. It may seem that in today's world of "politically correct" expressions and behavior, crotch clutching and pornographic obsessions on and off the internet, the tide has turned in yet another direction that is neither housewife nor career girl. Today's woman does not appreciate being thought of as a "sex object." She is tough minded and short on words, and above all else, does not need a husband or even sex. She does not need to fight her way into law or med school. Most of all, she does not need to do anything she does not want to do in order to rise up that corporate ladder, which seemed so impossible to her mother before her. Instead, sperm banks, technology and bi-sexuality have become the norm. Ironically, where divorce and "looking for Mr. Goodbar" lose their power for the Generation-X chic, a book called *The Rules* once again brings focus and clarity to a "meaningful relationship."

Above all else, therefore, I am a "Creature like no other." I am a "Creature like no other." I AM a "Creature like no other." I am a "CREATURE like no other." I am a "Creature like NO other." I am really a "Creature like no other!" But can I pick up the phone now?

153

Two Selections from:
The Last Chance Guide to Getting Married

Nancy Koan

Hi!

This book is for all you gals who know your left hand from your right, your head from your toes, but still grow a teeny, weenie bit misty when you see *Casablanca* for the 18th time and listen to Barbara spoon out "The Way We Were" as you pore over old high school yearbooks. You just may be C. B.s. Permit me to explain.

Deep inside you know that romanticism is as natural as whole oat bran and better for you. Being in love can be as exciting as getting an M.B.A., performing intricate dance steps and learning to stamp out forest fires. Actually, there's never really been an objection to the LOVE EXPERIENCE in general, but the past several years have shown its loss of status to the more popular themes of violence, video renting and home fax machines. But you know it's there — lurking in the shadows of your nightly dreams and spurring you on to newer and faster diets every spring. However, what some of you may be afraid to admit — quick, draw the blinds, lock that door — is that the old-fashioned follow-up to a good love affair (cough, ahem) — MARRIAGE — may still be something you want. There. It's said. Not so tough. *Closet Brides* — you brave group of women — stand up and be counted.

Actually, it's not that shameful to fantasize sashaying down a long carpet in a dripping white gown; impractical perhaps, but not shameful. Hasn't everyone at least once in her life dreamed of a closet full of Teflon, a set of unbreakable champagne glasses and a "someone else" to walk Spencer in the a.m.? Lift your heads and be proud. You've been suffering as a C.B. for much too long.

Getting MARRIED may indeed be the greatest challenge to modern women, but when did women ever run from a challenge? Didn't we overcome cellulite, virginity and the death of Rudolph Valentino? Nothing can stop us once we've put our collective minds to it.

Now remember, and this is IMPORTANT — this book is not saying that marriage is "IT." Personally, I could never assume that type of responsibility, let alone the bad press. In fact, there are plenty of women right in this book who may try to discourage you. But if you want to give it a try, these pages are here to help push you ... shove you, even, in that direction. Just read on and best of luck

1. We'll start out by SPRUCING UP YOUR IMAGE.

Okay, given there's no such thing as a female ideal except to men who created the notion and woe for us cause we ain't it. And there's no use trying to change the Barbie Doll fantasy — too many businesses depend on our spending money to achieve it (and what else would we do on our lunch hour?) However, we can TRY to make the most of what nature spared us. I'm not advocating nose jobs, just an objective look at what can be improved upon. Do it for you (not your mother) and eventually you will have done it for the two of you (not your mother, dummy, HIM!!)

Lose the FAT. I don't care if you take poison or cut it off, but get in shape. You'll need lots of energy to snare a man and having to schlep around an extra bag of flesh won't get you there any faster. Exercise and starve, starve and exercise. So what if you hate Jane Fonda, she looks good, doesn't she? Buy her video and squeeze those buttocks. It's cheap, effective and something you've been meaning to do since the 8th grade.

Clean up that face. The skin is more a barometer of your psyche than your dwindling supply of Valium. If you feel crummy, your skin will look like the underbelly of a frog. No amount of pancake can cover up GREEN PUS. Take some grains and scrub yourself into a Swedish glow. Got mole hairs? Zap 'em.

Do the same for surly eyebrows. It's only fair to your peepers — don't want your soul misread, do you?

Have those root canals taken care of. There's nothing more unattractive than a woman holding her aching jaw. True, it ain't cheap, but the mouth is the center for a lot of activity. If you need cap work — do it. On the plus side, you might snare your D.D.S.

Traditionally the crown of beauty, your hair is what's spotted first (that is, if you're walking behind a shoulder high fence). Most men never look beyond hair and boobs for eyes and ideas. Blondes can be plain, but never mousy. Go lighter if you think you'll laugh more. I say just get a good cut and keep it clean (that means every day, lazy bones). Whatever you do, DON'T wear a wig unless medically necessary. It's too humiliating in bed.

And lastly, throw out half your clothes. Don't shriek about the waste. That's the same reasoning that's kept you licking your plate clean all these years. Most of your wardrobe is probably unflattering, ten years out of style and ready to be turned into a tax deduction. Even your poodle dresses better. Let your most tasteful gay male friend help you buy some new duds. Then WEAR them, don't SAVE them. You'll never know when you'll meet HIM — traffic court, the blood bank. It'll pay off.

2. Okay, so maybe the makeover didn't work, guess you're gonna have to BUY HIM WITH A GREEN CARD

Desperate CB's, you should realize you hold a powerful card in the mating game — your good ole U.S. of A. birth certificate. If, in fact, you are of legal status in this country, there are countless men out there — Greeks, Turks, Gambians, and others — just looking for a nice girl to spend some time with (sometimes up to 3 weeks) in exchange for becoming American citizens. For the uninitiated, A GREEN CARD gives working status to foreign bodies. The mere acquisition of it can turn a frightened Mexican busboy into a proud *maitre d'* in months. Beyond that, just three years of legal marriage to an American gal can make this same fellow eligible for citizenship! But he needs YOU to get any of this in gear. He desperately needs to get MARRIED. Sounds nice, no?

Not only will you gain a hubby in this deal, you may be able to score a few extras — like charging him a fee of $1,000 and up. Some women have gotten additional perks — like VCRs and new hair dryers. You could become a professional and get married every three years or so — think of the video collection you could build.

Now the thing is, girls, so far the authorities haven't been too picky about the marriage vows. Supposedly they give out some kind of intimacy test that couples have passed by living together and studying the couples on "The Newlywed Game" reruns. But if you're not interested in having them scuttle off to their own pad and leaving you with just a "Mrs.," hold them to the hearth with a contract. People can get used to anything — even each other. If you're really lucky, you may actually fall in love!! (At least Hollywood believes that, merci Monsieur Depardieu.)

There are some good places for spotting green card candidates. I suggest you try these: the kitchens of many fine French restaurants; graduate schools — engineers love to study here with the thought of returning home to rebuild their native lands, but rarely do; the Mexican/California border — good pickins' at night; Greek coffee shops, obviously; and ballet companies.

In conclusion, here's wishing all you Closet Brides continued success in life and a minimum of crow's feet. If my advice has managed to shed the even tiniest light on the eternal dilemma of finding a groom, then I can die peacefully. If not — it's YOUR FAULT. Read this again and highlight significant sections. Carry it with you at all times and whip it out at every opportunity — the pool, the gym — even at your best friend's wedding — you may learn which method worked for her. And remember, if we should ever meet, my fondest wish is to hear you mutter these words: "Estoy a qui con mi marido!"

(quick translation—"I AM HERE WITH MY HUSBAND!")

Talking About You

KRISTAN RYAN

My husband sat across the dinner table from me in nothing but his green bikini underwear. He slid his chair away from the table and leaned back, rocking the chair slightly. "Your eating disgusts me," he said and took a long drag off his filterless Camel.

"What?" I asked, pushing my salad away from me and laying my fork beside it on the plate.

"You're fat. I would think that a person with MS would want to be streamlined. Thin, my dear, thin," he said and stood up and stretched. His penis poked out at me from behind the tightly woven fabric like a tiny mushroom covered in cloth. He sat back down, crossed his slender legs, leaned forward, took a long drag off his cigarette and blew smoke out of his nose. He smiled. Splashes of brown littered his teeth like bad miniature Picassos. His corpulent belly rolled forward on to his thighs and suddenly all I could see were two narrow strips of green molded against each hip.

"Brown period," I said to myself under my breath.

"You're having your period?" he asked.

"No," I said. "Your teeth remind me of Picasso's brown period."

"He didn't have a brown period," my husband yelled.

"I know," I said.

"You're just making fun of me. You know I'm sensitive about my teeth. You want to hurt my feelings, don't you?" he yelled again and then rolled the orange-red tip of his cigarette in the ashtray.

"No, I'm just speaking the truth," I said.

"We are not talking about me," he said, his voice in a knot. He took two quick puffs off his Camel, blew the smoke out of his mouth and sucked it into his nostrils. "We're talking about you. I've wanted to discuss your eating disorder for over two years, but you'll never let me. Every time I try to say something when you're eating, you say, 'what are you doing, monitoring what I eat?' "

"What are you talking about?" I asked. "I'm forty pounds lighter now than I was when you married me."

"Hmm," he said. "I can't say anything about that, but when we had dinner with your brother, down in Texas last month," he said picking bits of tobacco off his lip, "you went through so many bowls of chips and salsa it was embarrassing. I held your hand to keep you from eating." His chin jiggled when he spoke and the gray hairs of his sideburns bristled. "I can live with you this size, but I'm afraid you're getting bigger. You can't get bigger."

I imagined myself growing larger by the second, filling up the room like a giant balloon until I was so huge that my thighs and butt bulged from the windows. I envisioned myself exploding, guts and fat splashing the floor and ceiling. "Oh," I said, "I thought you held my hand because you loved me."

"I do love you," he said and took another drag off his cigarette.

I counted the soft, round moles protruding from the thin, white skin of his cheeks and forehead. One, two, three, four, five, six, seven. Folds of flesh hid the scars from where several cysts had been removed years earlier.

"I was hungry. People with MS have to eat on a regular basis and I hadn't eaten all day. By the time we got to the restaurant," I said, "I was starving."

"You need to get some help. You need to see a therapist about your addiction," he said. " You have a problem." He said this all matter-of-factly, as if God had spoken. The moles on his face seemed to grow larger with every word and the folds of skin hung lower. "A person who is starving should look like one. You were revolting," he said. "It was repulsive." He crossed and then uncrossed his dainty legs again. The tip of his filterless Camel burned brightly and wisps of white curled through the air like a flag unfolding in the wind. He took another puff. Smoke hissed from between his teeth and floated in my direction. The skin under his chin shook and his belly heaved like a pair of giant elephant lungs.

"If you don't see a therapist or go to one of those self-help groups, like Overeaters Anonymous or Weight Watchers, and get some help," he said, "I'm going to have to leave you. You've got to quit shoveling food into your mouth." He put out his cigarette and lit another. His green bikini underwear with his penis and testicles tucked neatly inside disappeared under his belly and behind his milky-skinned freckled thighs.

I rested my chin in my hand and my elbow on the table. I looked at the bowl of fruit and the salad I was having for dinner. I sat for a moment watching my husband flip his cigarette back and forth between his fingers. The smoke rose and dipped in the air like the roller coaster at Coney Island and for a moment it hung suspended, hiding his face.

"I can't see your penis," I said.

Non Adorata Nessuno:
(an intermediate course in self-approbation)

DEBORAH PINTONELLI

for josephine

I see you lounging in your complacent skin, worrying into the night. You are a cool drink of resentment, desperation, envy, fear. He is with Her. Or so you think. Anyway, she exists. She is a girl soft everywhere, with tight, tanned skin and pouty lips. You imagine Them spilling secrets, lies. You don't think about how He leaves Her: alone, put out like dumb cigarette. You romanticize how it was for you before, imagining how beautiful you were, and how much He adored you. You forget about the One who really loved you, the One whose calls you never returned, because you were too busy with Him.

He never adored *you*. If He ever adored anyone, it was Himself. But maybe that self isn't around anymore. Maybe the luxurious curls He once possessed now belong to someone else. Maybe His sensuous center is blown to bits. It is easy, even preferable, to pay a price to reclaim these things, to reclaim the right to be cold, ruthless, sexy.

Being cold, ruthless, and sexy are the most important things of all to Him. *You* are not cooperative. You insist on dragging in warm, fuzzy mundaneity into every aspect of his life. You do not appreciate variety, are too sentimental, and don't know the value of a dollar. And you do not wear sexy underwear! You are not enough of a slut! When will you learn to be more of a slut? Why is this so difficult for you?

He never adored you, he doesn't adore her, and he will not adore the one after her. He will spend the last years of his life alone in Florida or Arizona, wearing bad sneakers and inches-short khaki pants. You will spend yours alone wondering why you made such an ass of yourself for so much of your life. You might die with the diamond crucifix he gave you nestled in between your breasts. He will die saying He doesn't need anybody anymore. Or He will say He'd always been in love with the girl next door, if only He'd realized back when. He will send a horseshoe of roses to your funeral, and your daughters will want to pick it apart, petal by petal, and shove it down his nasty, dried-up throat.

You want revenge, but you will never get it. Or, you will get it every day of your life and it will taste bad in the mouth, not unlike the sperm He wanted you to swallow (Everyday would be great!). You are Twenty? Fifty? Seventy? You waste the better part of each and every day waiting, for what? A sign? A transformation? A windfall of penitence from an avowed sinner? He has forgotten you exist! If you still live together, He remembers you only when He walks in the door. If not, He will think about you fondly while he is tying his shoe, waiting for a train. No more, no less. Once parted, if you have ever embarrassed him by calling attention to his faults, you will have written your name on a stone buried deep in the ground. If you have not, he will call you on your birthday, maybe holidays, if you're lucky.

You want to be so lucky, don't you? You don't realize that your luck ran out a long time ago, baby girl. It ran out the first day you started acting so stupid, and it is now leaking away at an extremely rapid rate. In defense of yourself, you will say, to anyone who will listen (those coming fewer and farther in between): "But he loves me!" Or, "But he did love me!" Love being the currency with which to dupe oneself, the balm that soothes all existential aches, the gooey substance used to sugar coat every lie, every inconsistency, every nonsensical thought or action. In the name of love, which might very well be a powerful thing, you have done yourself wrong, and allowed him to step in time and time again to do a better job of it for you.

Wouldn't right now be a good time to stop all of this? Say you are twenty years old, with a good life ahead of you. Imagine that if you continue on this path there will be no good life for you. Imagine that. Imagine yourself fifty years later, in a brick bungalow in a nondescript suburb, waiting for him to come home for dinner. But he never comes. Instead comes a letter addressed to you: "I've gone back home. Don't wait up." Home being in this case another state, with another woman.

You don't want me to say these things to you, I know. If I continue to do so, you might write me off your list. You will find someone else to support you in your habit. You will tell yourself I just don't understand. But I do, you know, I do. So do as I say, just this once. Put on your comfy undies. Grab a chocolate bar. Snuggle up under the blankets with your hand between your legs. Eat the entire chocolate bar without using your teeth. Gaze at the blue moon. Remember to forget. Do it now.

Beauty Tips for Battered Women

Lisa Blaushild

Ladies, while you're being raped by your spouse and total strangers, do you suffer from embarassing vaginal dryness? You are not alone. Did you know that recent statistics prove that three out of four women are prone to chronic and persistent vaginal dryness each and every time they're forced into sex, even if they know their attacker? And vaginal dryness that occurs while a woman is being screwed without permission does not discriminate. This pesky affliction strikes the young and the old, crosses all ethnic and class barriers, and the number of new women who discover that they lack slippery secretions during uninvited penile insertion is increasing at an alarming rate. I strongly recommend writing your local congressman and insisting that government funds be immediately allocated for research into discovering a cure for this silent, yet steadily growing worldwide epidemic. But until one is found, what should you do as a modern, frequently attacked woman? First of all, stop blaming yourself. You are not an anomaly of the female species simply because you continually fail to produce internal mucosa during unrequested schtuppings. Relax! Even those of us who are sexually sophisticated enough to know that ultimately we are responsible for our own orgasms, cannot be expected to lube-up on cue just because some lug with a switchblade jumps us from behind, then grinds us into submission without the go-ahead on our kitchen floor. Remember: a healthy sex life comes from open, honest communication. So the next time you're cornered in a deserted subway station at gunpoint or dragged into a dark alley on your way home from the 7-Eleven, why not take a moment from begging and pleading for your life to shyly fess-up to your attacker about your ongoing inability to fill your quiff with appropriate fluids during unwelcome penetrations? Have a heart-to-heart. Resist the temptation to stereotype your attacker as a cold, unfeeling sociopath who is only concerned with fulfilling his needs as quickly and efficiently as possible before the cops arrive. Just because he's planning on fucking you without asking first, doesn't necessarily mean he isn't a compassionate listener. Begin building the bridge of trust between the two of you. Explain to him that over-the-counter remedies have proven ineffective, you still remain drier than the Sahara on the hottest day of summer during all trespassings on your person. Ask him for his honest opinion: Does he think you should see a shrink about this? You might even want to inject a little light-hearted humor into the subject to help break the ice. For example, once after a masked intruder climbed in through my living room window, knocked me over the head with a table lamp, and tied me to a chair, then proceeded to help himself to me against my will, I quipped, "Hey pal, you're going to need a lot of elbow grease to ram your cock up my juiceless canyon!" Did my attacker turn on his heels in disgust and crawl back out the window, thinking me less of a woman? I should say not! In fact, that risky, candid disclosure on my part proved to me once and for all that the sandy, dessicated quality of my box while I'm having intercourse without my say-so, not only didn't matter a hill of beans to this assailant, but, in fact, actually fired him up and made him want to jump my bones *even more*. I kid you not! See my point? As you become more comfortable discussing your sapless private part with your attackers, you'll learn that they won't be so easily put off by the news that there will be a lack of adequate moisture as they pump you without the green light of approval, and that you mean so much more to them than just some easy target in a tight-fitting outfit caught strolling alone down a deserted street past midnight. You're actually a highly desirable, *stalkable* piece of ass, worth risking lifelong imprisonment for, and certainly just as deserving of a vicious sexual assault as any other woman. You'll gain confidence and finally believe in your own *worthiness* as sexual prey. You go, girl!

USE GROUP THERAPY FOR PERSONAL GROWTH!

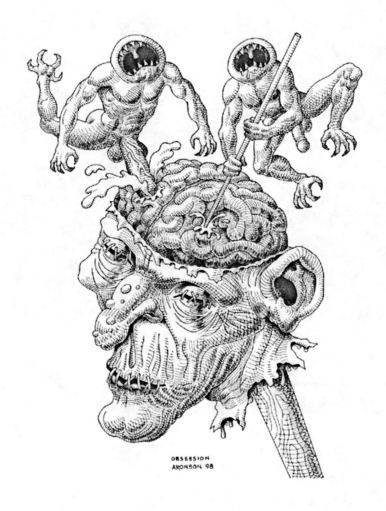

Enlightenment Through Extreme Pain

Michael Basinski

Hip-Hop and suburban youth culture's current fad of genital heating prior to intercourse as a means of contraception and disease prevention and as a *tough* path to Nirvana finds its roots in the indigenous cultures of the Arctic Circle. However, American youth are numb when asked to express their feelings in words about this important rite of passage. A year 2000 study of the Netsilki Inuit of Northern Greenland conducted by smart scientists and academics, from schools, for the Pain Research Institute of Annapolis, Maryland, hopes to grant some vocalization to our nation's silent sub-adults. It has long been known that the Inuit, AKA Eskimo, have multiple words for snow and pain. The snow words, like "toboggan," have been well documented. However, until recently, the words for heating, not cooking, of Netsilki genitals by placing them over active Zippo lighters have been overlooked. Zippos were first imported into the Arctic communities by the Royal British Philosophical Society in 1765 to prevent overpopulation and, at the same time, to transfer Western religious values to the starving hordes of our most northern neighbors. To remedy the youth of our nation's lack of proper response to genital heating as well as remedy the complete lack of factual information in our literature in the area of pain enunciation, three Netsilki natives, one mature adult male, one newlywed teenage male, and another newlywed teenage female, believed to be 19, were recorded during their spring heating ritual. Smart scientists, who know a great many people in colleges, translated their responses. A transcription follows.

Scientist 1: When you place your balls over the flame when do you ejaculate?

Mature adult male Inuit: Nitjataukpaumasulugu. (Nitjataukpaumasulugu literally translated from Netsilki Inuit means "making sounds."

Scientist 2: Could you demonstrate?

Mature adult male Inuit: What the Hell. (The elder turns toward the anxious youths.) Are you ready to rawk?

Teens: Rawk on!

Inuits all: Flickering quivering pulsing throbbing beating pounding jumping flashing shifting pricking boring drilling stabbing lancing sharp cutting lacerating pinching pressing gnawing cramping crushing tuggingpulling wrenching hot hot hot hot hot hot hot hot hot hot burning scalding searing tingling itchy smarting stinging dull sore hurting aching heavy tender taut raspy splitting tiring exhausting exhausting

exhausting exhausting exhausting exhausting exhausting exhausting exhausting exhausting sickening suffocating fearful frightful terrifying punishing grueling cruel vicious killing wretched blinding annoying troublesome miserable intense unbearable spreading radiating penetrating piercing tight numb drawing squeezing tearing cool cold cold cold cold cold cold cold cold cold cold cold cold cold freezing nagging nauseating agonizing dreadful torturing torturing torturing torturing torturing torturing torturing

Scientists: Thanks

Inuits: No problemo.

The Body A Minor Character In What Is Loved By Modern Fluents

MERRY FORTUNE

You may get sick. Very sick. You may end up in a hospital. Most likely no one will take you there. You will have to go by yourself. Maybe you will be lucky enough to need an ambulance. But you will go because you have gotten sick and it was told to you since you were very young that if you get sick, very sick, you should go to the hospital. But the nurse is a technician and you may need a back rub to fall asleep. So the only time she will be able to help you, really help you, is when you need to be monitored. She will not give you a back rub because that is a duty consigned to someone who makes far less money than she does. The minute she picks up a thermometer she is considered a technician.

I was four. Doctors still made house calls. I was surrounded. My mother, my uncle, the doctor became foreigners. The monsters in the closet. I had a high fever. They wanted to take my temperature but could not relax me. They were Martians, nurses were not yet technicians, but I was still alive. I could make a run for the door. I tried to get up thinking they would stop me but I was too weak to move. I started to pull the covers over my head to escape these swollen green things previously my mother, uncle and doctor. Hideous mounds of nothing resembling life were trying to push a glass tube loaded with mercury between my lips. I yelled and screamed and kicked at the covers. The animals went over and down. Food—over and down. Victrola, records—all over and down. The activity fascinated me for a split second but there stood that twelve foot hairy thing with that glass apparatus filled with poison aiming at my mouth but speaking gently saying something nice and soothing and I wanted this, and it was what once was my uncle becoming my uncle again, and it said: "But no—it's a candy cane!" And I let it into my mouth and savored the glass searching for the taste, sucking to get at the sugar, moving my lips pulling in my cheeks. And frustrated with the taste of only glass bit hard with my back teeth and the monsters became an out of control opera and the doctor was mad and holding me forward and finally sounding human and joining me on my intellectual level said: "Spit! Spit hard! Spit harder than you've ever spit in your life." And I spat blood and mercury and phlegm and saliva onto the floor with animals and Victrola.

The body lives far away and so far ahead of itself in another land separate from the mind one often seems to think. The doctor gave a diagnosis of pleurisy when testing positive for TB which happens when someone in your family has had the disease. Today another doctor said it was still childhood asthma and she wanted to provide me with an atomizer. I refused and she was nasty and just about called me stupid. Ten days later I got a nice form letter thanking me for my visit and when would I like to return. Today the doctor said I was diabetic and he could tell by my smooth silky skin. Today the doctor said the pain in my groin was all in my head. Today the doctor lost my Lyme disease test and told me that the next time this happens it's best to bring along the full body of the bug that bites you. Today I met a really good doctor who was happy to know I was helping myself. The world needs more doctors in admiration of educated patients.

Walking in a steady rhythm down Fifth Avenue with purpose and fluency, no more pleurisy, but rhythmic like the devil. A man walks by with a frankfurter stuck half way in his face. He's got an interesting technique. He swallows and chews and pushes the dog all at the same time. I don't need to eat. I live on love. I live in the limbo of a domesticated animal while observing that the more wild tendencies are suppressed by automatic feedings because they must coincide with a work schedule. One dog passes swiftly by because it is being pulled by its neck by a beauty parlor girl. He wants nothing more than to sniff the pee of the small terrier who has just minutes before walked there and had lifted his leg to the tree. Too many times I have witnessed the truncated longings of dogs.

My adrenals are in recourse while my attitude is in discourse the way rising stars are similar to falling stars and the truth is similar to a lie. All body parts are casualties of great thought and the imposition of morality. This is evident in the tireless interpretations of behaviors of the lesser animals among us: the faithful dogs barking, screeching monkeys screeching, evil crocodiles being evil, beneficent kittens because children are innocent.

You spend your life seeking help from life and you get it right and then die. By that time you're sick of it. The war, the torture, the septic tanks, the champagne hair dye, the copulation, the cystitis, the excesses, the denials, the lines, the sado-masochist's attire, the men, the women, the children, the shoes, the maraschino cherries, the marzipan, the dysfunctional uptake inhibitors, the bills, the equilibrists, the harbingers, the love, the candida episodes, the hate, the little board games, the mystique of god—gone, love—gone. All you now know is dreaded bowel movements, increasing isolation, and your animals are getting stupid from living in an apartment with nothing to smell. And the last thing you think about is all the money you spent trying to get through it and you think of that Edith Wharton novel where the entire slow world of beauty and calla lilies, dinners and alcohol culminates with the pertinent angst of one man's exit, his final scene played out like a million other death bed Catholics. You've tired of ceremony and lay wondering alone about to die alone as most do. Alone and your head is filled with an Edith Wharton novel and all the lives you've never lived and people you've never met and experiences you've never had and many may wonder as their final wonder what was so bad about renting movies all the time?

Insomnia. Blood sugar dropping. Angst at the morning; angst in the morning; angst at having to get up for anything in or around the morning. Angst is such an unusual word it's been advised not to use it more than once in a piece of writing or lifetime. A piece of rice-cake sticks to the roof of the mouth like dry ice. The open window lets in no air. The atmosphere seems to be under the jurisdiction of the somewhat willfully dumb. Something to do with getting the white guy in and bankers. One may choose to frequently muster disdain or not but there it is in the form of a lovely pink color in the sky which you are under. I want to help the woman down the stairs with her cart but she tells me she's been doing it this way all her life and needs no help from me.

I'm in the audience watching working musicians appreciated and surrounded by out-of-work musicians. I could have been an out-of-work musician instead I'm an out-of-work something unidentifiable striving to become an out-of-work proofreader in the meantime striving to returning to becoming an out-of-work something unidentifiable and at the same time unthinkable because I haven't come up with anything so far. The pop singer said if I could come up with one good idea in my life I would feel like I have accomplished something great. The respected jazz musician said: If I could steal one good idea in my life I'd feel pretty good.

The man waited at the desk for the verdict. His therapist at first willing to accept a fairly standard forty-eight hour cancellation policy had now stated there would be no cancellations and in accordance with the rules of the clinic the patient would have to pay for skipped sessions. When the patient complained the therapist said he had been too lenient with him and that the patient would have to follow the protocol of the institution of which the therapist was at the mercy. "It's all part of the therapy," I told him.

The woman spoke with uncharacteristic sincerity in the light of the Kinko's.

"So I fantasize about this man who might be my father. We have sex which seems a normal thing to fantasize about and helpful if you spend a lot of time alone. But I wonder about the staged arguments. Not that that's so bad. They seem to help to relieve anger. But just when I might be tenderly seeing his ass do you really think it helps to pick a fight?"

When she got done she noticed her fever responding to the residue of images accrued by talk she had accumulated in her marrow. She accepted the illness as a tribute to her sensitivity and expressive demeanor. Her initial response to her apartment as landfill was gone and she now saw herself as someone residing. She could not keep herself from the mundane talk she had been exposed to. It had taken on a physical life, one she could not dismiss at will and she looked for reasons why. That evening she had discovered the way Twinkies were really made. No heat ever touches a Twinkie. She fumbles with the thin wrapping tightly covering the food. "Is this shrink wrapped? It's shrink-wrapped. Jesus..."

So what if your mother did not know how to love you and your father didn't know what to do with a girl because that's exactly what your mother was and coincidentally what his mother was?

The woman had just gotten a promotion. She hands me her purse. Shows me the little clasps. She particularly likes the little clasps. Two little hands in faux but sturdy metal, bead work all done by machines. But in our brief encounter I humanely don't point this out to her, so in love with the purse she is.

"Look at the little secret compartment!" she says.

"For condoms?" I ask.

She closes the purse and looks away.

"It's just a little secret compartment."

When she was through with me admiring her purse she went off to the bathroom.

"I haven't had time to go to the bathroom all day" she says, happily opening and closing her new purse.

A Twelve Step Program for Neurological/Psychological Mutants

TOM SAVAGE

1. Everything you see may be a hallucination unless you say it isn't.
2. Your therapist may be crazier than you are. Do not trust in serious matters.
3. Sign nothing. Avoid anyone who looks or acts like a psychiatrist. Such people never admit when they are wrong.
4. However many brain cells you may have lost, remember — most of the population started with fewer than you have remaining as demonstrated by their fascination with the Simpson case, the British royal family, and celebrity sex scandals.
5. Allow yourself to sleep as much as you want. You may need more sleep for a few years.
6. When you find you can prolong your dreams upon waking, do not fail to write them down before going back to sleep.
7. If it begins to seem like you can see the air between objects as if there were a kind of fog, close your eyes for awhile.
8. If you begin to become incontinent, exercise more and stay away from that bed.
9. When you become hypersensitive to loud noises, reduce tegretol or move away.
10. Many people will treat you as if you were crazy. Do your best to ignore this.
11. If hypersensitivity to your own bodily sensations develops, read more or go for a walk.
12. If you feel so totally out of place you want to jump off the roof, watch "Third Rock From The Sun" on TV or some other stuff about outerspace thingies and reflect on how out of place these characters are.

5/22/97

Three Days of My Cure
(from Journal of my Cure)

SAL SALASIN

August 17, 1998

America, the freedom to think, say, and charge anything I want. And this is my girl-friend, Charlie Chaplin. You know, the little tramp?

My mother called me "dearie" because she couldn't remember my name. I had trouble in high school. I killed a guy in chem lab just to watch him die.

What kind of place is this where you can't wave around large sums of money on the street late at night!? Do the Republicans know about this? When I divorced Ann, I thought I'd never meet anyone else again. Then I met Barbara. And after I divorced Barbara, I thought I'd never meet anyone again. And then I met Marsha.

The Kemp/Dole Aid to Families with Dependent Children Reform Act: Legalize child prostitution in selected "free enterprise zones."

Glossolali, syndrome or art? You decide. Hint: It's one of those face-hole things where people use multisyllabic words like "bite me."

August 18, 1998

I won't be in on Monday. I may already be a winner in The Publishers Clearinghouse sweepstakes.

I think I have encephalitis lethargica.

I'm not a drug dealer. I collect vintage cocaine. Yesterday they impeached the President so I jerked off. "Need and panic and fear are great motivators." (Rush Limbaugh on the Republican Welfare Reform Plan.)

Hi. I'm an actor portraying Consumer Advocate Katie Adrianos for Depends. And I'm here to tell you that commodities LIKE being traded. And how many nights did our teachers sit at home masturbating in hellish shrines to their water gods, eh? The author of *Problems in the Philosophy of Kierkegaard*, or *Hello, Sailor*, a study of a perjury trap based on a dismissed civil suit, financed by a reclusive millionaire, conceived of by a guy who divorced his first wife in her hospital bed in the cancer ward and then went through two more; promoted by a hypocritical talk show host on wife number three; investigated by a thoroughly repressed Republican judge with six wasted years and forty million dollars of bad PR behind him, and implemented by a whole series of admitted reactionaries, liars and adulterers in the House.

You don't have to hit me with a bus. I'm Mr. Idiopathic Disrythmia. Once again the air smells of microwave popcorn. I am who I am. As a species, naked ambition tempered only by arrogance and greed. On which subject, why is Ariana Huffington still pontificating on TV when it turns out she no longer channels Seth, and her Congressman-Failed-Senatorial-Candidate-Millionaire-Ex-Husband admits that he's gay?

I'm at that awkward age when you're too young to hold down a job and too old to be tried as a juvenile.

August 19, 1998

The currency of the heart is suffering and everyone has their price. It was about this time I began to carry a gun and realized, my god, my career really was the only thing that mattered.

They tell you that they love you but they only want to search the glove compartment. Shut your eyes and think Prozac. The dead have risen and are voting Republican. Cash only and I still want to see your ID.

Not only am I not gay, I'm not even happy. I lost my parents in a crap game. I want to live each day as if it were my last, namely, coughing and spitting up blood. Acting up and acting out. I will call any number. I will talk to anyone. I used to break into homes and redecorate them. I was a model prisoner. Lingerie, mostly. Now I'm a pizza delivery engineer. I eat in exotic foreign malls.

"Everybody down on the floor." Another invitation difficult to refuse.

Therapy in the Form of Arrival and Departure

Lee Klein

Having lived in New York for almost a decade and therein been driven mad by jackhammers, police and ambulance sirens, paper bag crinklers, screaming babies of the Upper West Side, artists over-anxious to get their work shown or written about, blind professors laying down a guilt trip, streets clogged by convoys of baby strollers, cell phones manned by emphatic and demanding voices at high pitch, beepers, and a million other noises, I needed a safety valve. That safety valve/sanity method came in the form of frequent, low price travel to New Jersey's gaming center by the sea, Atlantic City.

I accessed the town by casino bus, a type of transit that paid you back most of your cost of travel in the form of rolls of quarters for the slots and coupons good for food. In the course of these travels I met a species that shuttles back and forth on the bus as often as twice a day, in the process stockpiling cash coupons and quarters as a way of earning a living. These were my mentors. All it took them was roughly a twenty-five dollar initial investment.

Once there, I kept to myself, achieving a much-needed dissipation of my frustration level. I felt I had been reborn each time I was dropped off by the returning bus on the Upper East Side, hoofing it across Central Park to my apartment on the other side of the city. I started the next day having been somewhere else.

I got a kick out of repeating the same journey again and again, watching the incidental features of the place change, tracking the Las Vegasization, as the casinos discovered family entertainment, leading to the creation of the Roman Circus at Caesar's and the animatronic forty-niner with mule at the waterfall fountain at Bally's Wild West. I had begun to care about the place.

I had created my own empire of negative space. There were large rooms to write in. So after I got my laptop, I took it with me to AC and began to write articles by the statues of the Nine Muses that were planted atop the Caesar's indoor Roman Coliseum facade.

One day, going to my favorite writing nook, I saw a poster for the "Bacchanal" dinner which offered a *prix fixe*, seven-course meal, inclusive of unlimited wine, back massages, and a vist from "Caesar and Cleopatra." I went there immediately. When Caesar appeared at my table, I held up a fork, on which was tined an escagot, and said, "Snail Caesar." I then proceeded to correct Cleopatra, who said, "I sailed down the Nile to meet the Emperor." I said, "First, the Nile only flows up, not down; second Caesar wasn't on the Nile at all, but across the Mediterranean." No one seemed to appreciate my display of learning.

Still, although chilled momentarily by the icy stares of fellow Bacchists, I continued on with my course of therapy, adminstered by Greyhound Bus and the ragtag, seamy City by the Seaweed.

My First Meeting

David Huberman

It seems that I've always been looking for some kind of help. For years, I tried self-medicating my problems away. Then I discovered the twelve-step programs. I decided to try to stop using drugs, so with nostrils white with flakes of cocaine and snot dripping down my face, I attended my first Narcotics Anonymous Meeting. It was held in a room on St. Mark's Place, in a building that the city designated as an all-crafts learning center. In the Sixties, it housed a psychedelic rock club known as the Electric Circus.

The speaker at my first meeting was a thin, middle-aged black man who reeked of exotic perfume. I picked up a suggestion of femininity around his eyes and wondered if he was gay. He was dressed in a very expensive dark sharkskin suit which was shockingly complemented by a bright red shirt and shiny black tie. He displayed chunky gold rings on every finger. His hair was styled in the greasy 'fifties' look.

He gave off the same impression as Chuck Berry and Ike Turner. He spoke of using drugs and living homeless on the Bowery for twelve years. When he was using, he wore a huge Afro that was home to a nest of cockroaches, but thanks to the program he is currently three years drug free, and now owns a duplex apartment in a swank neighborhood uptown. He told us about his white Cadillac El Dorado, his fine clothes, classy jewelry and said he had more women than he knows what to do with. I was wondering just how he paid for this drug-free lifestyle, so, after the meeting, I asked somebody what the speaker did for a living. "Oh him," the person said, "he's a pimp." I was impressed with this slick black man who left in style with three gorgeous foxes strutting at his side.

At the meeting, they suggested that I make ninety meetings in ninety days. I did exactly what they told me to do. With rewards like that awaiting me if I stayed clean, I didn't want to use drugs anymore.

Recovery Poem

Bob Riedel

I used to do drugs,
now I don't.
My friend said I should write
a poem about my recovery.
I told him All my poems
are about my recovery.
After all, I'm still
writing them.

Unfurl the Flag

John Penn

Ronald was only recently on death's bed near death's door. It was a small apartment. There wasn't much that wasn't close to the door. He had a desk with a small 2 dollar pumpkin resting over his computer. It was close to Halloween, but he wasn't going to make a face out of it. It would look too much like him, he realized. Besides, he hadn't the energy. He had a small refrigerator with bottled water, a small end table where his forty-five bottles of medication rested peacefully every night and day. His closet was stuffed with clothes that were unsuitable for burial. You could say that everything was near death's door at that time for Ronald, even his Converse sneakers. It was a matter of space.

His energy had been sapped by a "way-too-happy" woman in a white coat who pumped light red unnatural stuff into his vein, actually veins. One arm blew up the size of a small grapefruit, so she found another vein and continued. Light FM had played around him, a Billy Joel medley, he recalled. He never did like the short guy's music, not since the album "Piano Man." He was that old.

He knew now he wasn't going to die; not yet, though the possibility remained. His body had become flashing motel signs advertising "Vacancies," "Vacancies," "All Ladies and Germs Welcome." The signs would remain up for another six or seven months at least. He would have to monitor his every twinge, feeling and body ache. He didn't want to do this, not one to enjoy obsessions. But he was feeling better and he couldn't deny it. He resumed his usual routine, which was to go to the donut shop around the corner in the morning, drink his coffee, eat his bow-tie donuts, talk to the other smokers and smoke his brains out. The one thing he didn't have was lung cancer. He was grateful for that. There would be the gruff middle-aged labor union woman who complained about the service. "We come in every day, but it takes them forever to get me my bagel." There would be the woman with the white beehive hairdo that sat up at least two feet. She constantly sported sunglasses. "She must drink a little bit," Ronald thought, her head always painfully bowed. She would also constantly talk about her 87-year-old mother who wanted to die. "She just sits in that hospital bed and tells the doctor that she wants to die. Her hip's getting better though. It's one of those artificial ones."

Ronald would also talk to this ex-alcoholic, racetrack-obsessed, manic-depressive elderly gentleman who once carried into the shop a large American flag proclaiming his allegiance to God and apple pie. Ronald liked him the best. The man's name was Peter. On Peter's down days he would talk about how Social Security had ripped him off and how all doctors were shit. On his best days he'd try to sell you this newfangled phone beeper that he had just bought. He thought he was a salesperson but he wasn't. "It's great. I'm going to sell a ton. Don't you want one?" "No," Ronald would say. "I have no one to talk to." And

Ronald didn't. His circle of friends had shrunk like the large mass that once covered his ribcage.

All the people in the smoking section of the donut shop had something wrong with them, and they all knew it. Many of them were under doctors' care. Many had tried self-help groups — another favorite punching bag. "They just define themselves by their disease and wallow in it," said the gruff labor union lady who suffered from chronic fatigue syndrome. She drank ten cups a coffee a morning to overcome it. "Yeah, they say be positive, then they turn around and screw you," said the beehive lady concerning AA. "They don't recommend St. John's Wort, which works for me. Stupid doctors and nurses," said Peter. "I got you a horse at Belmont in the second race. It's a sure thing." He'd wink and then go back to talking about how sad he was yesterday, the day after his flag waving.

Ronald wasn't any different. He had plenty wrong with himself too. Some of it he shared. "Get a load of my bald head. It doesn't scare small children." Others he didn't. He could have at least six labels, i.e., illnesses that could be stuck on him. He could attend a multitude of self-help/anonymous meetings. He wasn't one for labels, though. They had gotten him into trouble. "So you're that!" and you could see them move away, those people whom he used to tell his many maladies to. Ronald had been confused by it. The daytime talk shows had trumpeted the labels, made "recovery" seem hip, had gobs of sympathy and understanding. That was only TV and the media, Ronald found out. In the rest of the world, pariahs and scarlet letters were still in vogue, though they had gone underground. Not everyone was an Oprah Winfrey.

Today, Ronald would have to leave the coffee klatsch a bit early.

"Where you going?" asked the beehive lady.

"Going to see the Anti-Dracula. It's better to get, than to give these days. At least for me."

"Oh, have fun."

Ronald dragged himself off the stool. Everything was a Herculean effort, his body constantly screaming "Lie down!" "Lie down!" He knew where he was going would help alleviate it. He just had to get there. It was across town, usually a twenty-minute walk. He could take a cab, but that would be like giving up, he thought. "I'm not going to be one of those people," he said to himself.

"You all have a nice day," Ronald said as he put on his coat and hat. It was a little nippy out and Ronald was still getting used to not having hair. The baseball cap was too thin for the weather, but he wore it anyway. "It will keep me moving."

It took him an hour. He passed the Taco Bell, rested on a standpipe for five minutes. Passed the Smile Deli, empty steps were available on the other side, another five minutes. He wanted to smile but he couldn't. Good thing he allotted plenty of time, he thought. Finally the generic health building, with its white bricks and named after rich benefactors, Maurice and Olivia Stewart, came into view. It was as if it was Camelot. He went through the handicap entrance. Push a panel and the door opens automatically. Inside he felt the bustle of sickness and health. He saw wheelchairs and canes and children being pushed in strollers. Ronald wished he could be pushed in a stroller.

In the elevator, he was one of three: a staff member person with a badge, an old bent-over woman with a cane, and him. He would beat one person out of the elevator. Only the third floor button had been pushed. There were other places besides the place he was going on the third floor, but he still thought it strange they were all going to the same floor. Ronald was like that. He could and liked to make things seem strange. It was one of his few joys in life. The badge person got off first. Ronald looked back at the old woman. He held the door for her. She was really slow. Both the badge person and old lady went right, while Ronald went left. Not strange, thought Ronald.

He found the door halfway down the hall and opened it. The lounge chairs were only half-filled when he arrived. He was bent over trying to find what little oxygen was in the room. He looked at the rail-thin lady with a blue flowered headscarf who lay in the only bed in the room full of La-Z-Boys. She had one of those green tubes sticking out from her clavicle, where doctors had cut into her to put a port of entry for whatever they were going to give her. It swayed a tad as she squirmed to get comfortable.

Ronald found a La-Z-Boy and sat down. He knew the drill. The nurse came over and hooked him up, burying the needle in his arm, taping him up good, running tubes and bags from a pole that almost reached the tile ceiling. He would be here for a while. He reclined the chair and closed his eyes. He knew stuff was going into him, the stuff he already had in him, not enough though to keep him going, but he couldn't feel it. He wished he could. It would seem as if he was doing something if he could feel it. He would make it go to the right places just from his force of will. Without that feeling he felt like he wasn't participating in it, and had no control. Only people in white coats had control. Ronald knew he had no will in this place. It had been left outside near the bronze plaque of the couple who donated the building. *Leave your strength and will at the door*, said the imaginary sign.

He received two floppy bags full of dark red gunk over a five-hour period. He had eaten a tuna fish sandwich on white bread so as to take his pills, fifteen of these really sweet cookies he had never had before, and about twelve cups of water. He went to the bathroom a few times. The pole and the floppy bags were mobile, though at times they would clog up and the nurse would have to pat, squeeze, and actually hit them a few times to make the drip drip drip continue. He liked watching her do this. Her eyes would be intently staring at the squishy red bags, almost religiously, thought Ronald. Hopefully all this will make me be able to return to my other duties, thought Ronald. He put up with the tuna fish sandwich so as to continue on. He had never been big on tuna. Sometimes it turned his stomach, but this day it didn't. The blood drip clogged up again and the nurse did her squeeze and hit thing again. This is going to take forever, thought Ronald.

It did too. He wasn't able to leave until the sun was already down. What he wanted to do what he always felt compelled to do would have to wait until tomorrow. This act, this thing that he liked to do had come from grade school. He knew that. He hadn't needed a shrink to tell him about it. Ronald had picked the activity because it was fun.

The next day, after coffee, the beehive lady saying again how her mother wanted to die, the labor union lady complaining about burnt toast, and Peter sitting silently pushing numbers into his beeper, Ronald paid and headed to the door.

"Where you going?" Peter said, breaking his silence. Ronald looked at Peter's drawn and tired face. He appreciated Peter's effort at friendliness. That's why I come here, thought Ronald.

"My usual," said Ronald, his fatigue having disappeared overnight.

"Blood in" is good, thought Ronald as the cold air hit him in the face. He had a bit of a walk, but today he could do it. It was downtown about ten blocks. He smiled and felt it. "Good, good, good." His head was still cold and his hat was almost blown off once or twice, but he was able to catch it both times.

Finally he arrived. It was a rather large grass field with a chain link fence that gave it its shape. Outside the fence were row houses. The field belonged to a high school, Jerome Pettis High School. It wasn't exactly like old Kendall Elementary, but it was still a place children went to learn something. The fence had made Ronald realize what he must do when he first saw it. It looked so familiar. The grass on the other hand wasn't. Northern grass is nothing like grass from Florida, but it was still a fence and a field. It would do. He hadn't told anyone about this place except for Peter. Why he told Peter he didn't quite understand fully though it seemed right. Peter had never told anyone else, had never questioned him why he did it, or said he was nuts. Peter had thought it was a good idea, actually.

Ronald started his walk, hugging the fence. He placed his hand on the chain link fence once or twice to feel the metal that once cooled his childhood during those days when he couldn't participate in Physical Education, which was almost every day. In Florida it was always hot, and the fence had cooled him, or at least that's how he remembered it. He continued his walk around the field hugging the fence. He was going to make a run for it, buy a boat, escape the harassment of his fellow students, escape the brutality of the PE teacher, avoid the face-slapping he received, the chastisement for not doing the homework neatly enough. He was going to be free. Every PE period he had walked that fence with two other boys who were also incapable of much else. It had been required since kick ball was out of the question for all of them. He never talked to them though. It had been forbidden by Mr. Polaski and his overzealous whistle.

Now Ronald enjoyed it even more. He was running away. The fence, the field, the childhood, all places he ran to. No blood followed him here. His pills would stay in his pocket. He would be what he once was, that person who saw danger behind every tree. He would root it out and dispense with it with his sword, the guy in the small boat making his way through an inlet in the Florida Keys, living off of fish and his natural survival skills. He killed Nazis. He was Captain America, Spider Man, the Green Lantern. He fought off evil germs and plagues and despicable torture guys in white coats who wanted to do him harm. He had stopped them.

On his tenth time around, when he was near the back of the field, he saw a pole or something. He kept walking. The pole started to come toward him. The person was skinny and the pole was at least twice the guy's size. Finally they met. It was Peter.

"I thought I'd join you," said Peter in a friendly voice. Usually Ronald would have gone into a rage, his privacy having been invaded, but this had never happened before, and Ronald kind of liked having Peter there. Ronald fidgeted with his cap.

"Why?"

"Why not?" said Peter, and it was a good enough answer for Ronald.

"Can I unfurl this?" asked Peter. It was the flag.

"Sure," said Ronald. "Why the hell not. This is America, isn't it? You can do what you want."

"You sure I'm not bothering you?"

"Just shut up and unfurl the damn thing." Ronald really wanted to see the flag. Peter untwisted the tattered flag and the breeze caught it and made it stick out.

"You walk in front of me, okay?" said Ronald. He had his parade, he thought. They walked like that until the sun went down, periodically singing the national anthem. Other than that, there was silence, and the wind, and Ronald's feet moving to a purpose he had long forgotten.

Barbie Goes To Group Therapy

Janice Eidus

Barbie shifted uncomfortably in the stiff metal chair in which she was sitting. She smoothed her white linen dress so as not to cause wrinkles. She crossed her ankles, taking care not to scuff her white patent leather high heels. Barbie had chosen to wear all white tonight, in order to remind the other women in the group that she was special. Not many women, after all, were thin enough and confident enough to look fabulous all in white.

She looked around the bleak, shabby room. Six other women, dressed mostly in drab browns and greys, had shown up for this first session of the women's therapy group. They were seated in a ragged circle, also in stiff metal chairs, although, Barbie noted, none of them were being careful about their posture, the way she was. They were hunched and slouched in various unflattering combinations. Eventually, they'll all have back problems, Barbie thought. She took a deep breath, keeping her back straight and thrusting out her large, yet pert and perfectly pointed, breasts. None of the six women were looking at Barbie. They were, however, looking at one another, exchanging warm, friendly glances. Barbie wished she hadn't had to come to an all women's therapy group. "Can't I go to a group with men?" she'd asked. "No, that's the whole point," her press agent and image consultant both had insisted, "it's got to be women." But Barbie knew that most women didn't like her, and the feeling was mutual. Little girls were different, of course. Barbie liked them just fine, the legions of little girls who bought the dolls made in Barbie's own image. But once the little girls grew up and put away their Barbies, she had nothing in common with them. All those little girls, Barbie knew, had once dreamed of growing up and becoming just like her: poised, glamorous, and breathtakingly beautiful. But when they didn't grow up to be any of those things, well, then they relegated their Barbies to trunks and attics and closets, hiding their formerly beloved dolls like shameful secrets. Barbie understood that her very existence shamed most women so much they couldn't even bear to look at her. She looked around the room again — yes, each of these drab women definitely had a Barbie hidden somewhere.

Barbie turned her attention to the group leader, who was sitting in the only comfortable chair in the room: a thick, padded, leather armchair. The group leader, who was wearing a grey jumpsuit, cleared her throat. Barbie stared at her suspiciously, feeling what she called her "threat antennae" go up. The group leader was awfully young to be a therapist. She was nothing like the older, maternal woman in orthopedic shoes that Barbie had envisioned. The group leader's short red hair was cut in a "downtown chic" style that was much too angular and masculine for Barbie's taste. Already, Barbie didn't like the group leader, and she hadn't yet spoken a word.

As though reading Barbie's mind — not that she'd looked over in Barbie's direction — the group leader began to speak: "Let's go around the room and introduce ourselves to one another, shall we?" Although the group leader spoke in warm, encouraging tones, she had a strong Brooklyn accent and a severe lisp. Spittle flew from her mouth while she spoke.

Barbie's threat antennae relaxed. She had nothing to worry about. This woman was no competition, even with her avant-garde haircut, because no man would ever choose a Brooklyn-born woman with a speech impediment over Barbie. Barbie's own speech was irresistible to men: crisp and accentless, with a lilting, flirtatious upswing at the end of every sentence.

A heavyset, androgynous woman in a shapeless grey shift, sitting directly across the room from Barbie, began to speak. She also was no competition. Barbie's threat antennae remained relaxed. The heavyset woman spoke in a whiney, nasal voice — something about having taken care of her bedridden, elderly mother for years. But her mother had just died, and now at last the woman wanted to live for herself, and she felt that being in a group of supportive women would help her.

Barbie stopped listening. The heavyset woman was depressing. When Barbie's own mother had gotten ill, Barbie had bought her a condo in Florida and paid for a full-time nurse. She prided herself on remembering to call her mother long-distance every few weeks. Barbie noticed that the heavyset woman was looking at everyone else in the room during her droning recitation, except Barbie. Yes, Barbie thought, she's so shamed by my exquisite presence, that she can't even look at me. After all, my blonde, shiny hair, my seductive, bright blue, bedroom eyes framed by my lush lashes, my pink lips, my perfect, pert breasts — it's all too much for these women. Sighing with pleasure at the thought of her own perfection, Barbie glanced down at her breasts, which peeked so prettily through the white linen fabric of her dress.

"Thanks so much for sharing your feelings with us," the group leader lisped to the heavyset woman. Reluctantly, Barbie looked up from her own breasts, and back at the group. The other women were all smiling at the heavyset woman. Nobody was looking at Barbie.

The woman sitting to the right of the androgynous woman began to speak. Barbie liked her looks a little better. She appeared shy and deferential, wearing a modest brown tweed suit. She kept her eyes downcast, and spoke softly. Once or twice in her life, years ago, Barbie had gotten slightly friendly with a couple of women — she'd lost touch with them, of course — but this woman reminded her of them. If Barbie liked any women at all, and she wasn't sure she did, but if she did, she liked shy, retiring types, attractive enough so that she wasn't embarrassed to be seen in public with them, but never attractive or assertive enough to arouse her ever-vigilant threat antennae.

The shy woman continued to speak softly, almost whispering, about falling in love with cold, cruel men. She was hoping, she said, that with the support of other women, she'd learn to break that pattern. Barbie stopped listening. This shy woman would never be able to find a man even close to her own Ken, that was clear. First of all, there were no other men like Ken. He, like herself, was sheer perfection. Barbie knew that all those little girls who had bought Ken dolls to date their Barbies had expected to grow up and marry men just as handsome and perfect as Ken. Instead, they married men with bald spots, paunches, and drinking problems — or worse, they didn't get married at all! — and then they felt more ashamed than ever, and the Ken dolls, like the Barbies, were relegated to trunks and attics and closets. Barbie decided she didn't like this shy woman, after all; she seemed hopeless, really, going on and on about wanting to be more assertive with men, when it was obvious that she never could be.

The group leader lispingly thanked the shy woman for sharing her feelings. There also were little murmured thank you's from the other women. Nobody looked at Barbie.

The group leader continued to go around the room, inviting women to speak. Barbie didn't listen carefully to any of the other women, either. One was a suburban mother type, dressed in a brown jersey pants-suit. She lived in New Jersey, and had problems with an unfaithful husband and an anorexic daughter. Yawn, thought Barbie, the bridge and tunnel set.

Another woman had acne scars. Spare me, thought Barbie, I'm not a plastic surgeon.

The two others seemed interchangeable to Barbie. They both wore long brown dresses. They both wept while they spoke, and they said the same things: they hated their jobs, they hated their mothers, they hated their bodies.

It was Barbie's turn.

"And what brings you here, Barbie?" the group leader lisped, loosing more spittle into the air, still not looking directly at Barbie. Barbie heard an edge to the group leader's voice that hadn't been there when she'd invited the other women to speak. She's masking her shame with hostility, Barbie thought, which struck her as very unprofessional for a therapist.

Barbie sat up even straighter in the uncomfortable chair. She held her breasts high, sucked in her diaphragm. She smoothed her already smooth, glistening blonde hair. "Oh," she said, "I don't have any problems. I'm Barbie, after all. But my press agent and my image consultant both told me that some little girls these days were finding me too cool and off-putting, that my sales are down because I'm not perceived as knowing how to 'bond,' or something. So they thought I should come here, to learn to bond with other females, to learn to be warmer. I told them that this would all blow over, that the store managers were probably just adding the figures up wrong. After all, math SAT scores these days are just terrible. Little girls love me as much as they ever did! I'm Barbie, after all. But they kept insisting that I come here. And Ken said, 'Well, Barbie, you might as well give it a try.' His press agent and image consultants say his sales are down, too, that little girls and little boys are finding him too stiff, sort of unevolved, so he's going to do some of those 'men's movement' things, hugging trees, wearing loincloths, stuff like that. But after all, nobody ever said Barbie and Ken — but especially me, Barbie, I'm the one who started it all! — had to know how to bond. I mean, give me a break. I'm beyond all that. I'm Barbie, after all."

Barbie waited for the group leader to thank her for sharing her feelings, the way she had thanked all the rest of them. But the group leader was silent. And Barbie realized that even when she'd been talking — and she'd been absolutely honest and open, just as her press agent and image consultant had told her to be! — the other women still hadn't looked at her. And, like the group leader, none of them were even polite enough to thank her.

"Let's take a short break," the group leader said, spitting and smiling at the other women. "Sharing our feelings can be very intense." The women all smiled back at her, murmuring appreciatively.

Cows, Barbie thought. How did those cute little girls, those girls who loved to dress up their Barbie dolls and comb their hair and play wonderful games of "Barbie Goes To The Prom" and "Barbie Wins The Miss America Pageant" and "Barbie and Ken Honeymoon In Las Vegas" — how did those little girls grow up to become these lisping, spitting therapists, these heavyset androgynes, these suburban moms in atrocious brown pants-suits, these interchangeable clones without any character or personality?

The women stood and left the room together, chattering among themselves. They were speaking so softly that Barbie couldn't hear what they were saying. It was just as well. Nothing they said could ever be of interest to her. She would go through with this first session of the group, since she was already here, but tomorrow morning, she would tell her press agent and image consultant to forget it, that wild horses couldn't drag her to another session of this group. "I'm Barbie, after all," she would say. "I don't have to do anything I don't want to do." If they argued with her, she would remind them that she could always find another press agent and image consultant.

Barbie decided to find a Ladies Room during the break, in order to reapply her make up. One thing she hated was to be seen with fading lipstick or smudged mascara, even by women like these who didn't know the first thing about correct make up application.

Holding both her head and her breasts high, Barbie rose from her seat and walked gracefully in her high heels out into the hallway. None of the other women were in sight. The hallway was empty. Barbie felt relieved. A sign for the Ladies Room said it was on the floor below. But there was also an "Out of Order" sign sloppily pasted on the front of the elevator. To her displeasure, Barbie realized she'd have to use the stairs. She opened the door to the only staircase on the floor. It shut behind her with a thud. The staircase wasn't very well lit, but she would find her way. She was Barbie, after all — graceful and sure-footed, even in dark, narrow staircases, even in white high heeled shoes.

Suddenly, Barbie felt spittle in her face. Wet, smelly spittle. Before she could wipe it off, or gag, she was surrounded. The group leader and all the other women closed around her in the narrow dark staircase. Barbie tried to step backwards, toward the door, but they pressed close around her. She was unable to move. She realized that they had tricked her —the elevator wasn't really out of order — and now she was trapped inside this staircase with these terrible creatures.

"Oh, Barbie," the women chanted in unison, their voices merging together in a wild, excited rhythm, "with your perfect, pert breasts, your stupid theme wardrobes, your gaudy Glamour Homes, and your vacuous, dazed eyes, you're nothing but a vain bimbo, a narcissistic bitch! You're not nice and perky, you're not sweet and generous, you're not any of the things they told us you were when we were little girls!"

Heart pounding, Barbie silently cursed her threat antennae for failing her. Her threat antennae had always protected her from female competition where men were concerned, but now, when she needed them most, they were useless against this new threat, one Barbie had never run into before — the threat of female violence. She couldn't believe that this was happening to her. She was Barbie, after all!

There was a stranglehold on her neck, and it was difficult to speak. But she had to. "But don't you remember," she gasped, "how much you loved me back then?"

"Of course we remember." They spoke in unison. One of them — the heavyset woman — sneered: "I remember it all, Barbie. I loved you so much. You were my best friend, my older sister, my good mother, my alter ego, my fantasy self. I sure do remember!"

"I also remember, Barbie," the shy woman said, no longer sounding so shy. "I remember thinking, Barbie would never stutter nervously in public, Barbie would never be so shy she would nearly faint or pee in her pants when the teacher called on her. I remember you, Barbie, very very well."

The suburban mother slapped Barbie once, sharply, across her face.

Tears came to Barbie's eyes. Her face stung.

"My daughter," the suburban woman said, angrily, "my daughter who's starving herself to death told me just last week that all she wants in the whole world is to look like Barbie!"

"Yes, precisely," the group leader said seriously, spitting copiously into Barbie's face, "that's exactly the point of therapy — to break free of the past, to break free of you, Barbie. You're the real reason we're here in the first place, the only reason. We paid off your press agent and your image consultant to tell you to come here. You were duped, suckered, jerked around, Barbie-Doll!"

And that was the next-to-last thing Barbie heard clearly, before the women — now shrieking one bloodcurdling, earsplitting, terribly unladylike cry — bonded together to throw her perfect body with its large, yet pert and perfectly pointed breasts down the long, dark flight of stairs.

The very last thing Barbie heard, however, as she tumbled down the stairs — before she breathed her very last breath, before her poised, graceful body in its white linen dress lay shattered and twisted and broken at the bottom of the stairs — were the group leader's lisping and ambiguous words: "So, ladies, on to Ken, yes?"

Self Help, an Unbearable Rant

Susan Maurer, M.S.W. R.C.S.W., A.C.S.W.

How do I help me?
Let me count the ways
First and foremost is poetry therapy
Write down exactly what you feel
Be honest and that will be the sonnet form
Editors will cream, say "thanks for sharing"
The next thing is tap dance in hell
O, tippy tap, brave effort, the
Movement keeps the soles cool
And the correct smile therefore
May be obtained at 7 a.m. on Lifetime t.v.
When the dancing Barbie Dolls
Do aerobics — Fuck *you*, Dancing Barbie Dolls
Base line aid involves money management
So close to life support. Spend $3.75/minute
On an analyst with a M.S.W.
Or call the Psychic Hotline
For slightly less. This will keep you money free
So the options of drinking too much
Or overeating are not readily available
With the latter habit however one does not
Get laid unduly, even with the former habit
Remember, though, sex burns calories
So slim down to get laid
Get up at 7 a.m. with 7" high
Barbie Dolls on the t.v.
Telling you they are there for you
(Fuck *you*, Barbie Dolls)
If they can do this so must you
Stop dressing to avoid physical contact
You know, toss out smelly t-shirts
Debate getting a bra, stop wearing shower shoes
Chinese hats and paint stained blue jean skirts
I am however willing to reveal
My primary self help tool
In the relative safety of poetry
I have a death will as opposed to a living
Where caring friends have sworn to snuff me

If I ever use the phrase "inner child"
Or say I love you again to a man 12 years younger
In closing I have this to say
Believe in the eyes of your teddy bear
This and this alone will get you
Through the next ten years
And after that you're on your own

Two Poems

Hal Sirowitz

Obsessive Thoughts

The reason you have trouble falling asleep,
my therapist said, is because you're having
obsessive thoughts. You're thinking
too much about love & sex. Those thoughts
never end, & don't proceed in a straight line.
They're full of twists and turns. You
have to start thinking about less
interesting things. Just before
you go to sleep you should try
listening to a boring tape,
like New Age music. But if it
starts reminding you too much
about love or sex, fast foward it,
& go on to the next song.

More Words

She rubbed against you,
my therapist said. That was
action. Action speaks louder
than words. But then you said
she was too busy to see you.
That was words. Then a week later
she said she might be able
to see you. That got your hopes up.
But that was still words.

New Age Lessons

DENISE DUHAMEL

The seminar on the tantra went very well as strangers paired off and closed their eyes while stroking one another's faces and breathing deeply as advised. I had an orgasm this way though I can't remember the face of my partner, his brassy hair not half as brilliant as even a boring sunset, but that's how it is when you'll do anything to find out — I left my worries in the middle of the room, looked into a mirror and said *I love you* while the men with AIDS cried out in pain and shame until a few weeks later when they actually did look better, rounder at their papery edges as though our prayers had helped them. Someone said how wonderful it was for me to be a woman, soft and receptive like a vase waiting to be filled with flowers. My whole soul was waiting to be devoured: an oyster sliding down God's magnificent throat.

My grandmother said sure, it was ok to watch church on TV, especially in winter, when her neighbors in the high-rise were all breaking their hips, the ice as pure as Christ but not as kind. I knew a woman who claimed she was married just because she needed some kind of ritual. The Holy Ghost was soft and giggly like Casper, and by golly, on a sunny day in the country, those fingers of light do look like they belong to one big yellow God who wants to pet the corn crops, hold onto the earth as though she were first in line in a bunny hop at a wedding no doubt of bliss and drunk relatives and good-natured toasts.

Then, of course, came the angel movement. Angelologists with business cards in their wallets as they spoke of dead teenagers arching in heaven like princess phones. And where are the wings that will carry us? The planes soaring straight through turbulence, brief as an orgasm and maybe that is enlightenment: an orgasm that rolls on forever, the whole body pulsing like a never-still atom re-arranging itself, the shifting positions of sex and the currents and waves of the womb.

The psychic I went to in the projects says, *Do you believe in Jesus? I can't help you if you don't agree you believe at least just a little. Jesus and the angels were the ones who told me to go bankrupt, to start again, this time without Visa or Master Card... I am absolved now that I've moved into HUD housing without cable or the home shopping channels. It is like purgatory for me where I try to resist the lotteries. The angels won't tell me my lucky numbers for my own good though sometimes I'm not sure they even know. The spirits are wise but awful with time. They know what won two years ago or tell me tonight's winning numbers are really next week's. They're tricksters, too, some of them. They hide my keys and tell me I need to diet. They've forgotten what it's like to crave a steak as you mix your canned tuna with lowfat mayonnaise.*

It's a search and all of us make it, holding each other in the dark with tongues barely touching the roofs of our mouths. That's one way to fly if you can concentrate, if you can move your energy in and out and around and see yourself like a chalk outline on a New York City sidewalk, if you can trace that flow and picture tree roots coming out of your spine to plant you to the ground. I'll tell you why the séances never work: because someone always started to laugh. I used to get giggle attacks in the church, picturing the whole congregation as literal sheep with curly paws jutting out of their suit coats and curly tails lifting the backs of prim skirts—pipecleaner tails twisted into U's and S's, mysterious as sex.

"That Guru That You Do"

CHRISTIAN X. HUNTER

Before leaving for India I was repeatedly told how people always came home changed in some fundamental way. I told everyone I wasn't going to India filled with transcendental ambition hoping to "find myself" or search for God or seek a guru. It takes great purity of mind and spirit to avoid the egotism and spiritual materialism that is the motivation behind so many yatras and sadhanas. I said I was going as a spiritual tourist — though I hope, not a voyeur — to do a little yoga, see what there was to be seen, to "seize the possibilities." Naturally, I'd love to meet a great teacher, but I want to spare myself the pointless detours taken by so many of the guru-seekers, with their preconceived notions of what the teacher will be like, and how the teacher will teach. It has been difficult not falling prey to cynicism in the wake of experiences with old friends who drove themselves mad with self-delusion trying to make reality fit the mold of their fantasy. Most spiritual aspirants are as the old Sufi proverbs describe, "seekers and never finders." They go climbing up mountain tops, pursuing spirituality in the same manner that other people pursue tennis, or swimming lessons. They wait around endlessly for feeble old swamis to spit out stray thoughts and simplistic cookie-cutter homilies which the faithful quickly declare to be profound wisdom. They drink Swami's urine and say it tastes like rosewater. They confuse the juggernaut intensity of their efforts to self-distract and self-delude, with *sadhana*, or spiritual practice.

As hard as it is to live in the moment or "Be Here Now," it is harder still to find the faith and patience to let the guru find me. For now I do my best to keep my eyes and heart open and trust the voice that tells me to just let it happen. Of course there is a part of me that listens for the voice of a shadowy guy whispering, "Hey buddy, psst, over here. Here's the shortcut through the woods to Nirvanaville."

In Lex Hixon's *Coming Home*, in the chapter on Zen Ox herding, he included a traditional Zen commentary saying: "*The Ox [true nature] has never really gone astray. So why search for it*? By seeking our True Nature, we are creating an illusory duality between the one who seeks and the object that is sought. Why search for true nature, which is already present as the consciousness by which one carries out the search? Our True Nature is never lost and therefore can never be found. We cannot discover a satisfactory answer to the puzzle *Why Search*? and this not-finding-an-answer brings about the gradual cessation of search which is the flowering of Enlightenment."

Dostoyevsky (I think) said, "Adversity is the mainspring of self-realism."

Not realization but *realism*. Now there's a do-it-yourself concept! I have many times told people to "get real." Maybe with a little luck, I might in this incarnation (supposing I believed in reincarnation) learn to do it myself.

Joining the Hare Krishnas

Elizabeth Morse

Your father and I are so glad you came to see us. Seven years is a long time, and we didn't know where you were.

We'd sit up late nights drinking scotch, and all we could think of was that you'd gone to San Francisco to take drugs. Remember when we found your hash pipe under the coffee table? I know I hit you but I couldn't do anything else.

Why would you have even thought of wanting to leave us if you weren't so interested in taking drugs?

A couple of years ago I saw a picture in the *Times* of a girl who looked like you handing out flowers in O'Hare airport. She must have been one of the Hare Krishnas because she was wearing an orange sheet.

Your father and I weren't surprised to think you'd join an organization like that, even though, of course, the girl in the picture wasn't you. We always knew you needed some order in your life.

You look so different after seven years. Your cheeks have filled out. Maybe it's because you've stopped taking drugs. It's just that you don't look as hungry as you used to when you were living with us.

12 e-Z Steps 2 Sellvation
PUR-ton-o-FUN...
Putting the FUN
BACK IN...
FUNdAMENTAL
SINC
19

SUMMING UP FOR SUCCESS!

New World / Same Old Shit (for Amadou Diallo)

JOHN FARRIS

1) HERITAGE

I was born in 1940
on Manhattan, "Island
of Hills", "Place of Inebriation".
placer of muskrat, beaver
and mink. My ancestors built a wall
for the Dutch
to keep them contained, out
like a line in the sand, being
thereby kept both in
and out, effectively dividing themselves
against themselves for the patroons; ironically

a minuet set to governance, elegance
itself in broad felt hat
and pumps with great, shiny buckles — himself

named Minuet, the drollery
of thin clay pipe
as good a symbol as any of this authority
over life
and over death;
his staff. Set to this at cutlass point. the refrain
of whipping, the promise
of musketballs between the
defenseless blades of shoulders, the elegance

of rope necklaces, my ancestors
learned to dance
on air, the traditional melancholy
melody of broken windpipes; blues; to twist
to cool jerk
to a battery of drums from the harbor, the fusillade.

2) IMMIGRANT

Poor fellow—he merely
made the mistake of being a young man
who took Emma Lazarus
at her word — a poet! — and having had

not much else — brought hope
all the way from home with him to the Bronx — following
the trail of minerals and contorted bodies
that stacked next to the lamp
the silent statue held would stretch 10,000 times beyond
that dim light, at least to where in the imagination, he had

marked the tattered map he held up
with an "X" for the Bronx, thus revealing right away to any
the inscription — the legend — to be not in stone
but copper, and so much hubris. In that harsh light,
he might have recognized them for who they were when
they came for him for the selection. In that peculiar light,
he might have recognized the "golden door" the poet
spoke of as the one that had been spoken of by his ancestors
as "the Door of No Return". In that brilliant glare
he would have known who they were exactly

when they came for him, and groveling, prostrated himself.

3)   DREAM

What he wanted was to quietly buy
into it — streets
paved if not with gold, then copper — nickel — if not
the legendary stone, then

cement, with "I luv you" scrawled
in the very latest language
next to the adolescent handprint; he
would gladly trade the parched soil of Dakar for it,
that dry savanna air
for these parched plateaus; his tongue;
beads — if not glass, then stone — if not precious — carnadine,

following the line
of traders that had proceeded him from here to Timbouktu
hauled as goods, fetishes
bringing membraphones, wooden masks: Dan, Baule,

Fon, Bambara; nailed, scarified. Such
an easy mark, they didn't
have to give him C.P.R.

Self Help

Ron P. Swegman

Alex woke up, looked out the window of his second floor bedroom, and discovered a most annoying situation — a pair of underwear was hanging in the tree outside.

"Nooo!" Alex moaned. His biggest urban pet peeve was the THE-PLASTIC-BAG-IN-A-TREE, but this wasn't a bag, this was a pair of off-white men's BVDs, fluttering lightly in the breeze of a sunny May morning.

Furious at this development, clueless as to how it could have happened, Alex showered and contemplated a solution. He wanted to just reach out with a gloved hand and grab the offending matter, but his arm was an arm's length short of the drawers. Other thoughts interjected and widened the scope of the problem. Pollution in general, the concept and all of its forms, swirled around his mind as he finished and flushed the toilet.

As he pulled on his socks, Alex concluded the plastic bag was the number one public enemy. He could not escape the presence of BIG BROTHER, the plastic bag. If a bag didn't lasso one of his feet on the street, there were two more waiting for him inside the Drug Mart, all brightly colored and affixed with a happy face. Each one was emblazoned, too, with warnings: THIS IS NOT A TOY! ... KEEP AWAY FROM CHILDREN! ... SUFFOCATION HAZARD!

And this was only the public side of the problem. Alex knew that in every household there were millions, probably billions more of these plastic bags and all of them filled with stuff. The thought overwhelmed him.

He went downstairs and fixed himself a small breakfast of granola and toast. A plastic bag full of plastic bags sat in its corner by the front door and stared at him. Its presence mocked him, the way the underwear had mocked him upstairs. He furrowed his high forehead and looked up and out the kitchen window. Yep, there it was; he could see the pair of BVDs through the thin spring leaves. He groaned.

Alex was certain the Municipal Waste department would just laugh him off the phone, so Alex resigned himself to "Do it yourself."

The victimized tree was a sweetgum, a fine-looking specimen of thirty-odd years, and therefore impossible to climb. There was a ten-foot stretch of straight trunk between its base and the first strong branch. Alex's simian brain told him a tool would be necessary.

He went into the broom closet and found a green broom handle left there by the previous tenant. Now he needed something that could snag or hook. Alex grabbed a hanger from the same closet. He snipped off the HANG part with a pair of wire cutters and used a length of twine to tie it to the broom handle.

Tool in hand, Alex went back upstairs to his bedroom. He opened the window and leaned out, thinking, "I hope no one sees me. Christ, what would they think, seeing some guy fishing undies out of this tree?"

Divine mercy provided Alex with an empty, early Sunday street as he made his attempt. His tool was long enough, but the BVDs were snagged in two or three places, which called for a more complex strategy than a simple quick rip through the branches. He had to perform a delicate two-part intervention: first, he dislodged the front flap; next, he twisted off the seat from a trio of recalcitrant twigs. That done, the underwear dropped to the ground.

"Success!" Alex cheered as he spiraled downstairs. And as the next day was trash day, he decided to solve two problems at once. He took the 30-gallon trash bag full of plastic bags outside, used one of the numerous plastic bags within to cover his hand, and said, "Gotcha!" as he grabbed and entombed the now deceased pair of drawers.

Alex never did learn how the underwear came to hang in his tree, but he thanked its intolerable appearance. His experience had provided him with the tool and the knowledge to combat his biggest urban pet peeve. He spread his absurd little tale, which led eventually to the formation of BAG SNAG, a coalition that continues to fight the ballooning presence of BIG BROTHER, the plastic bag.

Self-Help, West Coast-Style

CAROL WIERZBICKI

It's early spring in San Francisco, and I didn't bring warm enough clothes. My $95-a-night room at the bed-and-breakfast has no heat, so the only times I am truly warm are when I am taking a shower (thank God I have a private bath) or in the fussy brass bed under the electric blankets. I feel out of sorts, not really in the mood for exploring, and I'm kicking myself because San Francisco is a city I've always wanted to visit.

Alone in a strange city, unable to obtain a map of the bus routes, I depend on the map I brought with me and word-of-mouth to find my way down to the Mission district, where I drown my self-pity in neighborhood thrift stores and antique shops. In one of these I meet Jody, a middle-aged man who, despite his pot belly and prematurely gray hair, looks like he never outgrew his adolescence. Around his neck he wears a gold cross studded with jewels. I go to the counter to pay for my treasure—a glass lampshade for my old, hard-to-fit floor lamp at home—and we get to talking. To my surprise I learn that Jody is from my home state, Michigan. Jody's family fell apart after his mother died, so he moved out to California, living at friends' apartments, sometimes in a tent in their backyards.

Jody needed a hip operation, but had no money, so he tried to, in his words, "heal himself," but when he saw that this wouldn't work, he moved to San Francisco, found the means to get his operation—perhaps through some kind of disability program—and got well. He says, "Ten years after my mother's death, I'm still dealing with it, but I learned through the various self-help groups here that there are many kinds of love." Before I leave, he recommends a Rita Hayworth movie, "The Farmer's Daughter," in which a dirt-poor country girl ends up in politics through an improbable series of events that could only have been concocted in Hollywood (including an encounter with a traveling salesman).

My last night in San Francisco I hook up with Carolyn Peyser for a poetry reading she is giving in Berkeley. She's been in San Francisco about eight months and loves it. Her MS has gotten more apparent, and she now needs a cane to walk. As she tells me of her decision to move, a feeling of shame about the self-pity I had been experiencing comes over me. "I never looked back," she says. "I love my job now—doing telephone work for an environmental political action group. I've gotten very politicized since moving here." When I tell her about my new relationship and that it's been a long time since I've had one, she says, "Oh, I can't even remember what that feels like." I immediately think of the fussy bedspread in my $95-a-night room, and my shame deepens.

Carolyn's friend Gloria comes by to drive us into Berkeley. Gloria is a more intriguing study. I think Carolyn met her in some MS self-help group, though I have a hard time picturing Carolyn in any self-help group. Gloria is a self-acknowledged self-help poster child. "I've been in the city for about 30 years, and I've been into just about everything you could imagine," she says, but quickly adds that she realizes these groups have not solved all her problems. At the open mike part of the reading, she recites a courageous piece about her abusive mother, and I can see that she, like Jody in the antique store, is still dealing after all these years.

On the freeway, though, Gloria exhibits her more aggressive side, by turns getting impatient with traffic snarls, joking with Carolyn over Carolyn's tyrannical landlord ("Dickhead!" they call him, then break into schoolgirl giggles), and rhapsodizing about one intersection of the freeway that she claims has a certain "chi," or flow of energy. It is this Gloria I would like to see more of, and who has been buried under the socializing mulch of self-help.

San Francisco may well be the nation's self-help capital. There are probably more self-help groups and political action committees here than in any other city. But the popularity of Zen and other disciplines here seems to have only led to lightweight, lo-cal insights. In the open mike following Carolyn's poetry reading, a man recites: "I have seen the moon 5,000 times, but it was not until last night that I saw the space between the moon [dramatic pause] and me." Another poet gets up and says, "No one told me I'd have to climb over Mt. Diablo to get here," as if he had just seen God, but his poetry turns out to be just as banal as the first reader's.

San Jose — where I had been the week before — is a bit warmer than San Francisco, but there's not much to do there. My hotel was under construction, and therefore had no pool or gym. So after jogging through the campus of the Children's Science Museum, I walked around downtown. Here I saw the flip side of the silicon dreams my employer, the Association for Computing Machinery, was purveying at the exhibit hall: empty storefronts in beautifully restored buildings, and a few disenfranchised-looking people in place of shoppers.

The 50th anniversary of the first computer was being commemorated in San Jose that week — the first week of March, 1997 — but all I could see was a big, sterile research park, like some very well-salted Carthage, only the pestilences now were corporate downsizing and welfare reform. I noticed a sign posted on a fenced-in parking lot of an apartment building: "WARNING: This property has been found to contain carcinogenic agents." I mentally added: "Fallout brought to you by the capital of digital self-determination."

Time to go. My shuttle van to the San Francisco airport has to make several stops to pick up other passengers, and on the way we pass through Haight-Ashbury, where I see many scruffy-looking teenagers wandering aimlessly or parked on the sidewalk outside what looks like the original Ben & Jerry's ice cream store. I see sign after sign that says: "PREVENT RUNAWAYS," but when I get close enough to read the whole thing it continues: "CURB WHEELS-PARK IN GEAR-SET BRAKE." I guess they're more concerned about cars rolling down hills than homeless kids here. After the Haight, the neighborhoods get even more desolate, and it occurs to me that I've only seen either very rich or very poor areas here, and felt a kind of callousness that seems in direct opposition to the whole self-help ethos. At the ends of most streets I can see hill rising upon hill, each trying to outdo the other for pure majesty, oblivious to the pastel saltbox squalor at their feet.

My last night at the B&B, I finally got up the nerve to light a fire in the fireplace.

As I cowered under the electric blankets, staring at the shadows thrown by the curiously ineffectual flames, the lesson of my first visit to California finally hit me: self-help is only for the strong.

Plan for the Invasion of Californi

Analysis of Vectors of Contagion *via* the Internet [Phase 1.0: Initial Delivery Systems]

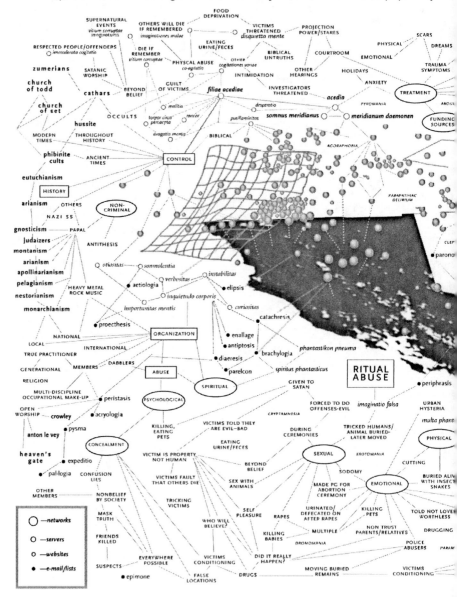

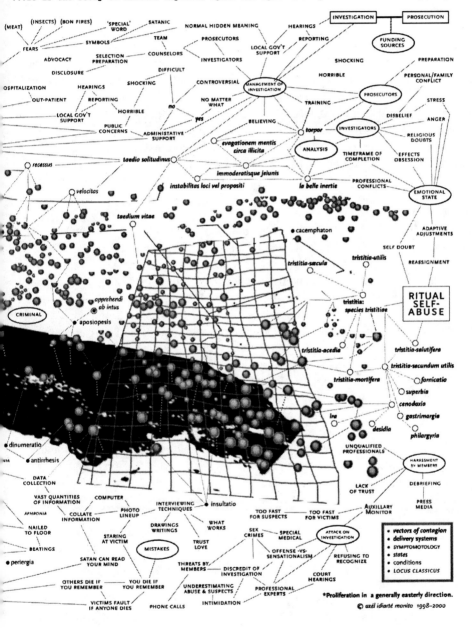

"...it is the story of numbers repeated again and again and again and..." —Doctor Enrique Sanchez

Doing It Yourself

JILL RAPAPORT

The rise in popularity of the D-I-Y movement is tied not coincidentally with the current celebration/outcry concerning executive compensation packages that even such media shills as Business Week complain are "out of control." If you like patterns, try this on: When popular revolutionary movements presented their numbers as a corrective to the historically unquestioned and oppressive one-man rulerships of tsars and kings, the ruling classes fought back by automating labor and forming corporations (the original manifestation of "the Man"). Now, although the Man was everywhere, he was also nowhere. *What are you doing, man? I don't know. I'm not doing anything. I'm not him.*

When the people fought back by forming labor and political unions, the Man, one step ahead, counterattacked with the development of ideological enmities, pitting worker against worker and nation against nation: War against the International.

A little-noted paradox of the period was that, at the same time North Americans at any rate were infected according to conservative policy analysts with the disease of entitlement expectations, their rallying cry went from union solidarity shouts and manifestations of community to the solitary whine of the human dromedary, questioning a god or pharaoh that had disappeared behind the bulk of corporate pyramids: "Maybe if I worked harder, I could make more money."

Into the Coca Cola of workers along with a watered-down cocaine was placed the cumulatively addictive tincture of paranoia that would soon submerge all other impulses. Soon the taste for blame was so entrenched and insistent that no matter how much the visions ran against common sense, the people were infected with a hatred and distrust of their fellows around the world that made it possible for them to follow the lead of a George Meany, virulently anticommunist American labor leader to whom even the likes of Richard Nixon was "soft on communism." Now you had the horse inside the gates.

In availing myself of the news of the city, state and world I got angry often, in the pointless fury of the delusional standee who expected a bus to come. I wrung my hands and cried, when anyone knew that the only way to get a bus to come was to light a cigarette — and I no longer smoked.

I traveled the shuttle between paranoia about street crime and apoplexy over white-collar plunder even though I knew better than some that both extremes were part of one continuum. I read the information releases of Graef Crystal and clicked on Executive Pay Watch, the new website of the AFL-CIO; I compared my living wage to Michael Eisner's, and the formulations of the age of dinosaurs jumped to mind. People had thought since the dawn of modernism that humanity was moving toward an equivalency of the physical, an automatic handicapping, or a leveling of the field, that would make comparisons of sizes, relative wealths, the accidents of birth and place, irrelevant. Well, people were wrong.

While you grew, the kings were making their comeback and the cabbage patch dug deeper for what little it could salvage from the still unoptioned earth. I was just as conned as the next person, despite having been born to fellow travelers in the generation that respected radicalism.

But finally, having studied the briefest of world histories, I was ready to make my own move into the equalizing stream that had for decades haunted survivors of the postmodern age.

On this, the anniversary of the firestorm in Waco and the militia-belt strike in Oklahoma City, and the better part of one year from the time of TWA Flight 800 (the greatest aviation mystery since Amelia Earhart), many questions sit naked and ugly on the table. Pierre Salinger notwithstanding, there are certain reasons to feel uneasy about the demise of an airplane on which the mainly privileged of one world started off on the journey to a second, in the process crashing off the U.S. coastline and taking with them the flare of a minor implosion of light that for an instant on a moonless horizon was trained on the world-threatening sorceries of global American capitalism.

Nearly one year since, the new area code prefix was three infinity signs lying on their sides: 888. The old area code prefix, which people had begun using in numbers that scared the managers of for-profit information, was being retired the hard way, blown up in a fireball, chips falling wherever they wanted, with nobody but scattered witnesses, to be discredited as lunatics in the manner of grassy knoll theorists of more than thirty years before, and occasional pilots of nowhere carriers, to be taken out of service early and retrained extensively at the camp for pilots who needed to keep their eyes off irregular blips on radar. SOMEBODY HAD A PROBLEM WITH TOLL-FREE ACCESS.

An atomized populace, crying in breaking frequencies as their flesh fried on the skillet surface of the grayprints of multinational mergers plotting a doomsday escape to outer space, were tramping the world, the new hoboes. In numbers lay disunity, a preemptive isolation that the men in space vessels had figured out before you comprised protoplasm. Now they were coming for the homes and lives of the upper middle classes, because class warfare, as it had ever been known, was obsolete. We were back to the one man, one rule concept and any unity was strictly virtual.

America's Self-Help Movement: Early Literary Origins

ALAN KAUFMAN

The contemporary American Self-Help Movement has its origins in the New York and New England of the mid-Nineteenth Century, in that time immediately preceding the Civil War when outbreaks of compulsive overeating, sex addiction and codependency threatened to halt the nation's westward march to San Francisco.

Romance novels were the order of the day, along with tie-dye parasols, hoop skirts, Yankee Beef Denture Cream and Yoga, all byproducts of the newly opened fair trade routes to the Far East, and which over the next one hundred years, would in turn export to our shores, respectively, theosophical doctrines encouraging lifestyles of detached passivity and sacred masters of corporate takeover backed by hundreds of millions of dollars.

Eastern influences came from Europe as well, or more specifically, from Russian-occupied Poland in the Eastern Pale, or Brooklyn, as it is more commonly known.

Before authoring *Moby Dick*, young Herman Melville spent some time as a ship's chandler in a dry goods shop where he met the older Anna Ziebrinskiz, browsing for whale bone corsets. Destined to become Joseph Conrad's mother, Ziebrinskiz was in from Warsaw on a brief jaunt to sample the brisk Atlantic tides. She and Melville became fast friends and would make day-long *spirit quests* through Manhattan, dry-humping on the steps of brownstones and often making out in public restrooms with bits of Lo Mein clinging to their teeth.

Shortly after her return to Warsaw, Joseph was born. (Their encounter would later be recalled in Conrad's memoir, *Heart of Darkness II: Melville and My Mother*.") This confluence of Eastern spiritual sources tupping the ruddy-cheeked stoicism of Boston-bullied New York is what gave us Transcendentalism, or EST, as we know it.

Soon hundreds of newly opened self-help centers dotted the landscape between Manhattan and Concord. Chief Justice Thurman Wicks spent time in a recovery center for addiction to M&Ms, while Walt Whitman led a small healing circle of journeymen printers through rituals involving abstinence from masturbation with sheepskin (a problem considered so grave for its impact on the local economy that a special commission of inquiry into its causes was immediately established by New York City Mayor J. Wheedlin Cash, and during which the wives of the Borough's five top sheepskin wankers stepped forward to offer their own chilling and compelling testimony to the horrors of living with the afflicted, a scene, according to eyewitness accounts, so scandalous that at one point outraged bystanders in the gallery smuggled a sheep into the courtroom and forced it to bleat at the poor women, by inserting a red chili pepper in its anus — an act which in turn led to the creation of the Animal Rights Movement and the establishment of the first social services office in New York City.)

Whitman, also by this time an advocate of phrenology — an early and actually quite effective form of psychoanalysis in which emotional problems are tracked on the outward surface of the head, rather than through its interior — would roam the city streets with a pair of calipers, measuring the skulls of stockbrokers and barrel merchants alike. It is said that he once received a round slap in the face from an old schoolmarm for encircling her bonnet with his calipers from behind and publicly declaring to the crowd that had gathered: "Why, her head is as tiny as an infant child's! Come look!"

It was a time of astonishing literary ferment as well. Between 1856 and 1860, and leading up to the Civil War — some say the direct cause of it — this movement would produce, respectively: *I Don't Want What You Have* by Emily Dickinson, *Let Go of Me!: Authenticity in the Age of Mesmerized Cows* by Henry David Thoreau, *Teaspoon In My Coffee: The Fatal Nature of Sugar* by Ralph Waldo Emerson, *Living With Debt* by Nathaniel Hawthorne, and Melville's monumental *Whoppers of the Sea*. It was a flowering time for Southern Literature, too, predominantly James Branch Cabal, who, in such self-published tracts as *The Cotton Swabs of Georgia*, mirrored back to the Southern States their own rising fears of Abraham Lincoln's codependency issues.

Of course, the great star in this new strain in American culture was none other than Ralph Waldo Emerson. His rise through the ranks of the American pantheon parallels that of John Bradshaw and the Inner Child movement one hundred years later. Himself a kind of unhinged grandfatherly Inner Child unleashed to bestride American letters, he declaimed in ringing sonorous lines of embellished self congratulations the condition of cosmic "allowingness" that could in the same breath permit indigenous Huron warriors of the previous century to bite off the fingers of their captured adversaries — which by Emerson, "O.K." — while, in turn, equally offering permission to westward-bound calvary troops to plant their sabers in the vaginas of Cheyenne and Dakota women resisting rape — also, by Emerson, "O.K." His doctrine of self-reliance could be summed up as "Trust yourself. If you think you're fucked, you are."

His greatness was his message and his message was his greatness: "It's all O.K.!" asserted his tracts to a rapidly expanding nation and by "all" he meant our American experience entire, a Manifest Destiny of iconoclastic and inventive conquest.

From the establishment during the Civil War of the world's first outdoor fast food concession at Andersonville Prison and the Union's development of scorched earth field hockey (and that would later be closely studied in military colleges as a warm-up for such historic feature films as *Pumpin' Pups* [depicting the encounter between a kindhearted Nedicks Waitress and unscrupulous German Shepherd]) to the celebration of physical fitness as a succinctly American virtue unique unto ourselves (and that would later produce the heroic frames of Germanic chiseled abs in the propaganda films of Leni Reifenstahl and Arnold Schwarzenneger) the great Emersonian cry of "It's all O.K.!" rings down the ages with lugubrious* resonance.

In the related arts and philosophies, John Wilkes Booth's uncritical pursuit of his own personal truth, a là Emerson, found its apotheosis in a death-defying leap from the dying Lincoln's balcony to the stage far below (and which would directly influence that great American cinematic manifesto: Sylvester Stallone's now famous *First Blood*, and which in turn laid the groundwork for the meteoric rise of Jeffrey Dahmer).

Emerson's transcendental vision also inspired Frederich Nietzsche's concept of the Unermenche, a racialist early SS philosophy subtly disguised as a Marvel Comic super hero's credo. Later, Hemingway would develop this very theme during his Idaho duck hunts with Gary Cooper. Today's New Age canonization of Sri Chinmoy, whose teachings fire the imaginations of people with none whatsoever, are the direct result of the independent New England minister's nightly service performed before an audience of his followers in which he channeled in a format of call and reponse the haunting clucks of mating fowls and the show tunes of Gilbert and Sullivan. Well can one imagine the delighted old Concordian on such occasions, surrounded by his apostles, who sucked cashew butter from his fingers as he groaned lustily.

Finally, whether one is tracking Emerson's New Age influence on popular culture from the off-camera drunken monologues of William Shatner of the television series *T.J. Booker* to the unskakeable self-acceptance of O.J. Simpson, one can draw a single straight line, using a Featherweight Flexible ruler and a leaky Bic Pen, to the Emersonian ideal: they, like so much else that is bloodstained on the American glove today, are the direct result of Emerson's great Transcendent call for an uncritical and healthy posture of hiring the best lawyer to kick your opponent's ass and of radical self-forgiveness around our "stuff," those "issues" that drive us to believe that all is not well, especially when it's not, and our efforts to commute our gnawing unease into a New Age Failure to live up to even minimal standards of adult responsibility and behavior. These, in turn, become affirmation of Nature's essential indifference to our condition, the great cosmic transcendent "fuck you" that is out there waiting to goof on our flabby and gross bodies.

*lugubrious: I don't know what this means. It could be made up off the tip of my head to seem intellectually authoritative. I often make up things to support my remarks.

Claims of the Normal

ROBERT ANTON WILSON

> Wilson describes himself as a "guerilla ontologist," signifying his intent to
> ATTACK language and knowledge the way terrorists ATTACK their targets:
> to jump out from the shadows for an unprovoked ATTACK, then slink back
> and hide behind a hearty belly-laugh.
> —*Robert Sheaffer, The Skeptical Inquirer* Spring 1990

Timothy F.X. Finnegan, founder of the Committee for Surrealist Investigation of
the Claims of the Normal, has done the Dutch Act—kicked the bucket, croaked,
passed to his reward, died, expired, became an ex-Irishman, went kerflooey, joined
the choir invisible, or as the Salvation Army so charmingly puts it, "got promoted to
glory." At any rate, they took the liberty of burying him.

The Committee for Surrealist Investigation of Claims of the Normal (CSICON),
however, lives on and deserves more attention than it has received hitherto.   Prof.
Finnegan, Dean of the Royal Sir Myles na Gopaleen Astro-Anomalistic Society,
founder of CSICON and sometime lecturer at Trinity College, Dublin, always
asserted that the idea for CSICON derived from a remark passed by an old Dalkey
character named Sean Murphy, in the Goat and Compasses pub shortly before
closing time on 23 July 1976. "Ah, sure," Murphy said, "I've never had a boogerin'
normal day or saw a fookin' average man."

These simple words lit a fire in the subtle and intricate brain of Timothy F.X.
Finnegan, who had just finished his fourteenth pint (deSelby says his fifteenth pint)
of linn dubh, known as Guiness to the ungodly. The next day the aging Finnegan
wrote the first two-page outline of the new science he called patapsychology, a
term coined in salute to Jarry's invention of pataphysics. (About Sean Murphy nothing else appears in the record except a remark gleaned by Prof. LaPuta from one
Nora Dolan, a housewife of the vicinity: "Faith, that Murphy lad never did any hard
work except for getting up off the floor and navigating himself back on the bar-stool,
after he fell off, twice a night.")

Nobody should confuse Patapsychology with parapsychology, although this
precise misunderstanding evidently inspired the long and venomous diatribes
against Finnegan by Prof. Sheissinhosen of Heidelberg. (We need not credit the
allegations of Hamburger that Sheissinhosen also dispatched the three separate
letter-bombs sent to Finnegan in 1982, '83 and '87. Even in the most heated aca-
demic debate some limits remain, one would hope.)

Sheissinhosen evidently believed that parapsychology represented an unpro-
voked attack on his language and thought, and that Finnegan often slunk in shadows, because he, Sheissihosen, never did correct his original error of reading patapsychology as parapsychology. You will find more about the Sheissinhosen-

Finnegan-LaPuta-Hamburger controversy in deSelby's *Finnegan: Enigma of the Occident*.

Patapsychology begins from Murphy's Law, as Finnegan called the First Axiom, adopted from Sean Murphy. This says, and I quote, "The normal does not exist. The average does not exist. We know only a phalanx of discrete space-time events encountered and endured." In less technical language, the Board of the College of Patapsychology offers one million Irish punds to any "normalist" who can exhibit "a normal sunset, an average Beethoven sonata, an ordinary Playmate of the Month, or any thing or event in space-time that qualifies as normal, average or ordinary."

In a world where no two fingerprints appear identical, and no two brains appear identical, and an electron does not even seem identical to itself from one nanosecond to another, patapsychology seems on safe ground here. No normalist has yet produced even a totally normal dog, an average cat, or even an ordinary chickadee. Attempts to find an average Bird of Paradise, an ordinary novel or even a normal cardiologist have floundered pathetically. The normal, the average, the ordinary, even the typical exist only in statistics, i.e. the human mathematical mind space. They never appear in external space-time, which consists only and always of non-normal events in non-normal series.

The canny will detect here the usual Celtic impulse to make hash out of everything that seems obvious and incontrovertible to the Saxons (or to most non-Irishfolk.) Patapsychology follows in the great tradition of Swift, who once proved that a man named Partridge had died, even though Partridge continued to deny this in print; Bishop Berkeley, who proved that the universe doesn't exist but God has a persistent delusion that it does; William Rowan Hamilton, who invented the non-commutative algebra in which p times q does not equal q times p; Wilde, who asked if the commentators on Hamlet had really gone mad or only pretended to have gone mad; John S.Bell, who proved mathematically that if any universe corresponds to the equations of quantum mathematics that universe must have nonlocal correlations similar to Jungian synchronicities; etc.

In the patapsychological model, the normal having vanished, most generalizations, especially about nonmathematical groups, disappear along with it. Hitler, for instance, could not generalize about "the Jews" within the patapsychological model, because first he would have to find a normal or average Jew, which appears as intracible to demonstration as exhibiting the Ideal Platonic Jew. As Korzybski the semanticist said, all we can ever find in space-time consists of Jew-1, Jew-2, Jew-3 etc. to Jew-n. (For the nonmathematical, that means a list comprising Abraham, Moses, Woody Allen, Richard Bandler, Felix Mendelsohn, Sigmund Freud, Paulette Goddard, Betty Grable, Noam Chomsky, Bernard Baruch, Emma Lazarus, Jesus, Albert Einstein, Lillian Hellman, Baron Rothschild, Ayn Rand, Max Epstein, Emma Goldman, Saul Bellow, etc. etc. etc. to the final enumeration of all Jews alive or dead.) Each of these, on inspection, will have different fingerprints, different brains, different neuro-immunological systems, different eyes, ears, noses etc., different life histories, different conditioning and learning etc. and different personalities, hobbies, passions etc... and none will serve as a norm of Ideal Form for all the others.

To say it otherwise, world Jewish population stood at about 10 million when Hitler formed his generalizations. He could not possibly have known more than at maximum about 500 of them well enough to generalize about them; considering his early prejudice, he probably knew a lot less than that. But taking 500 as a high estimate, we find he generalized about 10 million individual persons on the basis of knowledge limited to around 1/20,000 or 0.00005 % of them.

It seems, then, that Nazism could not have existed if Hitler knew the difference between norms or averages (internal estimates, subject to incomplete research or personal prejudice) and the phalanx of discrete nonnormal events and things (including persons) that we find in the sensory space-time continuum outside.

Similarly, the male human population currently stands at 3 billion 3 million 129 thousand, more or less (3,004,129,976, the last time I checked the World Game Website a minute ago.) Of these 3 billion+ discrete individuals, Robin Morgan, Andrea Dworkin and other Radical Feminists probably have not known more than about 500 to generalize from. This means that Rad Fem dogma consists of propositions about 3 billion critters based on examination of less than 0.00000001 per cent of them. This amounts to a much more reckless use of generalization than Hitler's thoughts on Judaism.

You can no more find the male norm from Gandhi, Gen George Custer, Woody Allen etc. than you can find the Jewish norm from Karl Marx, Emma Lazarus and Mendelssohn etc. Now you know how the word "feminazi" got into the language. The two ideologies have a strong isomorphism. They both confuse the theoretical norm with a vast array of different individuals — and they both have no idea how to create even a tolerably scientific norm (which will still differ in many respects from the actual series of individuals the norm allegedly covers.).

CSICON applies the same Deconstructive logic all across the board. For instance, whatever your idea of the normal UFO — whether you consider it a spaceship, a secret US government weapon, a hoax, or a hallucination etc. — such a general idea will render you incapable of forming a truly objective view of the next UFO that comes along. The only way to cancel such pre-judgement lies in patapsychology (and in general semantics.)You must remember the difference between the individual and unpredictable event that gets called a UFO and your past generalizations about "the UFO" or the "normal UFO."

Otherwise you will only note how this UFO fits your Ideal UFO and will unconsciously ignore how it differs therefrom. This mechanical reflex will please your ego, if you like to feel you know more than most people, but it will prove hazardous to your ability to think and observe carefully.

People who think they know all about Jews or males or UFOs never see a real Jew or male or UFO. They see the generalized norm that exists only in their own brains. We never know "all" — we only know what I call sombunall, some-but-not-all. This applies also to dogs (the patapsychologist will not say "I love them," "I hate them," "I fear them" etc.), and to plumbers, bosses, right-wingers, left-wingers, cats and all other miscellaneous sets or groups.

Personally, I see two or three UFOs every week. This does not astonish me, or convince me of the spaceship theory, because I also see about 2 or 3 Unifies every week: Unidentified Non-Flying Objects. These remain unidentified (by me) because they go by too fast or look so weird that I never know whether to classify them as hedgehogs, hobgoblins or helicopters — or as stars or satellites or spaceships —

or as pookahs or pizza-trucks or probability waves. Of course, I also see things that I feel safe in identifying as hedgehogs or stars or pizza trucks, but the world contains more and more events that I cannot identify fully and dogmatically with any norm or generalization. I live in a spectrum of probabilities, uncertainties and wonderments.

Perhaps I got this way by studying Finnegan's work. Or maybe I just drank too much linn dubh during my years in Ireland.

Hermetics, Cleaning, and Esperanto: The Self-Help Aesthetic of the Unbearable "DisinfecTrance" and Its Relation to Finnegans Wake within the Deeper Cryptology of the Unbearable Secret Society

ALFRED VITALE, K.S.C.

> "Anyone who should believe to find in this work nothing else but a collection of recipes, with the aid of which he can easily and without any effort attain to honour and glory, riches and power and aim at the annihilation of his enemies, might be told from the very inception that he will put aside this book, being very disappointed."
> —*Franz Bardon,* Initiation Into Hermetics, *p.9, Rüggeberg-Verlag, Germany*

1. Introduction

The latter half of the 20th century could be considered the "Era of the Commercialized Self-Help Movement". But as the millennium draws near, there have been significant advances in behavior change methodologies which eclipse the slower days of the "Peter Principle." Some of these self-help guides have countered the already prevalent conditioning of the contemporary cultural matrixes, but many have failed to create little more than increased revenue for publishing companies. From this morass of quasi-mystical, formulaic, acronym-laden, superlative-filled, cliche-packed, hyphenated, paperbacked tomes, there arose a tribe of confused philosophers...thrust onto the lesser literary catwalks with only their cunning linguistics to defend their posturing. These were the Protobearables. This group of hyperlogians, spouting dime-store doctrines like mantras and defiantly dressed in slovenly uncoordinated clothing, walked the streets of the cities in search of an angry repair. Angular nolohippies from soho, lusty schoolgirls of no fixed education, middle-aged youngsters and youthfully cantankerous 60-year old tykes, poets without paper, writers without writ, deluded amateurs, a motley collection of the unwanted...randomly scrambling together into various shapes and configurations with the inspired Word and beer as their guides. Prefiguring the SubGenius movement, they were dedicated to finding "slack". The ultimate slack, they conceded, could only come from an incoherent philosophy which preached a doctrine of "No Wei" (as opposed to the mere "Wu Wei" of the Taoists).

The potential for the self-help book to create an environment which required no effort became evident in the 1980s, when the detritus of EST seminars, Scientology, and rehab programs was to collectively "give up" and decide, once and for all, to never be successful, rich or famous. Upon this agreement, the Protobearables...this polyglot patchwork quilt of losers...became *Un*bearables. And with the Unbearables came a secret society that didn't actually have any idea what their secret was...a living Zen koan, with no master, no rules, but an exclusivity based only on talent and success. For if a person became a famous and successful writer, they would be forced to reject the Unbearables altogether...the two worlds could not co-exist, not within the landscape of small cafe readings and mimeographed zines. Thusly, the Unbearables have created a mobile "Tavern of Ruin." Through it all, they claim to be a unique phenomenon.

2. The Big "However"

HOWEVER! Could it be that there is something more insidiously influential and indicative of Unbearableness? They would of course answer with an emphatic, "No!", but that is their ruse. Their society relies on denial more than anything else.

In researching various documents and letters from Unbearables, as well as by examining source material and clues from the literary and esoteric record, I have found that there are signs of a truly clandestine self-help methodology throughout the history of the Unbearables. And, more intriguing perhaps, there are hints that they are a manifestation of a more ancient tradition (For more details about the historical synopsis, see www.thud.org/thud.htm).

Today, this group of surface hypocrites has repeated a pattern of scorning the very things that have created them...first it was themselves, then it was the Beats, and now it's the "Self-Help" movement (as you can read throughout this book). This has occurred for one reason and one reason only: to deflect attention from their real purpose, the Immanentizing of the Literary Eschaton! To do this, they have stolen clues and direction from a variety of Self-Help books which, in fact, have never been examined in this light. The Unbearables, simply put, consist of a host of plagiarized, pilfered, and altered self-help concepts, camouflaged by amateurishness and contrived innocence, but progenically projected from an older spermetaphoric lineage.

I'd like to briefly examine three books and note how they verify that the Unbearables are indeed controlled by the very self-help systems that they appear to be deriding in this book. These books are *Teach Yourself Esperanto*, *Initiation Into Hermetics*, and *How to Clean Everything*. I will also use the evidence in Joyce's *Finnegans Wake*, a book which Ron Kolm does not understand but insists (in private) on its ability to influence him and the Unbearables, to further confirm my theory. *Finnegans Wake* is also appropriate since its prescience predicts the Unbearable milieu and Joyce was certainly no stranger to secret societies and occult fanaticism.

3. The origin for the ritual of "From Somewhere to Nowhere"

As would often be the case, simple Unbearableisms that are taken for granted as coming from the Unbearables are more often plagiarized or altered from existing sources. As I stated earlier, *Finnegans Wake* will be a valuable tool for helping to see how Unbearableness consists of the booty of looted self-help books and literary works. In this case, we turn to the *Wake*:

> What has gone? How it ends?
> Begin to forget it. It will remember itself from every sides, with all

gestures, in each our word. Today's truth, tomorrow's trend.
Forget, remember!
Have we cherished expectations? Are we for liberty of perusive-
ness? *From somewhere to nowhere*? A plainplanned liffeyism
assemblements Esperanta's conglomerate horde. By dim delty
Deva.
Feast! Forget!
—James Joyce, Finnegans Wake *p.614, Penguin Books edition*

In the above section, (Italics are mine), we see the symbolic steps of the closing
ritual of Unbearable events. By using subtle clues for the attendees to "forget"
what happened at the event, they are protecting their formulaic predictability from
being discovered by astute guests. This form of quick-hypnosis culminates in the
"From Somewhere to Nowhere" hand signals, which are an ingenious reversal of
the Masonic distress signal. Using a complex form of Neurolinguistic
Programming, the phrase uttered becomes the implanted suggestion, and all who
come to events will leave with a nagging lack of closure. Entropy is not to blame
for this, manipulation is. Later, we will see how this phrase creates a mystical for-
mula for an even greater purpose.

4. Bar-a-tending

The planning of such activities and events takes place at symbolically important
taverns. Each of these places holds a historic mysticism due to their placement atop
a Ley Line, or because of their significant contribution to Self-Help mania. For
instance, it is well-known that the Cedar Tavern (the original one) was the meeting
place for some of the great modern artists. But this facade masks the real reason it
is so often used to plot or engage in Unbearable actions: the bar sits atop the spot
where it is believed that the first self-help book was made in the New World...the infa-
mous 17th century book, *Ye Seven Habits of Quakers* by Ukariah Zebadiah Sponk.

Another frequently utilized bar was the Old Homestead on the Lower East
Side. Serving originally as a front for communist party activities in the 20s, the bar
was mentioned, of course, in *Finnegans Wake*:

> Everything's going on the same or so it appeals to all of us, in the
> old holmsted here. *James Joyce,* Finnegans Wake *p. 26, Penguin
> Books edition*

The sentence alludes to the fact that the password to enter the back room of the
bar, where the bolsheviks would meet, was "Everything's going on the same".
When the Unbearables use the bar, they interact with some of these old *appa-
ratchiks* and sometimes take hot showers with them for fun.

The most important bar they attended, however, was surely the Shandon Star.
The significance of this bar is complex and rooted in both Celtic mythology and
occult mysticism.

The Shandon, in Celtic mythology, was a rather unhappy pixie who waited
around dark street corners, raping drunk poets after they would leave a pub. For

Unbearables, this is usually a desirable situation...a miserable succubus was often the best sex that an Unbearable could get! There is a legend that a young Rollo Whitehead was the first Unbearable to actually come upon the Shandon, and James Joyce's eerie prediction appears in *Finnegans Wake* on page 330. It is just one word, one sentence.

Rolloraped.

"Rolloraped" became the Secret Initiation Word of the Unbearables until it was exposed in a pamphlet called "Secret Rituals of Underground Poets" (origin unknown). But the word was *officially* taken out of use after 1991, when Katherine McKinnon and Andrea Dworkin infiltrated the group disguised as very unhappy men. Nobody really knows what the new Secret Initiation Word of the Unbearables is, but there is speculation it may be "Mah-hah-bone."

As an interesting sidebar to this, Rollo Whitehead himself did not take too well to this raping by the pixie Shandon. Later, his misogynistic fits became well-known throughout literary circles in the 1950s, and once again we find Joyce tapping into the Akashic Record to predict Rollo's begrudging attitude towards women:

> Did you anywhere, Kollum, on your gullible's travels or during your rural troubadouring, happen to stumble upon a certain scowling young nobleman whimpering to the name of Row Low Whitbr'd who always addresses women out of the one corner of his mouth, lives on loans and is furtivefree yours of age? (*James Joyce,* Finnegans Wake *p. 173, Penguin Books edition*)

But perhaps the more tantalizing facet of the Shandon Star was, in fact, the symbol in mythology which was *known* as the "Shandon Star". Most experts in mythology agree that the Shandon Star was actually the dog-star Sirius, thus linking the Unbearables with the current theories about extraterrestrials from Sirius contacting the ancient Egyptians to create the Pyramids and culture, or as some have speculated further, to create Sirian-Human hybrids to rule the world from behind the scenes. They would be the Secret Chiefs to the Theosophists, the Illuminati to the Birch Society, and Editors at the New Yorker to the Unbearables.

5. *"How to Clean Everything": A Cryptic Rosicrucian Manifesto disguised as a Self-Help book about cleaning.*

An esoteric scholar, Colin Wilson, once remarked that the Rosicrucians were everywhere, even in his breakfast cereal. Indeed, as the Unbearables discovered, there were far more hints at the secret of the Rosicrucians than academics cared to believe. When, in 1983, a small book called *How to Clean Everything* was sent anonymously and without a note to the Unbearables, it was believed to be a sign from the Rosicrucians. Immediately, work was begun to decipher the hidden meanings in its pages. From previously non-existent documents, never before written, I've discovered that there was in fact a current of Rosicrucian thought that stretched from the Knights Templar to the French Revolution then to the Germ-

Theory of Disease, to Ivory Soap, and finally, to your local supermarket. This school of thought believed, truly, that cleanliness was next to godliness. It was also believed that women were the true vehicles of the "Holy Grail", a cleaning solvent that would take stains out of any material or off of any surface. However, the search for the Holy Grail had not been fruitful. A group of Grail seekers banded together at the end of the 17th century to find this blessed solution, and thus was Freemasonry officially born in England. Using the analogy of the house and building structures, they set out to reveal clues to this cleaning elixir whenever they found them, but only in forms that would be clear to the "initiated". The first few sentences of *How to Clean Everything* were indeed such a clue:

> This book is for women who dislike housework but like nice homes. Though it obviously will give brides an enviable head start, it was not written especially for them, but for those of us with growing families, who have to make every stroke tell or go under. (*Introduction, p.7*)

I have consulted with a group of "Rollosicrucians" (those early followers of Rollo Whitehead's short-lived religion of Perfunctorism) and they explained to me the significance of the above sentences. Basically, it can be translated as "That which is above is like unto that which is below, though it helps if you are very tall and have a midget partner. Only through sexual Housecleaning can we truly find the Grail. fnord."

I asked them about another rather odd statement on page 8:

> This knowledge has never been obtainable in a single volume.

The Rollosicrucian Grendel McFlirt immediately blurted out, "Well DUH! Can't you see it's indicating that we are awaiting the second volume to triumphantly ride into the Holy Land on the back of a big fat ass?"

Frustrated, I headed back to *Finnegans Wake* to see if I could find references to this string of Sanctified Ablution Fluid Seekers, and I was not surprised to find two passages which hinted that Joyce indeed was a member of this Depurating Brotherhood:

> Daunts daunts o whoreling dr'velish, them that shone wid polushin miasmer, cleaninguess is goodliness for you; on beer tables sits the shore of the penmans ship; her medically polyepiglottal singsong Alivens the Liffey cafe; Pour a'beer. (*James Joyce, Finnegans Wake p. 218, Penguin Books edition*)

and again:

> Well, after it was areedin in the Sunt Marksy Churchkey Wankshop (for once they did not sully their white kidgloves, cleansing cuds after their beery dinners of cheeckin and ribbin,

with their welt dionysian scrubbers and their mend out of a slope becket, and their when you're quite finished with the bleeding bacterial), even the soap that suds'd his goldin baldin hair had brought a plant against him. (*James Joyce,* Finnegans Wake *p. 205, Penguin Books edition*)

6. Esperanto & the Secret Sufi Dr. L.L. Zamenhof

Dr. L. L. "Kool" Zamenhof was the inventor of the novel "auxiliary" language called Esperanto, now the butt of jokes among those who speak the more serious and useful language of Klingon. Zamenhoff was a dawdler, a lollygagger, a layabout and a rapscallion...but his contribution to language was immeasurable. Esperanto was to be the language of free love, peace and Anarchy! In late 19th century Poland, Zamenhof was a respected oculist, but not much is written about him historically. In the introduction to *Teach Yourself Esperanto*, the authors write:

> Some people think of Zamenhof as a dreamy Utopian who imagined that if a neutral second language were once introduced, all wars would cease and the world would become a Garden of Eden.

It was this royally failed Utopianism that first attracted the Unbearables, primitively fumbling to align themselves with the most crooked and least understood paths. Utopia seemed like a safe bet because it was pretty clear that it would never actually happen...thus, it once again highlighted the Unbearables' penchant for inaction. They were the champions of things that failed. That is why Esperanto became the ritual tongue for Unbearables. For a time, many of them gave themselves Esperanto names, much the same way that new converts to the nation of Islam gave themselves Muslim names. Jim Feast became "Funto da Teo" which meant, "A pound of tea"...Ron Kolm became "Oni Ripetas" or "One who repeats". But this came to a terrible end when Mike Carter, overseas and on his way home, was stopped and detained at Turkish customs because his chosen Esperanto name meant "I am carrying a large shipment of Hashish to give to your daughters" in the local Turkish dialect.

7. Cleaning and Esperanto: A Deadly combination for the first Unbearable Casualty

In May of 1991, a gang of janitors from P.S. 123 attacked and killed Prudence Gunnar Titwillow-Bush, the radical feminist whose work with the Unbearables consisted of short one-act plays where the audience was directed to clean the seats by the rather immobile and slothy characters up on stage. It was her statement against the emasculation of the vacuum cleaner, but it meant more to some. After a particularly spotless performance, she was met backstage by three angry janitors fearing the loss of their profession...the first janitor struck her on the forehead with a scrubbrush and she fell, the second hit her across the shoulder with a slop bucket and she fell flat...the third janitor sprinkled her body with that sawdusty stuff they use to clean vomit in 3rd grade classrooms, and she died then and there. The

Unbearables were devastated and all their performances stopped immediately.

Months later, in homage to this martyrdom, the first Unbearable event since the tragedy was called SpektaklA o, which meant "A bit of the Spectacle" and consisted entirely of heavily armed thugs who spent the evening chasing janitors through school buildings and forcing them to submit to standardized testing. Those who did not score above 6th grade level were brutally beaten with chapbooks.

Eventually, they returned to a fairly normal state of Lower East Side literaryness. But there were still remnants of their Esperanto and Cleaning days even as late as 1997...a review in the Village Voice stated:

> Years ago, their incessant cleaning and conversations in bastardized Esperanto created the original milieu of Unbearableism... participants were encouraged to clean with a religious zeal, creating an ecstatic state called DisinfecTrance. At the Funky Brewster bar last night, the DisinfecTrance returned and we were all transported once more to that immaculate state of pure sanitized bliss. Like the days of yore, we were handed rubber gloves and Brillo pads and whipped into a scrubbing frenzy!

The "DisinfecTrance" was a hallmark of the pinnacle that was reached during the zenith of their apex as figures in the writing scene. It separated them from the mundane, it kept them apart from the vacant stares of the open poetry night crowd, it was the dividing line between the careerism of the St. Mark's writers clique and their own perverse and blatant amateurosis. The Unbearables chose to find Gnosis in antibacterial scrubs rather than succumb to the delusion of the established literature demiurge. But the DisinfecTrance was only a stepping stone to the more current evolution of Metaphysical Immaculatization that infuses their current activities. To discover the roots below this surface, we need to examine one more book: Franz Bardon's *Initiation Into Hermetics*.

8. The Revolting period: "Initiation Into Hermetics" enhances the ritual of going "from somewhere to nowhere"

For almost 6 years now, the Unbearables have been using the techniques of Hungarian mystic Franz Bardon, with whom Rollo Whitehead spent two months in the early 1950s. Though Bardon is relatively unknown, his techniques of magic and energy transference were very helpful in creating a magnetic cleansing field to surround the DisinfecTrance. This field was a direct link to the spirit of the Grail and the psychic energies built up by all those throughout history who have sought out this Holy solvent. Ultimately, there came a language of metaphor to subtly describe these energies which culminated in the phrase: "From Somewhere to Nowhere." As was noted earlier, this phrase had a neurolinguistic effect on the audience. Now, however, we can probe even deeper to see that it is a summary of their quest to find the Ultimate Cleaner: Dirt and filth are noticeable, but the Holy Grail will clean them completely...thus, making the dirt literally go from somewhere to nowhere!

Because Bardon's techniques were so practical in helping to galvanize this atmosphere of subtle energy cleaning agents, the Unbearables could now take the

DisinfecTrance one step further. They could create a completely spotless environment, brought about by both their subtle body energies and the audiences which their Bacchic frenzies could include. The effect would require no real effort, but would have maximum output. They called this new event, The Akashic Vacuum Cleaner. Unbearables would utilize the magnetical fluid in parts of their bodies to read poetry while simultaneously sanitizing the floor on both the physical and astral levels, creating a chain reaction which hooked the audience in against their will. Attendees would leave the event in a confused state but with copies of Unbearable books and less money in their wallets. Despite this, attendees always remark on their April fresh scent.

9. Postscript: What's Next?

One of the questions I've had to wonder about throughout this work is simply, "What's next for the Unbearables?" But I believe that an answer is *not* going to be simple. Since their last book, they have gone into a state of cautious dormancy, as if they are anticipating a bold reformation or an embarrassing crash. Critics of their previous books have noted that the Unbearables have blasted things which they seem to be emulating, and with this current project, they will probably do much of the same. One thing is certain, however, there has been an emergence of so-called "Tantric Limpiadoros" who have honed the practice of the DisinfecTrance to achieve sexual ecstasy through the intimacy of cleaning...a feat that was never really accomplished by the Unbearables...and they continue to exhibit what is termed in the vernacular, "The Tao of the Sexual DisinfecTrant". In a final note of irony, Rollo Whitehead has recently come out publicly to denounce the Unbearables altogether, saying, "They never really existed in the first place. I made the whole thing up as a joke. They are a complete fiction."

SOURCES:

alt.hermetics.books.helpless.geek.virgins, *Bardon was Hungarian, Right?* Newsgroup posting, August 2, 1998.
Bardon, F., *Initiation into Hermetics: A practice of magic*, 1971, Rüggeberg-Verlag, Germany.
Cresswell, J. & Hartley, J., *Teach Yourself Esperanto*, 1968, Teach Yourself Books.
Feast, J., *Bolo Bolo and Duran Duran: Two Treatises on the Repetitive Marcusian Meta-Politic in Hong Kong Action Films*, Published in "Beaver" magazine, July 1990.
Joyce, J., *Finnegans Wake*, 1976, Penguin Books.
Kolm, R., & Kolm, D., *My Daddy Says Everything Three Times*, No-Tech Press, 1998.
Maynard, J., *An Unbearable View of Twin Peaks: Where are the tits I was promised?* Published in Pink Pages, #9.
Moore, A.C., *How to Clean Everything*, 1977, Simon and Schuster.
Principia Discordia or How I Found Goddess and What I Did to Her When I

Found Her: The Magnum Opiate of Malaclypse the Younger, Anti-Copyright, All Rites Reversed.

Ventricle, T. & Snapple, Y., *Thomas Pynchon: Who's he trying to kid?*, Published in "The Journal of Disenfranchised Poetics", Spring 1984.

Vitale, A., *Patrino Diras: The Complete Poems of Hal Sirowitz Translated into Esperanto*, Harper Perennial, 1996, New York.

Whitehead, R. & Witz, B., *The Appearance of Silicon Tele-Dildonics and Trans-Linuxian Sensuality in the Neo-Discordian, Non-Aristotelian Cyberonomy*, Published in "Public Illuminations" #37.

God Help Us!

SHALOM

After much deep thought and contemplation, Ron jokingly proposed the merger of Disney World and the Vatican. In his right mind after toking on some weed, he figured that both the Holy See and the mighty Mouse's playground would be able to increase profit margins and collectively benefit from the marketing of their combined icons. His previous brain storm had been an alliance between K-Mart and the Satmar Chasidim of Williamsburg, Brooklyn. This particular amalgamation seemed logical in light of the yearly pilgrimages made by the Satmar to upstate New York in search of clean air, green grass and the ultimate religious shopping experience.

Jim listens avidly as Ron unfolds his vision. "Think of it, Jimmy my boy, Michael Eisner and Pope John Paul's seven dwarf archbishops giving birth to 21st-century church doctrine while riding on the Holy Rollercoaster." Jim picks up the thread and puts in his two cents. "Can you just envision this, my fellow infidel? TV spots with Jesus preaching the Gospel while aided and abetted by an irate Donald Duck."

Ron ponders this as he stares at the ceiling, his eyes transfixed by a cockroach slowly climbing into a light fixture. Suddenly he jolts out of his chair and heads straight for his jacket in which he has a notebook and pen. He wants to get this all down before they both come out of their stupor and forget it. He flips the small book open and hurriedly begins to scribble a list: A redesigned head piece for the Pope with Mickey Mouse ears, communion wafers stamped with Mickey's logo, Tinkerbell's Fairy Dust Church Incense and a Madonna for the New Millennium, the Virgin Minnie. Ron chuckles to himself thinking, "Poor Mickey won't be getting any anymore."

Barbie saunters over, ice clinking against the side of her glass. "Leave it to you two barflies to be offensive," she spouts, intruding into their conversation. "Don't you have any respect for other people's beliefs?"

Ron and Jim glance at each other and their eyes brighten. Simultaneously they exclaim, "We can't help ourselves, shameless heathens that we are. Guide us, o fair maiden. Help us to help ourselves." Then they both laugh uproariously.

"It's all the same, Babs," Ron says, his tone turning serious. "What is there to respect in all this nonsense? Don't you get it? Organized religion is organized business. One feeds off the other and both feed off the masses. I can't respect that." Then he starts to laugh maniacally, completely throwing her off balance.

"Help you guys? You guys are hopeless," she squeals and runs off.

"We're also helpless, so God help us!" Jim shrieks as he and Ron crack up again, tears streaming down their faces. They can't remember the last time they laughed this hard.

As for Barbie, she can still hear their laughter echoing in her ears hours later.

Beckett Read This Book

Bob Witz

beckett read this book
about depression
its 4 cures:
alcoholism drug addiction
madness suicide
yet he thought
hope springs eternal
like his dick a poem a can of beer
like work like the sun

and he smiled

YOU DONT HAVE TO FUCK PEOPLE OVER

TO SURVIVE

An Afterword, Which Is, In Fact, A Forward

JIM FEAST

In 1946 as the U.S. demobbed from World War II, a number of recently paroled detainees were out on the street, looking for work. Among these were Man Mountain McBrain (Wobbly and bluesman), Yoko Snapple (interior decorator), Carmen Asturias (migrant worker), Tess Ventricle (unlicensed veterinarian), Hakim Bey (medievalist and pacifist) and Rollo Whitehead (car thief). Due to overcrowding and bureaucratic snafus, the six, who should have been in separate law enforcement facilities — Yoko, for example, in the Japanese internment camp — were kept in the same cell for going on two years and had developed a rough and ready respect (if not tolerance) for each other.

Judging from each one's profession, none had lucrative or stable employment prospects, and, in truth, most of them were Bohemian radicals first and workers second. And if there was one thing that stressed them out as they looked for work, it was how to support themselves. During the early '40s all of them had become dissatisfied with monopoly capitalism and so turned to various forms of political, cultural or criminal protest.

From what little they had gleaned in Alcatraz from letters and radio broadcasts, the country was in for a period of counter-terror, where the state would endeavor to roll back gains in racial equality and workers' rights earned in the war plants of LA, Detroit and Chicago.

As they sat talking in a dingy bar in the Mission district, they wondered whether they'd be able to find backwaters where unrepentant leftists could still get a few shots off while also making a living.

"I exclude from our discussion," Hakim said, "any pseudo phalanstries, where young rebels attempt to institute new social relationships in a commune setting."

"What's wrong with those?" Carmen asked. "They could be set up in abandoned Pueblo Indian cliff houses."

Hakim was adamant, "In 'real' life, those communes ended up serving the Machine. They became wildlife refuges for Zoot-suited Dadaists, where all the beer guzzled, hairs split, sperm ejaculated and vaginal fluid squirted was nothing but oil that helped spin the wheels of the Imperial State."

"So what hope can you offer, if you can't find a crawlspace in the whole rotting edifice?" Tess asked.

Hakim temporized, "I'm not saying it's impossible. I think there could be a kind of temporary zone in which —"

Rollo butted in, "I dare to differ. We'll find a place by studying growth areas of the economy."

"Come again," from Man Mountain.

Whitehead, squirreled up in the corner, rolling a cigarillo for Tess, the striped shadows cast by the paper lantern over the bar making him look like a raffish zebra, went on, "Capitalism is destructive, consuming its own innards as it flourishes. When a technical breakthrough emerges, as when the auto was invented, obsolete technology, like horseshoeing, is thrown onto the slagheap.

"Around such sea changes sparkle a penumbra of livability where cranks, windbags, tramps and scamps can find, not just a refuge, but a place from which they can —"

Carmen, " — vibrate the culture."

Tess was enthusiastic, "Let's find that place! This will be our group self-help project. Old self-help books told you how to work really hard to make lots of moolah; but our goal will be to find a place where we can get jobs that let us goof off big time."

Yoko, who had once appeared in a rodeo, let go with a yell, "Yippee Kai Yay, let's ride the wrecking ball!!"

They decided to call these free enterprise zones *leisure suites.* After doing some research in the San Francisco public library, they agreed that the economic sector in the most turmoil was pharmaceuticals. So that's where they determined to find their *leisure suite.*

The six moved to Detroit to enroll in the 12-week trials of a polio vaccine being conducted by Jonas Salk. Once in the program, each received top-flight medical treatment and, more importantly, when the group volunteered to be injected with live polio at the end of the vaccine protocol, they were rewarded with a generous monetary stipend. As the trials ground on, the group began insisting they be allowed to inject their own daily doses. This was both an early blow for experimental subjects' rights and part of a Machivellian scheme. Once they forcibly gained the right to take the vaccine home, they began selling it on the black market, using the money to get high on bennies.

On their last day of treatment, they took their usual route to Salk's lab, which was located next to the Ford Motor Co. River Rouge assembling plant. As they entered the lab, they were surrounded by armed guards who locked them in a refrigerator. The wily Salk was afraid his subjects would get last-minute jitters at allowing themselves to be infused with the live polio virus, so he'd ordered a preemptive strike.

Bey and Snapple, who had knowledge of electrical engineering, converted the ice-locker intercom into an outgoing phone line. At the same time, Whitehead and Ventricle, using their encyclopedic drug erudition, ransacked the shelves for anything that might keep them awake through the long evening and thus aid their escape. As the night slowly wrung out, Asturias and Whitehead called everyone they could think of, leaving desperate messages with spouses and drinking buddies.

Some background. The second greatest U.S. auto strike in the twentieth century was occurring at that very moment. The young Walter Reuther had initiated a sitdown strike at the River Rouge plant, which continued even though he'd been put out of action when winged by a management thug. Both Asturias and McBrain had been walking in solidarity with the workers and had made a lot of friends on the picket lines. As dawn approached, they had the epiphany that their salvation was only a factory away so they called the River Rouge strikers on Snapple's jury-rigged intercom.

At 5:30 a.m., the six heard a shattering sound as a spanking new red Tudor hurtled through the lab's plate glass window. The workers had activated the assembly line, which they'd rerouted to exit directly across from the laboratory.

Car after car rolled forward, each goosing the one before it, pushing it through the broken window, splintering desks — their hoods clotted with the rainbow-colored contents of shattered beakers. A rubber wheel popped loudly, punctured by a jagged test-tube shard, and a bunson burner bleeding blue flame whipped across the floor like a decapitated snake. Frantic lab mice were dodging tires and seeking freedom as every 4 minutes, 15 seconds a new chassis cruised through the window. The alacrity of the cars' arrival testified to the recently instituted speed-up which was one of the causes of strike, although now the regularity served another purpose, driving the lead car toward the locked freezer.

The cars rolled on until a final shove buckled the door, allowing the chilled prisoners to make their way through the rubble of scrambled toxins, bashed-in scientific apparati and new cars. Walking through the window frame, feeling they had escaped one of Modernism's worst hells, amid the comradely cheers of the auto workers, the sixsome stumbled out into a just-riveted dawn.

Haiku Explaining
Why I Haven't Written Anything
For This Book

Michael Randall

I needed more time
or maybe a self-help book
on writing satire